Please return or renew this item by the date shown. There may be a charge if you fail to do so. Items can be returned to any Westminster library.

KT-169-334

Telephone: Enquiries 020 7641 1300
Renewals (24 hour service) 020 7641 1400
Online renewal service available.
Web site: www.westminster.gov.uk

QUE

WITHDRAWN

City of Westminster

VICTORIAN LONDON, 1851.

Queen Victoria is on the throne and the Great Exhibition is about to open!

Lucy Locket lives with her father, the New Mother and the New Baby. They sent away Lucy's beloved Nurse and replaced her with a horrid governess. Lucy desperately wants someone to be kind to her, and to have some fun – but there's very little of that in her house.

Kitty Fisher is a street performer who earns tin for her supper by tumbling. She has always lived on the street and by her wits, with only the kind Gaffer to help her. But now Gaffer is gone, and Kitty is all alone.

When Lucy runs away from home, Kitty shows Lucy how to survive – including where to find the best picnic leftovers in the park, and which trees make the best beds. Lucy learns quickly and shows Kitty her own skills – befriending families to get free meals and singing beautiful melodies for the crowds.

But the streets of Victorian London are dangerous and soon the girls find themselves under threat from thieves – and, even worse, the workhouse!

Jacqueline Wilson

Illustrated by Nick Sharratt

THE RUNAWAY GIRLS

CORGI BOOKS

CORGI BOOKS

UK | USA | Canada | Ireland | Australia
India | New Zealand | South Africa

Corgi Books is part of the Penguin Random House group of companies
whose addresses can be found at global.penguinrandomhouse.com.

www.penguin.co.uk
www.puffin.co.uk
www.ladybird.co.uk

First published in hardback by Doubleday 2021
Published in paperback by Corgi Books 2022

Typeset by Jouve (UK), Milton Keynes
Printed and bound in Great Britain by Clays Ltd, Elcograf S.p.A.

The authorized representative in the EEA is Penguin Random House Ireland,
Morrison Chambers, 32 Nassau Street, Dublin D02 YH68

A CIP catalogue record for this book is available from the British Library

Paperback ISBN: 978–05–525–7863–9

All correspondence to:
Corgi Books
Penguin Random House Children's
One Embassy Gardens, 8 Viaduct Gardens
London SW11 7BW

Penguin Random House is committed to a
sustainable future for our business, our readers
and our planet. This book is made from Forest
Stewardship Council® certified paper.

In memory of lovely Sophie Nelson –
my wonderful copy-editor for many years

1

The smell of Sunday dinner stays in the house all afternoon. It seeps into the velvet curtains and floral wallpaper in the dining room and wafts all the way upstairs to the schoolroom. Roast beef, golden Yorkshire pudding, gravy, crispy roast potatoes, carrots and peas, and then rose-red plum tart with vanilla custard.

I don't get to eat it, of course. The New Mother insists it is far too rich for a little girl. I have a small portion of minced beef and a scoop of mashed potatoes. They stick in my throat without gravy. I am allowed custard for

1

pudding, but not plum tart. I have prunes. They are plums that have died, horrible wrinkled black things that stain the custard a dirty brown. They have stones inside. I put them in a ring around the rim of my bowl and count them.

Tinker, tailor, soldier, sailor, rich man, poor man, beggar man, thief!

Nurse told me the rhyme and said I would end up marrying one of these men when I grew up. I imagined them all crowding into the nursery: the tinker with his pots and pans, the tailor with pins in his mouth, the soldier with a musket, the sailor dancing the hornpipe, the rich man greedily counting gold coins, the poor man in his threadbare suit, the beggar man with his cap held out, the thief snatching my gold bangle.

I decided I didn't want to marry any of them. I'd prefer to be a single lady like Nurse.

I sometimes played the tinker, tailor game with my marbles too, scooting them across the slippery nursery oilcloth. Nurse used to kneel down and play marbles with me, but Nurse isn't here any more and I am not allowed to play with any of my normal toys on a Sunday.

I am only allowed my Sunday doll. She lies in a long brown cardboard box like a little coffin the rest of the week. She is too valuable to play with daily. The New Mother gave her to me when she came back from Paris with Papa. She is a grown-up doll in an elaborate blue silk costume and a miniature matching parasol. She wears tiny white gloves on her hands, and kid boots on

2

her feet with buttons like pinheads. Her blonde curls are mostly hidden by her bonnet. I am not allowed to take it off to brush them. I mustn't undress her either, but I've peeped up her skirt to check she's wearing drawers. They are white and edged with lace.

I've called her Ermintrude. She looks very haughty, as if she doesn't like me touching her. She has a beautiful wax complexion, pale with pink cheeks, and blue glass eyes that stare at me.

She is staring at me now. I think she is as bored as I am. I stand her on the windowsill in the sunlight so she can look out into the garden. I am not allowed to go down and play there while it is so very hot. This is Sunday rest time.

Why do I always feel so rest*less* when it is rest time? Miss Groan is certainly resting. I can hear her snores from her room next door. The grandfather clock downstairs in the hall chimes the three-quarters hour. Why does time go so s-l-o-w-l-y on a Sunday?

I'm not allowed to read any of my storybooks either, only the Bible. I have had enough of the Bible already today. I have spent two endless hours in church this morning, fidgeting on the hard pew seat, with Miss Groan digging me in the ribs to make me sit still. She made me learn ten verses of the Bible by heart this morning before breakfast, though I think I have forgotten them already.

I am sure Miss Groan chooses the hardest verses deliberately. Miss Groan is my governess, and my goodness she makes *me* groan. She signs her name Miss J. M. Groan.

Those initials filled me with delight when she first came to our house. I so hoped she was called Joan Moan Groan! She's actually boring Jessica Mary.

Jessica Mary sounds attractive, like a jolly little girl in a story, but there is nothing jolly or little or girlish about Miss Groan. She is a plain woman with a big nose and a big chin. Have you ever seen a Punch and Judy show at the seaside? Miss Groan is the spitting image of Punch. She has a little stick just like Punch's too. She prods me with it when I am too slow to learn. When I am naughty she hits me with it. She does, truly. Well, a little rap across my knuckles. That's hitting, isn't it?

I am sure nursery governesses are not allowed to hit their pupils. I plucked up my courage and told Papa when he was next at home – he has to go away a lot on business. He sighed and said, 'Oh dear, Lucy Locket! Have you been behaving badly? Still, it's not Miss Groan's place to chastise you. I'll have a word with the wretched woman.'

I am not really called Lucy Locket. My name is Lucy Alice May Browning, but Papa calls me Lucy Locket after the girl in the nursery rhyme.

Lucy Locket lost her pocket
Kitty Fisher found it
Nothing in it, nothing in it
But the ribbon round it.

He used to sing the rhyme to me when I was very little. He still repeats it sometimes, when he can't think

4

of anything else to say to me. We don't really know each other very well. Papa is away on business a good deal, and when he is home he stays in his study most of the day. Sometimes when he passes me on the stairs he seems surprised, as if he's forgotten he has a daughter.

When we went to the seaside this Easter I was allowed to play on the beach with three other little girls. It was such a treat for me because I'd scarcely played with other children before.

I met the girls when we were all queuing for a donkey ride. I was quivering with excitement as I waited. I'd never seen such beautiful animals, so quiet and docile, with big brown eyes and huge ears. My donkey was called Neddy and he seemed to like me, snuffling quietly when I stroked his neck. I wanted to stay on his back for ever.

The other girls loved their donkey rides too, and so we all drew donkeys with our tin spades in the damp sand. The other girls were all barefoot with their drawers rolled up to their knees, so I kicked off my shoes and stockings too, and bared my own legs. Perhaps Papa thought this immodest, because he came hurrying up to us when we started paddling in the sea.

'Come along at once, Lucy Locket. Your mother is getting chilly,' he said.

But he wasn't looking at me. He was talking to one of the *other* little girls. He thought *she* was his daughter. We weren't even especially alike, though we were both fair and wore our hair in ringlets. If I hadn't protested he might have taken that little girl back to our lodgings instead of me. Perhaps he would have preferred her. The New Mother certainly would.

She's not *my* mother. My mamma died when I was a baby, which is very tragic for me – and of course for her. I miss her terribly even though I didn't have a chance to get to know her very well. I am sure we would have loved each other more than anything in the world. I don't love my stepmother. I detest her.

It is a sin to detest a parent. I have learned the whole of the Ten Commandments over many Sundays and there it is on the list: *Honour Thy Mother and Father*. I honour my father, but it's impossible to honour the New Mother.

I have very vivid memories of the day I first saw her. Papa said he'd met a lovely young lady who was going to be my new mother. We didn't get off to a good start.

'Hello, Lucy, dear! Won't you come and give me a kiss?' she said. I was wary of this beautiful lady with her dark shining hair and her piercing eyes and her fine satin dress. I ducked my head and wouldn't go near her.

'Beg pardon, madam, sir! She's just a little shy,' said Nurse.

'Or perhaps a little wilful,' said the New Mother silkily. 'I think she needs a firm hand.'

I think I knew from that moment on that I was doomed.

When she came home from her honeymoon with Papa she changed my life for ever.

'You're getting to be a big girl now, Lucy. You don't need to be molly-coddled by that old nurse. She's not really suitable – she's far too lax. You can wind her round her little finger. I shall find you a governess.'

So Miss Groan arrived and dear Nurse had to leave. We both wept bitterly.

'Where will you *go*, Nurse?'

'I'll try to find another position – but it's going to be hard at my age, and I'm not sure your stepmother will give me a good reference. I suppose I'll go back to my village in Sussex. I've got family there,' she said, dabbing her eyes.

'You're my family, Nurse, and I shall always love you. When I am a little bigger I will come and find you and we will stay together then for ever and ever,' I said, sobbing.

'I will always love you too, Miss Lucy, and never ever forget you,' said Nurse.

After she left I cast myself down on the floor and cried for hours.

'Really, Lucy! You're far too old for these temper tantrums!' said the New Mother. 'Such a fuss about a silly old nurse. I daresay you'll have forgotten all about her in a couple of months.'

As if I could ever forget Nurse! She looked after me from when I was born. She was almost like a mother to me and I loved her very much. She was satisfyingly plump so I could nestle into her. She was soft and yet she gave support, like a pillow. She smelled a little like a pillow too, of freshly ironed linen and lavender water, with her own warm Nursie smell underneath.

When I scraped my knees or had a stomach ache or woke up in the dark after a bad dream, Nurse would pick me up and cuddle me and it would all be better in an instant. I didn't mind that I didn't have any friends my own age to play with. I had Nurse instead. She played with my dolls with me, making them talk in tiny voices, and she marched all my Noah's Ark animals up and down, roaring and neighing and trumpeting. She even once had a turn on Rufus my rocking horse, though he creaked in protest.

Nurse kept her own big pot of jam in the cupboard and gave me a spoonful after I had to swallow any nasty medicine. She also spread it on our bread and butter and flavoured our bland bowls of rice pudding and semolina and tapioca with great dollops of raspberry conserve.

She didn't ever punish me severely. If I was clumsy she'd say something comical like, 'Whoops a blooming buttercup!' If I was naughty she'd tut with her tongue and say, 'Really, Miss Lucy, you're a bad little girl today. Let's put you back to bed and then get you up again so it'll be tomorrow and you'll be a good girl again.'

It worked too. We acted it out, and I made little snorty noises pretending to be asleep, and then Nurse woke me up and she'd say, 'Are you my good little girl now?' and I'd yell, 'Yes!' and then we'd burst out laughing. Nurse and I spent half our time laughing.

I don't have anyone to laugh with now. I moped about the house when Nurse left and I was sitting glumly on the stairs when the doctor came to visit the New Mother.

She wasn't exactly ill, but she was tired all the time, perhaps because she was getting surprisingly stout. The doctor bent down and shook his head at me.

'You're looking very peaky, little one,' he said. 'So pale and wan! No wonder you're not thriving in this sooty old city! I think I shall prescribe some sea air for the whole family.'

So for Easter Papa took lodgings at the seaside. I had never been before and I loved it there. It was wonderful, especially because Miss Groan was not invited! She went to stay with her sister while Papa and the New Mother and I had our holiday. The New Mother's maid Jane came too, to help me button and lace all my underclothes, and to unbutton and unlace each item at night-time. She tied up my hair into curling papers at night and brushed my ringlets in the morning, but otherwise she left me alone and concentrated on the New Mother.

The sea air didn't seem to agree with her, and she spent most of her time reclining on the sofa in the lodgings with the blinds drawn. Papa kept her company or went out fishing with his gentleman friends. He decided we must go home early. I didn't get to play with the girls on the beach again. I didn't get another ride on Neddy.

'I wish we didn't have to go home,' I said miserably when we were on the train. 'I haven't got anyone to play with there.'

'For heaven's sake, Lucy, stop moping,' the New Mother snapped. 'Why do you have to make such a fuss about everything? Oh, dear lord, why does the carriage have to jerk about so? And the seats are so uncomfortable even in First Class. My back is aching terribly.'

'There there, my dear,' said Papa, patting her tenderly. 'We will be home soon.'

When she dozed off at last he turned to me and whispered, 'I think you might find someone new to play with very soon, Lucy Locket.'

I didn't understand what he meant, not until a few weeks later. Suddenly the house was in turmoil, the servants running up and down the stairs, and the doctor arriving in his carriage.

'What's the matter, Miss Groan?' I asked.

'You will find out soon enough, Lucy,' she said. 'Now, let us apply ourselves to our arithmetic. We'll start with simple addition.'

There was a simple addition to our family that day. The New Mother had a New Baby!

I was taken to see her late that afternoon. The New Mother was lying back on her pillows in bed, her black hair about her shoulders, looking beautiful in a new white lace nightgown. She actually smiled at me.

'Come and meet your little sister, Lucy,' she said softly. 'Hush now, because she's asleep!'

I crept forward towards the bed. The New Mother was holding a white shawl. I could just see a glimpse of pink head through the crochet stitches. She seemed a very *little* sister.

'What's her name?' I whispered.

'Angelique,' said the New Mother proudly.

'She's our little angel,' said Papa, his eyes brimming with tears. 'Isn't she beautiful? Almost as beautiful as her mother.'

The New Mother uncovered the baby's face. Beautiful? She looked very red and wrinkled to me, but I knew it wouldn't be tactful to say so.

She came with an enormous amount of possessions for such a tiny person: endless sets of white clothes, plus bonnets and booties and mittens, and even a tiny white fur-trimmed coat. It was nearly summer when she arrived so she didn't really need it, but she wore it for her first outing in her perambulator and Papa laughed delightedly and called her his Baby Bunting.

She does seem exceptionally sweet in her tiny clothes, but she looks a nightmare when they all come off. She doesn't wear drawers – she has to have napkins, and they get in an alarming state. I've watched, astonished, while Nurse changes her.

She is not *my* Nurse. She is a new nurse, just for the baby. She's not a bit like my own dear Nurse. This one is gaunt and pinched and wears a starched apron that crackles when she walks. She sleeps in my Nurse's old bed. Angelique doesn't sleep in my bed in the nursery; she has a brand-new cot with lace curtains by the window. The walls have a new wallpaper – tiny pink rosebuds in a pattern. There are new floral curtains and a fluffy white rug on the floor. It isn't my nursery any more. It belongs to Angelique now.

I have a new schoolroom instead. It is pale green and beige, with a desk for me and another for Miss Groan, and a blackboard with chalks. It used to be a spare bedroom, very dull. It still is. The tiny room next to it is my new bedroom. I have my books and my dolls and my Noah's Ark crammed in with me, which is cosy, but there is no room for Rufus my rocking horse. He's to stay in the nursery. I had to give him to Angelique, though I protested fiercely.

'He won't like it at all! He needs to be exercised every day and Angelique is still far too little to ride him,' I said to Papa and the New Mother.

Papa chuckled. He likes it when I say childish things, but it irritates the New Mother.

'Really, Lucy dear, you're too old for such nonsense! You know perfectly well that the rocking horse isn't real. You must stop this silly fancy now you're a big girl.'

'Then could I perhaps ride a *real* horse?' I asked. 'I've seen girls my age riding ponies in the park.'

Papa looked at the New Mother enquiringly.

'Oh, please, please, please, Papa!' I said, jumping up and down.

'Calm down, Lucy dear. I think you had better concentrate on your lessons with Miss Groan for the moment. We shall think about riding lessons in the summer,' said the New Mother.

She always calls me Lucy *dear*, but it certainly doesn't sound like an endearment. It's as if she's calling me Lucy nuisance, or Lucy naughty, or Lucy plague. And now it *is* summer, but the riding lessons haven't started.

It is so so hot today, but Miss Groan will only allow me to have the schoolroom windows open a crack. I think she fears I will hurl myself out onto the pavement below. It would be wonderful to be riding my own pony in the shade of the trees. Perhaps we could gallop and I would feel the wind in my hair and cool down a little.

I wandered over to the blackboard and started drawing a white pony. I couldn't make his legs go the right way, but I hoped he'd still be able to gallop. He had a very long mane and a wonderful tail, and I coloured him in all over, using up a lot of white chalk. I liked him so much I couldn't bear to rub him out with the duster, although I knew Miss Groan would be very cross when she saw him and consider him a criminal waste of chalk. I think writing endless numbers that rarely add, subtract, multiply and divide themselves accurately, is much more a waste of chalk.

I'd like chalking numbers to play hopscotch. I saw some children playing this game down an alleyway when Miss Groan and I walked to the park. I liked the way they hopped swiftly on one leg for the single squares and landed on two feet in the double ones. It looked a very easy game, but great fun. All the children were laughing and shouting.

One small girl with short black curls saw me staring and grinned at me. 'Come and play,' she called.

'Oh, Miss Groan, may I?' I begged.

She looked astounded. 'Of course you can't play, Lucy! Have you taken leave of your senses? They are street children,' she hissed, pulling at my arm to try to make me walk right past.

'Well, I am in the street and I am a child, so I can't see why I can't join them,' I said, though I knew perfectly well what she meant.

I could see that the children weren't very clean and their clothes were skimpy and ragged, and some of them were barefoot. I wished *I* just wore a short petticoat and didn't have to cram my hot feet into stockings and kid boots in the summer time. But I was a rich girl, and they were poor girls, like the counting game.

'Come back and play with us!' the little girl called after us.

'I'm sorry, but I'm not allowed,' I called back, horrifying Miss Groan even more.

'You mustn't talk to children like that, Lucy!' she said.

The curly-haired girl had sharp ears. 'Don't take any notice of that old goat, Lucy!' she shouted.

It was so wondrously rude that I burst out laughing. Miss Groan practically tore my arm from my shoulder dragging me away. She smacked me hard for insolence when we got back home, though *I* hadn't called her an old goat.

I hoped I would see the hopscotch children again, especially the girl with black curly hair, but Miss Groan took another route to the park after that.

I did a little hopscotch dance on tiptoe in the schoolroom, landing as lightly as I could because I didn't want to wake Miss Groan. Her snores didn't falter. I wondered if every person in the house was also fast asleep, as if they were all in a fairy story like *Sleeping Beauty*. I imagined Papa and the New Mother lying side by side on their bed like those marble people on tombstones in churches. Even little Angelique must be sleeping too, because when she was awake her cries were ear-splitting. Her nurse would be lying on my Nurse's old bed, only taking up half the room.

Jane and Maggie the maids would be sharing a bed upstairs in the attic. Little Lizzie the kitchenmaid would be lying in her truckle bed in the attic too. Cook never seemed to struggle upstairs on her swollen legs. Perhaps she slept under the big scrubbed table in the kitchen. Mr Barnaby the butler had his own room in the servants' quarters. Billy the boot boy didn't have a room at all. Perhaps he had to cram himself into a cupboard when he fancied forty winks.

I never ever slept at rest time. I didn't always sleep at night either. I'd lie wide awake, tossing and turning, wishing Nurse was still here so that I could go and curl up with her. I wondered where she was now. She cried when we said goodbye, though she tried very hard not to, her chin wobbling, her eyes squeezed shut. She still wasn't sure whether she would find another child to nurse. The New Mother hadn't given her a very good reference.

I begged her to write to me to let me know how she was getting on, and she promised she would – but she hasn't yet. Maybe the New Mother instructed Mr Barnaby to tear up any letter addressed to Miss Lucy. I wouldn't put it past her.

I often peered out of the window, wondering if Nurse could possibly be outside in the street, looking up for me. I went to the window now, leaning my forehead on the glass pane. It was so hot it scorched me.

'I expect you're hot too, Ermintrude,' I said to the Sunday doll. 'Perhaps I'd better put you in the shade.'

I picked her up – and then nearly dropped her in shock.

2

Something dreadful had happened to Ermintrude's face! Her eyelids sagged over her blue glass eyes, her nose dribbled down past her lips and her cheeks oozed to her neck. Her wax had melted in the sunlight!

I held the doll at arm's length, tilting her this way and that, hoping her ruined face might just be some trick of the light. She stayed grotesque, her eyes staring at me from beneath her swollen lids. I thrust her back in her cardboard box face down, crumpling her parasol in my haste. Then I backed away from it, terrified she might somehow climb out and point a tiny finger at me accusingly.

When Miss Groan awoke at last I was sitting bolt upright at my desk, turning the whispery pages of my Bible. She was always nagging me about my posture and threatening me with a back-board.

'Ah, Lucy!' she said, impressed. 'Which passage are you reading?'

I didn't have a clue. The little black words had been waving up and down, refusing to make any sense.

'It's all about God,' I said, which seemed a safe guess.

Miss Groan nodded approvingly. 'And you've put your lovely doll back in the box yourself!' she commented.

'Yes, I grew a little tired of playing with her,' I said.

'Well, you are growing rather old for such childish pursuits,' said Miss Groan. She yawned without bothering to hide her gaping mouth, her long face growing even longer. 'I feel parched after my nap. Let us ring down for some tea – and perhaps a sugar biscuit too. I think you deserve a little treat for being such a good girl.'

I ate the sugar biscuit but felt as if it might choke me. Miss Groan had put poor ruined Ermintrude in her usual place at the top of the cupboard without checking on her. I was safe for now – but what was I going to do next Sunday?

I was tormented by the thought as the days went by. If only I could reach the box, smuggle it outside and throw it in a gutter up an alleyway then perhaps Miss Groan and the New Mother and Papa might think we'd had a burglary. I could even snatch a few trinkets too to make it seem more convincing. But I was under Miss Groan's surveillance nearly all the time, and remained helpless in the brief moments she was out of the room.

I opened the cupboard, but no matter how I tried I couldn't leap high enough to reach the big cardboard box. I tried teetering on a chair but still couldn't reach. I attempted climbing up the cupboard shelves like a monkey, but slipped and banged my shin most painfully. I needed a ladder, but the only one I could think of was in the garden shed, and I knew I couldn't possibly drag it into the house and up the stairs without being seen.

I was so haunted by the dilemma that I must have seemed like a little ghost. Miss Groan was pleased that I was so quiet and unusually obedient, and the New Mother was so absorbed in her beloved Angelique she wouldn't have noticed if I'd disappeared altogether.

Papa was home from business. He adored the new baby too, and was forever gurning at her and going cootchy-coo in her face. I wondered whether he'd ever made such a fuss of me when I was a baby. Of course he would have been in mourning then. It suddenly occurred to me that he might blame me for my mother's death.

'Why are you staring at me like that, Lucy Locket?' he asked.

'I'm sorry, Papa,' I said quickly.

He peered at me closely. 'You're very pale! I wonder if you need some more sea air?'

'Oh, yes please, Papa!' I cried. The Sunday doll didn't accompany us on holiday. I was only allowed a couple of storybooks for rainy days and my tin bucket and spade.

'That's not a good idea, dearest,' said the New Mother. 'Little Angelique is too young for a spell at the seaside. Her skin is far too fine and tender. She would burn no matter how we protected her. Is that not right, Nurse?'

'Yes, madam,' said the new nurse smugly. 'I never recommend it for my youngest charges.'

'Then perhaps just you and I could go on holiday together, Papa?' I said hopefully.

But he shook his head. 'Don't be silly, Lucy Locket. I could never leave my family,' he said.

I'm your family too! I protested silently in my head.

So I had to wait it out, madly hoping that after Monday, Tuesday, Wednesday, Thursday, Friday, and Saturday the world would suddenly twirl double-fast on its axis and speed past Sunday altogether. But it dawned as always, and I had to endure it. I was still being so unusually good and subdued that Miss Groan gave me the most interesting and easy set of Bible verses she could think of, about Jesus curing Jairus's daughter.

I learned the verses quickly. If Jesus could cure a child, then surely he might be able to give a little doll a new face? Miss Groan caught me kneeling by my bedside praying fervently and seemed astonished by my new piety.

'That's enough prayer for now, Lucy. You will have another chance to pray in church this morning,' she said, giving my shoulder a little pat.

For the first time in my life I wished the interminable service would go on even longer. But it was finished at last and we walked home for lunch. Even Cook seemed to have got wind of my sudden change of character. She didn't quite stretch to giving me my own Yorkshire pudding and roast potato, but she added a pat of butter to my mash and gave me a spoonful of vegetables too.

I still had a serving of sloppy milk pudding instead of pie, but I found I had an extra prune.

Tinker, tailor, soldier, sailor, rich girl, poor girl, beggar girl, thief, **doll-destroyer.**

'There now, rest time,' said Miss Groan. 'I'll get your Sunday doll.'

'I suddenly feel very sleepy, Miss Groan,' I said quickly, giving several artificial yawns. 'I think I will have a proper lie-down. I won't need my Sunday doll.'

'My goodness, Lucy! Well, by all means try to have a nap. I will loosen your dress at the back and help you with your boots. You can just lie on the top of your bed in your undergarments,' said Miss Groan.

'Thank you very much, Miss Groan,' I said fervently. But then I saw she was going to the cupboard and reaching upwards.

'I don't need Ermintrude!' I said. 'I mustn't take her to bed with me, as I don't want her pretty clothes to get spoilt.'

'What a thoughtful girl! We'll just stand her carefully on your bedside table so she can keep you company,' said Miss Groan.

'No! Please don't get her out! I don't want her looking at me when I'm sleeping!' I said wildly.

'Now now,' said Miss Groan, taking no notice. She opened the box, and gasped. She pulled Ermintrude out, held her to the light, and screamed at the sight of her new gargoyle face.

'What on earth is the matter?' It was the New Mother, bursting into my small bedroom in her petticoats, a shawl round her shoulders. 'Why are you screaming?'

Miss Groan handed Ermintrude to the New Mother wordlessly.

'Oh my lord! The doll's face is ruined and it cost an absolute fortune. It comes from the finest toy shop in Paris. How did it *happen*?' the New Mother demanded furiously.

'I have no idea, madam! It came as such a shock! The doll was like that when I opened the box just now,' said Miss Groan.

The New Mother was frowning. 'And are you saying the doll was in perfect condition when you put it in the box last Sunday?'

'Yes, madam, I swear it,' said Miss Groan. Then she put her hand to her mouth. 'Well, I didn't actually tidy the doll away myself, as far as I recollect.' She looked in my direction. I squirmed, clutching the sheets. The New Mother looked at me too. I had to fight to stop myself pulling the bedcovers right over my head.

I looked back at them as fearlessly as I could, although my heart was beating so fast I thought it would burst right out of my camisole.

'Why are you looking at me? *I* haven't done anything to poor Ermintrude,' I said.

'I think you have, missy!' said the New Mother, and she seized me by the wrist and yanked me to my feet. 'How *dare* you! You've done it deliberately to spite me!'

'Oh, madam, I can't see how the child would do anything quite as bad as that,' said Miss Groan. 'Not under my watch. To do such damage to the doll's face she'd have had to attack it with a knife, and I'd never let her keep such an object about her person.'

The New Mother was peering closely at Ermintrude's face. 'There are no sharp marks. I think the wax has melted.' She turned to me. 'Did you snatch matches from the kitchen to *burn* her, Lucy?'

'No, no, of course I didn't! I swear not, on Papa's life!' I said.

'But you did something, didn't you,' said the New Mother, sticking her face right into mine, staring deep into my eyes. 'I *know* you're hiding something! Confess it at once, or I will whip it out of you!'

'You're not allowed to whip me! You're cruel and hateful and I wish Papa had never set eyes on you!' I shouted.

'Lucy!' It was Papa himself, standing in the doorway in his unbuttoned shirt and braces.

'See what this child has done to the doll I bought her!' said the New Mother, brandishing Ermintrude.

'Whatever has got into you, Lucy? How could you destroy such a precious gift? And I will *not* have you talking to your poor mamma in such a rude disrespectful manner. *And* on the Lord's Day!'

'She's not *my* mamma,' I said, and I burst into tears. 'I don't want a new one. You might have forgotten my real mamma, but I haven't!'

'Come with me,' Papa commanded in a new cruel voice.

I shrank from him, but he took hold of me, pulling me off the bed and marching me to the door. He took me downstairs to his study. His braces were still trailing but he didn't look remotely comical now.

I was not allowed in Papa's study. As far as I knew the New Mother didn't go there either. The servants were only permitted to dust and sweep the carpet once a week, and they knew they mustn't shuffle any of Papa's papers or move anything by so much as an inch.

I had dared peep inside once and seen Papa's big mahogany desk with its green leather top. He had pens and ink bottles and fine cream paper laid out neatly just so. I'd longed to play at being a writer, but had had the sense not to dare. It would be so easy for my hand to jerk, a pen-nib to break, a bottle of ink to spill all over the top of the desk. I would be in very serious trouble.

It seemed I was in very serious trouble now. Papa strode into his room, pulling me after him. There was the desk, still set out in precise order. I peered round at the bookshelves of leather volumes, at the etchings of London scenes on the walls, the cabinet of filed papers, the big green ashtray for cigar stubs – and the cigar box itself with an exotic lady on the lid – and the glorious great globe in the corner.

In normal circumstances I'd have longed to take down several books and read a page in each, to peer at the pictures, peep in all the cabinet drawers, take a fat cigar from the box and pretend to smoke, tapping it into the green ashtray, and navigate my finger through all the blue patches on the globe until I'd swum the whole world.

But now I just stared at Papa, terrified. He opened the biggest drawer in his desk and I thought he was going to whip me himself. I was in such fear that I very nearly made a puddle on his Turkish carpet there and then. But he wasn't holding a whip. He was holding a photograph in an ornate silver frame.

'I haven't forgotten your mother, Lucy,' he said huskily. 'Here she is.'

He held out the photograph to me. I held it very carefully, peering at the lady in the picture. She wasn't quite how I'd imagined. I'd thought she'd have exquisite features and long fair hair down to her slender waist, and she'd wear embroidered silk dresses like the princesses in my fairy-tale book. This lady was wearing an ordinary frock and had her hair tied up neatly in a bun. She had dimples in her cheeks, smiling at me as if we were being introduced.

'Hello, Mamma,' I whispered very softly.

She seemed the most beautiful woman in the world to me then, her simple dress with the little lace collar finer than any ball gown. I ached for her to step out of the photograph and put her arms round me. I felt tears trickling down my cheeks.

I tried to see some resemblance to myself. 'Do I look a little like Mamma, Papa?' I asked.

'Alas, no, child,' he said.

'Why haven't you ever shown me her photograph before, Papa?'

'I didn't want to upset you, Lucy. I feel very sad when I look at her photograph. I have to keep it in a drawer or I might very well start crying myself,' said Papa. 'I loved your mother dearly. I still do. I will never ever forget her. But now I am lucky enough to have a new beautiful wife and I love her very much too.'

'As much as Mamma?' I said, clutching her silver frame.

'I love them both,' said Papa. 'And now I have two little girls, Lucy and Angelique, and I love them both too.'

'Which one of us do you love the most?' I asked shakily.

'I love you equally,' said Papa. He paused. 'At least I *did*.'

I looked up at him, trembling. My eyes were so watery I saw double, two Papas, both of them stern strangers.

'What do you mean?' I whispered.

'I find it very hard to love you when you behave appallingly to spite poor Mamma, who has tried so hard to please you. How could you have wilfully damaged that beautiful French doll?' he said.

'I *didn't*!' I cried.

'Will you still persist in telling downright lies, Lucy?' said Papa.

'It's not a lie! Well, not exactly,' I sobbed.

'Aha!' said Papa.

'I suppose it was my fault that Ermintrude's face got spoilt – but I didn't mean it to happen. I stood her on the windowsill last Sunday when it was very hot and she melted in the sun!' I said.

'You stood her directly in strong sunlight? How could you have been so foolish? What happens when you light a wax candle, child?' Papa demanded.

'It starts to burn,' I said.

'Did your mamma and I not warn you that the doll must never be sat too near the nursery fire?'

'Yes, but that was fire. I didn't think the sunlight could possibly harm her,' I said.

'Where does the sunlight come from, Lucy?'

'The sun, Papa.'

'And what does the sun consist of?' he continued sternly.

'I suppose the sun consists of flames,' I whispered.

'Exactly,' said Papa.

'But I didn't realize at the time. I didn't mean her face to melt. It looks so horrible and scary now. Please forgive me, Papa,' I begged. I put my head on one side and looked at him pleadingly.

'It's a great shame you were so thoughtless about such a special doll, but I can forgive you for such childish carelessness. However, I can't possibly forgive you for saying those terrible words to your mamma. You said she was cruel and hateful!' said Papa. 'You sounded as if you really meant it too!'

I swallowed. Could I force myself to say I had just been in a passion and that I truly loved the New Mother? It was so unfair. I knew full well she didn't love me. She might put on a soft simpering voice when she spoke to me in front of Papa, but she was often curt and unkind to me behind his back.

'She threatened to whip me!' I burst out.

'What wicked nonsense,' said Papa.

'She did, she truly did, just before you came in the door. You ask Miss Groan,' I said.

'I will do no such thing. I cannot believe you can invent such a wicked story to justify your own base behaviour. I can scarcely believe you're my own little girl. Go back to the schoolroom. I cannot bear to look at you any more,' said Papa.

He took the photograph from me and gave me a little push away from him. I slunk away.

Then I heard a dismal wailing. For a mad moment I thought it was *me* making the sound, but then I realized it was Angelique. I peeped in the nursery. She was all on her own: no Nurse, no New Mother.

She heard my footsteps and increased her wails, clearly calling to me. I went over to her beribboned cot. I didn't know how to prepare her bottle of milk. I certainly wasn't going to attempt to change her napkin. But I couldn't just leave her when she sounded so miserable. Perhaps she had a tummy-ache and needed a cuddle. I certainly did.

I leaned over the cot. She was on her back, red in the face, flailing her little arms, but when she sensed my shadow she opened her eyes wide and looked at me.

'Hello, little sister,' I whispered. 'Are you unhappy too?' Her tiny starfish hand clutched hold of my finger.

'Do you want me to pick you up?' I asked her.

She hung onto me tightly, which seemed to mean yes.

I leaned over and put my hands carefully under her armpits, ready to lift her, when there was a shrieking behind me.

'Don't you *dare* touch that baby!' the nurse shouted, dashing over so quickly I could see her thin ankles in her black wrinkled stockings.

'She was crying,' I said.

'Did you pinch her?' the nurse asked.

I stared at her, shocked. 'No, of course not,' I said.

The nurse elbowed me out the way and picked Angelique up herself. She peered at her little face. She even lifted her nightgown and examined her scrawny little body.

'Why are you doing that? Of course I haven't hurt her. She's my sister. I was just going to pick her up to comfort her,' I said.

'Well, you're not allowed to, in any circumstances. Madam's just been giving me her orders. You mustn't even set foot in the nursery,' said Nurse.

'But that's so unfair! Angelique likes me, you know she does. When I play Peep-bo with her she laughs,' I said.

'You're not to be trusted now, not when you've destroyed that lovely dolly deliberately,' said Nurse. 'I was so shocked when Madam told me. I've never heard of a child acting so viciously before.'

'It was a total accident,' I protested. 'The doll's face melted in the sun. I'm not going to sit Angelique on the windowsill and wait for the sun to melt *her*.'

The nurse gasped. 'How could you even suggest such a thing, you little child of Satan!'

'I *didn't* suggest it. I didn't mean I'd *do* it, I was just saying,' I told her, but she didn't understand.

'Get out of the nursery this minute,' she said, wrapping Angelique's shawl round her protectively. 'Do you want me to call Madam?'

No, I didn't want her to call the New Mother. Then I surely *would* be whipped. I trailed back to the schoolroom. Miss Groan was there, a Bible in her hands.

'Oh, Lucy!' she said, shaking her head at me.

'You know I didn't deliberately spoil Ermintrude, don't you, Miss Groan?' I said with a sob.

'I'm not sure I know any such thing,' said Miss Groan. 'You've behaved atrociously, and shocked us all. Your bad behaviour reflects on me too, even though you haven't been in my charge very long. That old nurse of yours must have spoiled you dreadfully.'

'No, she loved me wondrously,' I insisted.

'Defiant to the last. Sit down and read the Bible. Then you might at last repent,' said Miss Groan.

She gave me a long passage to read about Hell. It was very gloomy reading. Many hours seemed to go by before tea time. I always looked forward to Sunday tea because it was the only day I was allowed cake. Sometimes it was jam sponge, sometimes yellow Madeira, sometimes seed cake. I wasn't very keen on seed cake because the little black specks looked worryingly like tiny insects. I knew they *weren't*, but I tried to avoid them all the same.

But today it wasn't seed cake. It wasn't any kind of cake. It was plain bread and butter, just one slice, with half a glass of milk. I was clearly being punished.

I looked at Miss Groan's tray. She had a buttered crumpet and a slice of fruit bread and a large portion of jam sponge, my favourite.

'Stop staring at my food, Lucy,' she said.

'But I'm so hungry,' I said mournfully.

'Well, you shouldn't have been such a naughty girl,' said Miss Groan, licking butter from her thin lips.

'My tummy hurts I'm so hungry,' I said, rubbing it. I put my head on one side. 'Dear Miss Groan, mayn't I have just two bites of your sponge? You have a very big slice.'

'No, you may not!' she said, and she took her tray and went off into her bedroom with it where I couldn't plague her.

I very much hoped things would be back to normal on Monday, but I found myself still in deep disgrace. I wanted to see Papa to beg him to forgive me, but Miss Groan said he had no wish to see me. The New Mother didn't wish to see me either, but I didn't care about that. I wasn't even allowed to see my baby sister any more, not even a peek around the nursery door. Angelique's nurse glared ferociously if I even came near now.

Oh, how I missed my own lovely Nurse. I ached for her to take me in her arms and cuddle me close. She wouldn't ever shun me. She would understand. She would still love me.

Now I only had Miss Groan, and she made it clear she found my company abhorrent now. She set me endless general knowledge and geography and scripture tests and delighted in correcting me when I made mistakes. She savoured her teatime treats in front of me this time, biting so greedily that blobs of jam dribbled down her big chin.

'It's bread and butter for you,' she told me sternly. 'No sugar biscuits for bad little girls. Madam won't allow it.'

Tuesday proved terrible too, and Wednesday was equally woeful. It was Thursday now and I *still* only had a solitary slice of bread for my tea. It was gone in four gulps. I sighed and wandered over to the window to look out. It was very warm today but sultry, the sun behind grey clouds. If only the weather had been like this on that Sunday! Then Ermintrude would still have a fine face and Papa would still love me.

I heaved another great sigh and idly watched the passers-by below me. I saw a mother and father walking along with a little girl between them. She was holding their hands and chatting merrily while they smiled fondly at her. I wondered if there was any magic spell that would make us change places, so that she would be stuck up here in disgrace while I trotted happily between my fond parents, most likely going home to a splendid tea with two slices of sponge cake with jam *and* cream. I wished it hard, my eyes tight shut, but when I opened my eyes at last I was still in the schoolroom and the little girl and her parents were almost out of sight.

There was another woman going past now, small but bulky, her bonnet faded, her frock plain with several patches at the back, not quite the right blue colour for her dress. Nurse had had a blue dress like that.

It was my own dear Nurse walking right past the house! She might well have looked up to see if I was at the window. She might even have waved to me hopefully – but my eyes had been squeezed shut when I was wishing.

Now she was walking past, her head bowed, thinking that I hadn't even recognized her. I wanted to bang hard on the window and cry her name – but then Miss Groan would come running. Instead I gathered my skirts so they would not rustle and crept in my kid boots to the door. Then I was out and along the corridor, past the nursery, down the carpeted stairs, creeping across the gleaming black and white tiles of the hall, tugging hard at the bolt on the big front door, peering round all the time in fear that Mr Barnaby would spot me and call an alarm . . .

Suddenly I was outdoors, on the doorstep, in the street! I didn't bother to try to shut the door. I simply ran and ran and ran, seeing Nurse in her blue dress far in the distance now.

3

It felt so strange to be out all by myself. I wasn't even allowed to go down to the end of the road to post a letter in the big red box. When I was little I'd happily held Nurse's warm hand. Miss Groan always gripped me with her bony fingers when she took me to the park. It was a dreary outing, because I didn't have a hoop to bowl down the chalk paths or a boat to sail across the little pond. These activities weren't considered suitable. I had to walk along daintily like a little lady.

I certainly wasn't being dainty now, charging down the road like a steam train, my skirts hitched up around my knees. Miss Groan would have a fit, but I couldn't help it. I simply had to catch up with Nurse!

I ran and ran and ran, my ringlets bobbing wildly without a bonnet. My frock was very tight about the chest so I was finding it hard to breathe. I was glad I was still considered too young for stays. I had once peeped round the door of the New Mother's dressing room and seen her sitting in her stays in front of her looking glass. She looked very comical, but I wondered how she could bear to wear such vicious-looking garments. Her flesh bulged over the top of them in the most uncomfortable way.

Still, it meant that she had a very small neat waist when she was fully dressed. Papa often tucked his arm about her waist admiringly. I was pleased to see her waist increasing enormously in the months before baby Angelique was born, though it was subsiding again now. Perhaps she had purchased new stays made of cast iron.

I felt as if I were encased in iron myself and was forced to stop for a moment to bend over and ease the stitch in my stomach. I panicked when I stood up properly because Nurse had vanished – but then I saw she had crossed over the busy road and was walking hurriedly along the other side of the pavement.

'Don't run away from me, Nurse!' I shouted, and plunged into the traffic myself.

There was a shout and a dreadful curse and a frantic neigh as a horse reared up in front of me, nearly setting his cart tumbling.

'You wretched little varmint! Why don't you look where you're going? You nearly got yourself trampled to death!' the carter shouted, his bulbous face red with fury.

I felt my own cheeks burning. How dare he talk to me in such a way! He was shaking his whip at me too!

I bolted further across the road, dodging another cart and a hansom cab, and reached the other side at last, trembling. I badly wanted to lean against a wall to recover, but Nurse was getting further away again.

'Please slow down, Nursie!' I called, but I knew she couldn't hear me for the rattle of the vehicles.

I hurried on, gasping, conscious that people were staring at me. Indeed, one elderly gentleman in a frock coat and top hat actually caught hold of me by the shoulders.

'What's the hurry, child?' he demanded.

'Please, sir, I need to catch that lady up there,' I gasped.

He peered ahead. 'That's not a lady! She's simply some old beggar woman!' he declared.

I was outraged. 'She's not a beggar woman; she's my dear Nurse,' I said, and when he wouldn't let me go I pummelled his chest.

He said some very vulgar words then, for all he was a gentleman, but his hands lost their grip on me. I tore myself away and continued my pursuit. My rage gave me new strength and I ran even faster. Then I saw Nurse pause near a horse trough and take a drink from the water fountain.

'*Nurse!*' I cried, tearing along, until I reached her at last. 'Oh, dearest Nurse, I've caught up with you at last!'

I tugged at her blue skirts and she peered down at me, perplexed. But she wasn't Nurse! She was a complete stranger, with weather-beaten cheeks and a wart on the end of her nose.

'What are you saying, little missy?' she asked, twisting her face to one side so that her ear poked out of her battered bonnet. 'Begging your pardon, but I'm very hard of hearing.'

'You're not Nurse!' I said, and I started crying.

'What's that? You want your nurse? Don't cry now, I'm sure she's nearby,' she said.

'Oh, how I wish she *were* nearby,' I said, crying harder. 'I miss her so.'

'Don't take on now,' the False Nurse said. 'Here, have a nice drink of water.'

She offered me the drinking cup on its chain. I shrank away from it. Miss Groan had warned me never to go near one. She'd drummed it into me that poor folks used them, and I would catch something horrid from them. She'd never specified what sort of horrid it would be. I peered up at this poor lady. I wondered if warts could be catching.

'I'm not thirsty, thank you,' I said.

She shrugged her shoulders, took another drink herself, and wiped her mouth with the back of her hand. 'Well, suit yourself, dearie. But try to calm down. Folk are starting to stare,' she said, looking round.

I saw two ladies peering at me, looking concerned.

'What's the matter, little girl? Is this person upsetting you?' one asked, glaring at the False Nurse.

'Be off with you,' said the other lady, brandishing her parasol.

'I ain't done nothing!' poor False Nurse protested. 'I was simply trying to comfort the little lass.'

'A likely story,' said the first lady. 'I think we should call for a policeman!'

I thought she was bluffing, but said hurriedly, 'No, she's right, I promise. She hasn't done me any harm at all.'

'That's right, missy, you tell her. I may be poor but I'm a decent woman. I'd never upset anyone, especially a child,' she said. 'Don't you go calling no policeman. I'm not ending up back in the workhouse, not for nothing!'

I didn't understand what she meant, but I felt very bad that the two ladies were being so mean to her, when she truly had done nothing.

'It's not her fault she's not my real nurse,' I said.

'So where *is* your nurse, little girl? You're far too young to be out on the streets unaccompanied,' said the first lady.

'I don't *know*,' I wailed.

'Well, she should be sent packing for not keeping a proper eye on you,' said the parasol one. 'I think we'd better accompany you home and tell your mamma.'

'I haven't got a real one of those either,' I said.

'What on earth does she mean?' said the first lady to her companion.

'Heaven knows. Perhaps the child is a little simple. But anyway, we cannot leave her roaming the streets, talking to common folk,' said Parasol.

'Tell us your address, little girl,' said her friend.

I hesitated, biting my lip. If these two interfering ladies marched me back home I would be in even more trouble. Miss Groan would hit me with her stick. The New Mother would be furious. And Papa might actually whip me.

'I don't know my address,' I fibbed, though Nurse had taught it to me when I was as little as three or four, just in case we were ever accidentally parted. She made up a little song so I'd always remember: five Yewtree Crescent.

Number Five, Snakes Alive,
Yewtree, you and me
Crescent like the moon
What a merry tune!

The *Snakes Alive* line had given me nightmares, seeing pythons peeping out the windows and a big boa constrictor winding itself round the chimney, but I never forget which number house I live in.

'I told you she was simple!' the first lady murmured to Parasol.

I burned with humiliation. I turned my back on both of them, and tugged at the False Nurse's skirts again. She might be common folk, but she seemed kindly.

'Couldn't you look after me?' I begged her.

The two ladies gasped at the thought. The False Nurse looked frightened.

'I wish I could, missy, but it's not my place,' she said.

If she couldn't look after me then I simply had to look after myself. I couldn't stand there dithering. I had to get away.

'Goodbye,' I said abruptly, and then ran for it.

They were too taken aback to try to stop me. The two ladies were wearing wide crinolines, so running was beyond them. The False Nurse could certainly walk as fast as I could, so perhaps she could run fast too, but she stayed where she was. I think she wanted me to get away.

But where was I going? I didn't want to go home. I supposed I would have to go back eventually, but it was too frightening a thought for now. I might as well make the most of my new-found freedom.

I deliberately walked in the opposite direction from Yewtree Crescent. I could go to the park – but it was probably the first place Miss Groan would come looking for me. Besides, some of the other nurses and governesses knew me by sight. They'd wonder why I was out on my own. They'd be sure to try to catch hold of me. Anyway, the park was a very boring place. It was flat grass, with a winding chalky path that powdered my boots. There were occasional flower beds but they had scarcely any flowers, just ornamental shrubs in varying shades of green. There were trees, but little ones, not tall and stout enough to swing from – and as if Miss Groan would ever let me do such a thing.

The only pleasing thing about the park was the pond. It was small and round, but Nurse and I used to pretend it was the seaside. When it was very hot Nurse would unbutton my boots and unroll my stockings and let me have a little paddle. She once came in the water with me, exposing her strange flat feet with their crooked toes.

'Why are they all twisted sideways?' I asked.

'Because I never had the right size of boot as a child,' Nurse said matter-of-factly.

'Why not?' I persisted.

'Because we were too poor,' said Nurse.

'Are you poor now, Nurse?'

She laughed. 'Well, let's say I'm not rich.'

It seemed dreadful to me that some people were too poor. I supposed that meant *I* was too rich.

'When I'm grown up and have lots of money I shall share half with you, Nurse,' I said earnestly.

But how could I keep my promise when I didn't know where Nurse was? If only I could run to her now. She said she might go to Sussex. I had looked it up on the map of Great Britain in the schoolroom atlas. Sussex didn't look very far from London on the page, but when I'd asked Miss Groan she said it was more than a hundred miles away. I asked her how far it was to the park and she said she supposed it was half a mile away. I always felt tired when we'd walked there and back. That was only a mile all told. How could I possibly walk all the way to Nurse's cottage in Sussex? It would take days and days and days and days. I'd wear out my boots. I'd wear out my *feet*.

It was so hot too, the sun glaring though it was past five o'clock. The air was so still and heavy I struggled to breathe. I needed to find a cool alleyway out of the sunlight where I could recover.

There was a little alley on the other side of the road. I wasn't sure I had the nerve to make another crossing – but perhaps the alley was the one where the street children played hopscotch? I longed to watch them again. The little brown girl with the wild black curls might talk to me again. Perhaps we might make friends?

I steeled myself, looking this way and that through the traffic. I kept nerving myself to dart, but the carriages and carts and omnibuses were so big, and the poor old horses were forced to pull them very fast, their iron-clad hooves pounding along the road. They often left steaming deposits behind. I'd have to hold my skirts high and jump over them.

I watched to see how the ladies managed, as their skirts were even longer than mine. They waited until they got to a crossing where a ragged boy brushed away the dirt. Gentlemen gave him a coin and then steered their ladies across the newly swept pathway.

I didn't have a gentleman companion or indeed a coin, but I scuttled along behind a smart couple and followed in their wake as if I were their little girl. I couldn't help staring at the poor crossing-sweeper. He wasn't much taller than me and yet he must weigh lots less, because he was just skin and bone. It didn't look as if he had enough to eat. His clothes were torn and he didn't have any boots at all. It must be awful to be barefoot on that dirty road.

I wished I had a coin to give him. I gave him a sympathetic smile instead but he glared at me and stuck out his tongue. I wished I dared stick out my own tongue at him, but Miss Groan would faint if she saw me. But of course she couldn't see me, because she was inside number five snakes alive, and I was out in the streets of London all by myself.

Still, at least I had crossed over the busy road without being mown down, my skirt hem and pantelettes still clean and my boots free of mud. There was the alleyway. I couldn't see any children, but perhaps they were at the other end.

I stepped into the alley. It didn't smell very nice at all. Perhaps this wasn't such a good idea. I took another couple of cautious steps, trying to peer ahead, but my eyes weren't used to the shade.

I thought there was a patter of steps behind me. I stood still, listening hard. I heard the rumble of traffic on the road outside, and a *drip drip* of water somewhere, and a dog barking far away. The footsteps had stopped.

'Hello?' I said uncertainly.

My voice sounded strangely hollow within the close walls of the alleyway. Nobody answered, but I heard a stifled cough. My heart beat fast. I decided to run back to the main road as quickly as I could.

I turned and ran – straight into someone behind me! Then hard hands were gripping me, holding me fast.

'Help!' I shouted, and a ghost-me echoed my words around the alleyway.

'Shut your mouth, child, or I'll give you what for!' the person said roughly.

I didn't know exactly what she meant, but it sounded very threatening.

I twisted my head to see them properly. It was a woman without a bonnet, her hair tied back untidily, her frock hanging limply. Her face was gaunt, her eyes gleaming. She didn't look at all kindly.

'Please let me go at once or I'll tell my papa!' I said.

She cackled with laughter. 'Ooh, how frightening!' she said, mocking me.

'How dare you talk to me like that!' I said.

'I told you, shut it!' she said, giving me a shake. 'Now stand still, little Miss Muppet, while I just . . .' She was fumbling at my pinafore, her dirty hands on the crisp white lace.

'Stop it! Whatever are you doing?' I said. 'That's my pinafore!'

She untied the bows at the back and had it off me in a second. Then she pulled me even nearer, her hand at my throat, trying to undo the buttons on my frock!

'Get off me!' I cried, and I kicked at her hard.

'Ouch! You little madam!' She raised her hand and slapped my face so hard my head wobbled. I'd had several smackings since the New Mother came to live with us, but never such a fearsome blow as this. I started crying and covered my face with my hands. She wrenched them

44

away, making me hold my arms out. She was taking off my dress, my lovely blue silk frock!

'You mustn't do that! You can't take off my dress!' I sobbed.

'Can't I, miss? Oh, begging your pardon, but that's exactly what I'm doing,' she said, still mocking me. 'Just pretend I'm your nursie and behave yourself!'

'Don't you dare mock me! And I don't *have* a nurse any more,' I said, struggling with her, but she had the dress up and over my head in a flash.

'Lovely stuff! Silk, is it? That'll fetch me a bob or two down the market,' she muttered.

Was she actually going to sell my dress and pinafore? I could scarcely believe it. Did she mean to go off with them and leave me here in my petticoats?

It was even worse than that! She took my petticoats too, all three of them, and she even took my pantelettes, though I kicked her again, and got another horrid slapping.

'You can't take them! Please, please, you mustn't!' I begged her, but she took no notice of my pleas.

'Fine soft cotton with a lace trim, such pretty little garments!' she said. 'There now. Might as well make a proper job of this!'

She pushed me hard so that I fell over on the dirty ground, and then took off my boots and stockings too. I was so stunned I couldn't struggle any more. She even took my shift, stripping me right to the skin.

'There now, like a little babbie,' said the vile woman, laughing at me.

She bundled all my clothing together, wrapped them in her apron, and then started walking away.

'You can't leave me without a stitch on!' I cried.

'Can't I?' she said over her shoulder.

'But how will I get home? I can't go out into the street stark naked!'

'Yes, you'll look a right figure of fun!' she said, laughing again.

I stood up and lunged at her, trying to snatch my clothes back, but this time she kicked me, her boots horribly hard on my bare skin. I fell again and she hurried off while I lay there, crying.

I sobbed and sobbed until I was exhausted. I couldn't believe what had happened to me. Surely I must still be asleep? All I had to do was open my eyes and then I'd be back in my clean soft bed at home. I'd still be in disgrace, with a New Mother and no Nurse, but even that seemed preferable to lying in a filthy alleyway where mad women attacked you.

I strained my eyes wide open, clenched my fists and willed myself back home – but no matter how I tried I stayed stuck in this dreadful alley. I clasped myself and felt bare flesh rather than cotton and silk. I was still naked.

What on earth was I to do? I was only a few streets away from Yewtree Crescent – and yet it felt as far away as Timbuktu. How could I ever get there without any clothes? If I prayed to God, would He smite everyone blind for half an hour so I could run back home without anyone seeing me? It seemed unlikely.

I would have to wait until it was pitch dark in the middle of the night, when all the gin palaces and taverns were closed and everyone in their beds. Then I could sidle through the streets, huddling in shop doorways if I heard anyone approaching. But evil robbers and murderers might be lurking in the darkness!

'Oh, Papa, come and rescue me!' I prayed desperately.

Would he sweep me under his great coat and carry me back, overjoyed to find me? Or might he still be very angry with me? He didn't seem to love me much any more. He preferred the New Mother and little Angelique. Perhaps he didn't care that I was missing from home. Maybe he was relieved to be rid of me?

This set me off crying again, so I didn't hear fresh footsteps until someone was nearly upon me. I screamed in terror, convinced that the evil clothes-stealer had returned.

'Hey, hey, don't be scared! I won't hurt you!' It was a child's voice. I blinked away my tears and saw a ragged small girl. A dark girl with wild curls. The girl who had played hopscotch and called Miss Groan an old goat!

4

'**H**ello!' she said, squatting down beside me.

'Don't look at me!' I said, trying to cover myself with my hands.

'Oh my goodness, you're in your nothings!' she said, and chuckled.

'Don't laugh at me! It's not my fault! Some dreadful woman came along and stole all my clothes! She hit me terribly and left me for dead!' I declared.

'Did she now?' said the girl. 'You were wearing some good smutter, then?'

'If smutter means clothes, then yes, I was wearing a lovely dress. A pretty blue silk frock with my lace-trimmed pinafore. She took them, she took my kid boots and my stockings and she even took my undergarments!' I said.

The girl giggled again and I hung my head in shame.

'Oh, don't be so upset! It just sounded so funny. But I can see it's not funny at all for you, and I'm very sorry. But I daresay you have other fine frocks in your wardrobe and more boots and I expect you even have another set of . . . undergarments,' she said, pronouncing this last word in an overly affected way. I realized she was copying my own accent. She was trying hard not to laugh now, though she did still splutter a little.

'Of course I have more clothes!' I said indignantly. 'But how will I get them? I can't walk home naked!'

'Don't take on so. I'll get you a dress,' she said.

'Really?' I said. I blush to admit it, but I thought she meant she would go to a dressmaker's and order me a new frock. 'It doesn't have to be very expensive, and when I am home I will ask Papa to reimburse you and give you several pennies for your trouble.'

This time she laughed out loud. 'Are you a crackpot?' she asked. 'Where would I get the sort of cash for a fine frock, you ninny?'

'Don't call me horrid names!' I said.

'Well, don't be so silly. Cheer up, I'll get you a new frock for nothing, and you don't have to pay me no pennies.' She stood up and pulled her own ragged brown dress over her head. 'Here you are,' she said cheerfully, holding it out.

I hesitated. It was too dark to see it clearly, but it seemed in a terrible state. There were tears everywhere in the coarse material and it smelled of her own warm body. I couldn't possibly wear such a garment – could I? But it would seem so churlish to refuse, when she'd left herself wearing only a crumpled shift.

'Thank you,' I said humbly, and I took a deep breath and let her drop her dress over my head. It felt horribly uncomfortable but I supposed I was at least fairly decently covered, although showing a lot of bare leg.

'There you are! A perfect fit!' she said delightedly, clapping her hands.

'But don't you mind not wearing it?' I asked.

'My shift covers my bum, don't it?' she said, twirling round. 'And it's white, or near enough, so we can kid on it's Sunday best!'

I knew bum was a very rude coarse word, but dear Nurse had used it several times when she was pretending to be vexed with me, threatening to smack me on my b-u-m.

'You're very kind,' I said. 'What's your name? I am called Lucy Alice May Browning, but most people call me Lucy.'

'I'm Kitty,' she said.

'Are you really called Kitty?' I asked, and I actually laughed myself, in spite of my dilemma. 'Not Kitty *Fisher*?'

'Who's Kitty Fisher?'

'You know, like in the nursery rhyme. "Lucy Locket lost her pocket, Kitty Fisher found it, nothing in it, nothing in it, but the ribbon round it!" My papa calls me Lucy Locket.'

She stared at me blankly. 'I've never heard that rhyme,' she said. 'But Lucy Locket is a sweet name.'

'So what is your surname then, if it isn't Fisher?'

'Ain't got one,' she said.

'You must have! Everybody does. Your last name, the one that comes after Kitty,' I told her.

'Nope. Nothing comes after Kitty. That's all I've got. Kitty kitty kitty. Miaow!'

'What is your papa called?'

'Ain't got one,' she said cheerfully.

'Are you sure? What about your mamma?'

'Ain't got one of them either,' she said.

'You must have had one *once*,' I pointed out in a superior fashion. 'I haven't got a mamma now because she died when I was a baby, but everyone has a mother to start with.'

'I didn't,' she said, shaking her head so that her curls bounced. 'But I did have a Gaffer.'

'What's that?' I asked.

'Aha! Got you there!' she said. 'Fancy not knowing what a Gaffer is!' She was copying my superior tone exactly.

'Well, what is it then?' I asked more humbly.

'It's not an it, it's a *he*, and there's only one and he's mine,' said Kitty proudly. 'He found me when I was a baby in a bush in the country, mewling like a kitten, he said, so he called me Kitty. And he picked me up and wrapped me in his neckerchief and tucked me inside his shirt where it was warm and told me he'd look after me.'

This was so surprising I could barely believe it. I leaned against the dank wall, trying to take it all in.

'What were you doing in a bush?' I asked.

'I was born there,' said Kitty.

'Oh!' I said, suddenly remembering that Miss Groan had told me newborn babies were found in gooseberry bushes. Then the doctor came along, put the baby in his big bag, and brought it to their new home. She said Angelique had been brought that way to my New Mother.

It had seemed unlikely at the time, as if something didn't quite add up, but now Kitty was telling me the same story.

'So Gaffer is a doctor?' I asked.

'Of course he isn't a doctor, silly. He was the Gaffer of all the gentlemen wayfarers. They all looked up to my Gaffer. He had pride of place in any tavern, and so did I,' Kitty said proudly.

I stared at her.

'You're telling fibs. Little girls aren't allowed in taverns,' I said.

'That's all you know! When I could walk a bit Gaffer would lift me onto the bar counter and I'd dance a jig for all the men and they'd each give me a penny, and Gaffer would let me buy any trinket I fancied when we went to market,' said Kitty. 'And I'd sing for them too. Gaffer said I trilled like a little canary.'

'Our Cook kept a yellow canary in a cage in the kitchen. She taught it to sing and it made the maids laugh,' I said. 'But then its feathers started falling out and it looked so sad. I knew it hated being kept in that tiny cage. So one morning when Cook was busy at the range I opened the little door. I only meant the canary to have a quick fly about the room to stretch its wings, but the window was open a chink and it flew right through and never came back. Cook gave me such a whack with her soup ladle.'

'Gaffer never hit me once, no matter how naughty I was. He just chuckled at my antics,' said Kitty.

'Like my Nurse!' I said. 'But she got sent away. Did your Gaffer get sent away too, Kitty?'

'Yes,' said Kitty. She looked suddenly very sad and serious. 'He's gone away. I don't want to talk about it.'

'Oh dear, I'm sorry,' I said. 'So who looks after you now?'

'No one,' said Kitty. '*I* look after me.'

'Little girls can't look after themselves,' I said.

'Who says?' Kitty demanded. She stood up straight, elbows out. 'I can.'

'You can't possibly,' I argued. She only came up my shoulders, and I was considered small for my age. 'How old are you? Six? Seven?'

'I don't know,' said Kitty. 'Gaffer never told me. I can be any age I want.'

53

'But who gives you your meals and helps you with your clothes and puts you to bed?' I asked.

'I get my own food and I tuck myself up,' said Kitty. She shook her head at me pityingly. 'And as if I need anyone to put my own dress over my head!'

'Yes, but what about tying bows at the back and buttoning boots? I'm sure you couldn't do that,' I argued.

'Why would I want to fuss with bows and boots?' said Kitty. 'Only rich helpless girls have them. Only you haven't at the moment, have you?'

I hoped she couldn't see me blushing in the dim alleyway.

'Oh, don't look like that. I was only teasing,' said Kitty, taking my hand. 'When you get home you can tell all your servants to put your frock and boots on – not forgetting your undergarments!'

'I wish you wouldn't keep mentioning them,' I said. 'It's very rude of you.'

She laughed, not at all belittled or offended. I was baffled by her attitude. I was rich and she was poor. It was like the hymn: *The rich man in his castle, the poor man at the gate, God made them high or lowly, and each to his estate.* She was definitely lowly. Shouldn't she be calling me Miss Lucy and acting humble? She was acting as if she were superior to me.

But perhaps she *was* superior if she really could look after herself when she was so little. And she was being kind to me, for all her teasing. She'd lent me her own frock and was standing there in just her grubby shift.

'I'm sorry,' I said. 'If you come home with me I'll give you your dress back and get Papa to reward you handsomely.'

'I don't need no reward,' she said. 'But I will have my frock back. It's my best-ever dress because Gaffer gave it me.'

I thought this Gaffer had very poor taste in clothes, but knew it would not be polite to say it.

'You're a funny girl,' I said. 'Well, come with me then.'

'Wait a second. Turn your back,' she said.

'Why?' I was suddenly anxious. What was she going to do to me? Was she going to play a trick on me?

'Because I need to tinkle! That's why I came into the alley in the first place,' she said.

'Oh!' I said, fearfully embarrassed.

I turned my back at once and she relieved herself. I very much wanted to do likewise, but couldn't dare do such a vulgar thing in semi-public.

'That's better,' Kitty said cheerfully. 'Right. Let's take you home.'

We walked towards the main road – but I stopped dead when I stepped out of the alleyway. I looked down and saw myself properly in my coarse borrowed frock. The stains were worse than I thought. *I* was stained too, from falling in the grime and mud of the alley. And I felt almost naked in spite of Kitty's frock. It was so short and I felt so bare and vulnerable without drawers and petticoats. My poor feet curled up at the thought of walking on the greasy pavement, and crossing that filthy road.

'What's the matter?' asked Kitty, stopping too.

'I look so awful!' I said.

'No you don't!' said Kitty indignantly. 'You look like me in that frock – and Gaffer always said I was the prettiest little girl-child he'd ever seen.'

I supposed Kitty might be considered pretty if she brushed her hair and had a good scrub and wore proper clothes, but out in the daylight she looked like the little street urchin she was. She was scarcely decent too in her short shift, but that wasn't her fault.

'People are staring at me,' I whispered.

'Then stare back. Waggle your tongue if they pull a face,' said Kitty.

I couldn't manage it. I slunk along so close to the walls that I kept banging myself on the hard brick. I saw the wary glances of the passing folk, the sway of the ladies' skirts as they twitched them away from me, the glare of the gentlemen – as if I were polluting the very pavement. Kitty held my hand and I clung to it tightly.

'So we're going the right way?' she asked. 'You do know where you live, don't you?'

'Yes, of course I do. Number five Yewtree Crescent,' I rattled out, grateful to dear Nurse.

'A yew tree!' Kitty said. 'When we came to a city Gaffer took me into every churchyard we passed to see them.'

'Was he a religious person, your Gaffer?' I asked, surprised.

'We didn't go *in* the church. We went to see the yew trees outside. They are very old and we must respect them. Don't you know that?' Kitty seemed incredulous.

I nodded, as if to say of course I did, but to be truthful I only had a hazy idea of what a yew tree looked like. I didn't really bother to look at the trees when we went to church. I did look at the gravestones though, especially in the children's corner. I imagined all those babies curled in little boxes under the grass, sucking their thumbs. Perhaps the great dark branches above them belonged to a yew.

I couldn't think of a similar tree in the Crescent, though there was a big dense tree in the gardens that kept out the sun. I had once tried to eat a pale berry, hoping it might taste like a white currant, but Nurse had struck my arm to make me drop it, saying they were poisonous.

'Did you know that yew tree fruit is poisonous?' I said, wanting to show Kitty I knew more than she did.

'Of course it is. That is why they are planted in churchyards, so animals will keep away,' said Kitty.

'I knew that too,' I fibbed, trying to keep my end up.

But when we turned off the main road and approached the Crescent Kitty suddenly seemed overawed.

'This is never where you live?' she said. 'You're kidding me.'

'Look,' I said, pointing to the sign at the start of the Crescent.

Kitty squinted, trying to spell out every letter.

'My goodness, can't you *read*?' I asked, shocked.

'I can a little, but Gaffer said we had no need of book learning,' said Kitty.

Kitty spoke of this Gaffer as if he were God Almighty. It was starting to be irritating.

'I love to read,' I said. 'My storybooks are my favourite possessions.'

'I love stories too. Gaffer used to tell me a different story every night,' said Kitty. She was looking this way and that. 'These are very grand houses, Lucy.'

'I suppose they are,' I said. It had never really occurred to me before. Number five was just the house we lived in. I stared across the road at it.

It had changed since the New Mother came. The front door was painted a shiny black with a big lion door knocker right in the middle. The steps were kept snowy white, though the poor housemaid had bright red hands from all the scrubbing. There were new earthenware pots either side of the steps, with large green spiky plants that looked as if they could scratch you.

I wished with all my heart that the house was back the way it used to be, before the New Mother and Angelique, when it just belonged to Nurse and Papa and me. I looked up to the first floor schoolroom, fearful of seeing a silhouette with a big nose and chin. Miss Groan was going to be so angry with me. She would surely whip me this time. The New Mother would whip me too. Even Papa might take a turn, as he didn't love me any more.

'What's the matter?' Kitty asked.

'I'm thinking about the whipping I shall get,' I said.

'But it will soon be over,' Kitty said, trying to comfort me.

'Did your Gaffer whip you?' I asked.

'Never!' said Kitty. 'But after he was gone a bad man came along and I lived with him and lots of other children, and he beat us if we didn't do as we were told. But I beat *him* when he was sleeping and then I ran away.'

I blinked at this. I couldn't ever imagine beating Papa. Not even the New Mother or Miss Groan. I was wondering if I might run away again. But where would I go? And what would I wear? How would I get food? Where would I sleep? Kitty seemed to manage, but I didn't have her spirit.

The tears started rolling down my cheeks.

'That's right!' said Kitty. 'Cry a little harder if you can. Look extra sad and sorry. They will welcome you back with open arms. And if you like, you could tell them that I rescued you from the wretched clothes-stealer and lent you my very own frock and then they might be very grateful and give me some little reward.'

'Yes, all right,' I said, squeezing her hand. 'But I'm very frightened.'

We crossed the road and I started up the white steps, still hand in hand with Kitty.

'Perhaps we should have gone round to the back?' she said.

'Of course not. I *live* here,' I said.

'But we're making a mess of these steps,' said Kitty.

I looked down – and saw our muddy footprints on the snowy stone.

'Oh goodness!' I said. 'The poor maid will have to scrub them all over again – but I shall say I am very sorry.'

I reached up for the brass lion door knocker. He snarled at me, hot under my hand from a day of burning sunshine. I knocked timidly, and we waited. Nothing happened.

'Perhaps we should knock a little louder,' said Kitty, and she rapped hard upon the front door.

We heard scurrying feet and then the new nurse appeared, her cap awry, looking flustered.

'What on earth do you two ragamuffins want?' she demanded, outraged. 'You can't come to our front door!'

'Where are all the maids?' I cried. 'It's not your job to answer the front door!'

'How dare you talk to me like that! Be off with you, or I'll call the Missis,' she said.

'Nurse, it's *me*, Lucy!' I said.

'What nonsense is that? What do you know about her? She's gone missing and the whole house is in uproar!' she said. 'Mr Barnaby's fetching the police.'

'You don't need no police! Look, she's come back now!' said Kitty. '*She's* Lucy.'

The nurse stared, and then suddenly grabbed Kitty's shoulder by one hand and mine by the other.

'I know your game!' she said. Then she shrieked at the top of her voice, 'Missis! These two guttersnipes have come about Miss Lucy. I think they're holding her to ransom!'

'Don't be so foolish, Nurse. *I'm* Lucy. Look at me!'

She looked at my tousled hair, my swollen face, my ragged dress, my filthy feet, and she shook me hard. 'Stop this nonsense, you brazen brat,' she said.

The New Mother came to the door, clutching Angelique so tightly she started shrieking.

'Oh, my lord, get away from my front door, you horrid dirty creatures. Call for the Master!'

I opened my mouth to call her 'Mother', but I couldn't say the word even now.

Papa came running, with Miss Groan following, wringing her hands. 'Stand back, my dear. Keep Angelique well out of their reach,' Papa warned, glancing at Kitty and me in horror. 'Barnaby will be back with the constables any minute. They'll drag the truth out of these two wretched children. What have you done with my little Lucy?'

My chest was so tight I couldn't speak. It was the seaside nightmare all over again. Papa didn't recognize me!

'Don't you know your own daughter?' Kitty said incredulously.

'Stop this wicked charade!' Papa cried, grabbing her from the nurse.

'Look, Lucy, never mind any reward – I'm out of here, if the traps are coming!' said Kitty, struggling to free herself.

'Stop it, Papa! You're hurting her. Kitty *rescued* me!' I gasped.

But he wasn't even looking at me now. 'Barnaby!' he bellowed.

Barnaby was marching purposefully down the road in his black butlering outfit, flanked by two police constables.

'Hurry, gentlemen! Arrest these two ragged girls! One is masquerading as my daughter!' Papa shouted.

They started running fast.

'I'm off!' said Kitty, punching Papa in the stomach and wrenching herself free.

She darted away, and the police pursued her, blowing their whistles and waving their rattles, making a terrible noise. One of the policemen threw himself at Kitty and knocked her to the ground. Then he tried to pull her up by her hair, making her scream.

'Stop it!' I cried, and I ducked away from the new nurse, and started running to Kitty.

The constable had his fist clenched and started beating her about the head. His rattle had fallen to the floor. I picked it up and hit him hard on his back, using all my strength.

'Lucy?' It was Miss Groan, on the doorstep now. 'Sir, sir, I believe that little girl *is* Lucy!'

But I wasn't staying now. I grabbed Kitty's hand and we ran away together.

We ran and ran and ran. Kitty was smaller and her legs shorter but she was much faster than me. I hung onto her grimly, glad now that I wasn't trussed up in all my petticoats and frock and bonnet. My feet stung on the hard hot pavements but my limbs moved freely in Kitty's ragged dress.

She seemed to be running with purpose, though not in a direct way straight down every road. She dodged down alleyways and back closes and once sprang over a brick wall. It was not a very high one, but I had to take three runs at it before I managed to hitch myself over, and then I landed badly with straight legs so that I jarred my whole body.

I would normally have stopped and cried bitterly, but this was a desperate situation and I simply had to keep on going. My breath was rasping now, my chest hurting, and my stomach knotted with pain, but I gritted my teeth and carried on. On and on and on.

Then at last we came to a park – not the trim little park near the Crescent, but a bigger, wilder place. There was a gated entrance with a park keeper consulting his pocket watch, a set of keys in his other hand. Kitty ignored him and ran further down the pavement beside the railings, while I staggered after her.

She followed the railings round the corner and then found two iron posts that had buckled, leaving a small gap.

'Through here,' she said, demonstrating.

She was through with one squirm of her small body, and then she ducked down and tunnelled through the thick hedge until she was out the other side, in the park, out of sight.

'Kitty!' I cried, terrified that she was going to run off and leave me all alone.

'Ssh! Come *on*!' she hissed through the hedge.

'But the gap's too small for me!' I protested.

'No, it isn't. You can do it. Try!' she commanded.

I bent down and put my head through the gap in desperation, ramming it fiercely between the two posts. But then I was trapped. I couldn't get any further because my shoulders were too wide. I tried to pull my head back, but it wouldn't budge now.

'I'm stuck!' I gasped. Oh, help help help! I was going to be stuck there for ever, half in and half out. I was horribly conscious that a lot of bare leg was showing now, possibly even my behind!

'No you're not!' said Kitty, scrambling back to look at me. 'Go sideways. Twist round, stupid!'

My eyes filled with tears now, hating her calling me stupid when she was a street girl and couldn't even read properly – and I'd rescued her from the horrible constable and run away from my own papa to be with her.

'Don't cry,' said Kitty, and she wiped a tear away gently with the back of her hand. 'Move your shoulders and squeeze round slowly. You can do it, I promise.'

I tried moving inch by inch, slotting one shoulder through the gap and then the other. Kitty seized hold of me and pulled with a sudden jerk. I shot through the railings like a cork out of a bottle.

'There!' she said. 'Now, creep under the hedge.'

'But it's all dirty,' I protested, though I was filthy already and a little earth wasn't going to make much difference.

I crawled alongside her and then straightened up, every single part of me sore and aching. But even so, I was overcome with the beauty of this park. It was wild and overgrown, with yellow and white and purple flowers scattered throughout the long grass, not planted in rows in specially dug earth. I could see there were more formal gardens further away, but I liked this part much more.

The gardens were very empty. Where were all the people you usually saw in any park, the strolling couples, the elderly ladies walking their dogs, the children with their hoops and balls? Then the significance of the keeper with the keys dawned on me.

'This park's closed!' I said, peering all around.

'Yes!' said Kitty. 'Great timing!'

'But we're not supposed to be here. We'll get into trouble!' I said.

She burst out laughing.

'Stop it! You're forever laughing at me and it's very rude,' I said.

'Well, really! Just listen to you. We'll get into trouble indeed! We're in far worse trouble already. Well, I am. If those constables get me they'll lock me up for kidnapping,' said Kitty.

'But that's ridiculous. We simply tell them the truth,' I said.

'And they'll believe you?' said Kitty, eyebrows raised. 'For goodness' sake, Lucy, your own family didn't believe you, didn't even *recognize* you! How come your papa didn't know you? Don't he give a fig about you?'

'Of course he does! He loves me very much! He's just a little short-sighted,' I said fiercely. Papa certainly did wear little spectacles when he read his newspaper. Oh, perhaps that really was the truth. Of course he'd know me if he could only see me properly. Maybe I'd just been a blur to him. It was wondrously comforting to think it.

'Is there something wrong with his hearing too?' Kitty asked relentlessly. 'You spoke to him loud and clear. "*Stop it, Papa!*"' She was imitating my voice and I hated it.

How dare she mock me! What was I *doing*, running away with this dirty mocking girl?

'Why are you being so horrid to me when I rescued you from that awful constable pulling your hair?' I demanded.

'I'm not being *horrid*. I don't mean to be anyway. And I'm very very grateful you rescued me. He was a real brute!' Kitty rubbed her wild curls ruefully. 'Look, he must have yanked out a whole lock! I've got a bald patch now, see!'

She parted her hair and I saw a circle of scalp as big as a farthing.

'Oh my goodness, you poor thing! It must have hurt dreadfully,' I said.

'I can take it,' said Kitty, swaggering a little. 'That bad man used to beat us and I never cried out once.'

'I know I'd cry,' I said. 'What are we going to do if the park keeper catches us here?'

'He won't. He'll have gone home to his family. There's nobody here but us now. And all the animals,' she said.

'Animals?' I said, alarmed. I peered round, imagining bears and wolves and wildcats.

'Rabbits and squirrels! And mice and stoats and hedgehogs and weasels and badgers and rats,' said Kitty.

I didn't mind rabbits and squirrels but I wasn't at all sure about the others, especially the rats.

Kitty saw my face. 'They'll be hiding in the grass. You won't see them,' she said reassuringly. 'And we'll be high above them anyway. Let me show you my special place.'

'So you know this park already?' I asked.

'Of course I do. I come here lots.'

'With those other children? The ones playing hopscotch?'

'No, this is my secret place when I want to be on my own. It's like the real countryside. I pretend I'm with Gaffer sometimes, just like the old days,' Kitty said softly.

'You don't mind me coming here with you?' I wondered. 'Am I . . . am I your friend now?'

Kitty shrugged. 'Sort of. Only you're rich and I'm poor so we can't really be friends, can we?'

'Yes we can,' I said. I didn't care if she mocked me. I wanted a friend so much.

'Then I'll be Lady Kitty and I'm inviting you to my summer dwelling,' said Kitty grandly.

'And I'm Lady Lucy Locket and I shall be delighted to say yes please!' I said.

'Then pray come with me,' said Kitty, giggling.

She led me along the wild edges of the park into a little wooded part. I thought she was going to point out a yew, but these trees were very different to the ones in the Crescent.

'They're oaks,' said Kitty. 'And very old. Gaffer always said they are the King of trees. It's where the fairies live. He used to show me the little fairy hats.'

'Oh, those little cup things on the acorns!' I said. 'I tried to eat one once because it looks like a nut, but Nurse said it was poisonous.'

'And the fairies wear them when they go out at night,' said Kitty.

I stared at her incredulously. 'You surely don't still believe in fairies!' I said.

'Of course I do!' said Kitty. She put her hand over my mouth. 'Shush now, or they'll hear you and take offence!' she whispered. 'Gaffer said you must take care never to insult a fairy or they'll torment you dreadfully.'

She seemed to be serious. She was such a strange girl. She seemed so much older than me in many ways, and yet so much younger too. Perhaps this was another pretend game. It was so lovely to find someone to play with. Nurse had done her best but I could sense she was only making things up for my benefit. Kitty's eyes were dark and dreamy as she told me all the tricks a fairy might play on me if I annoyed it. Their favourite game was sticking their victim all over with their green spears.

'Like this,' she said, and she picked a hairy green head from a hedgerow plant and aimed it at my hair.

'Hey!' I said, laughing, trying to comb it out with my fingers.

Kitty did it for me, and then wound her finger round and round inside one of my ringlets.

'I like the way your hair curls,' she said.

'It's not like this naturally,' I said. 'I have it in curling papers every night. Nurse used to do it for me and she

69

was quite gentle, but Miss Groan pulls dreadfully and makes my whole head ache.'

'If you put these curling papers in my hair would it go smooth and shining like yours?' Kitty asked.

'Well, it might,' I said, a little doubtfully. 'But I think you might need to wash it first.'

Kitty was in need of a very thorough scrub all over, but it didn't seem to bother her.

There was something else that was bothering *me* dreadfully. 'Lady Kitty, does your dwelling happen to have a closet?' I asked.

'A closet?' Kitty asked, looking puzzled.

'You know. Where you can relieve yourself,' I whispered, blushing.

'Oh! Well, of course, Lady Lucy. Here we are,' she said, gesturing to a clump of ferns. 'They need watering!'

'Yes, but I can't go outside like this. Someone might look,' I said.

'Oh yes, this park is very crowded now, with people all around us,' said Kitty, gesturing at the grass and the paths and the flower beds, all deserted.

'*You'll* look!' I said.

'Yes, I might,' said Kitty mischievously.

'Stop teasing me!'

'Well, stop being so silly.'

I walked reluctantly to the ferns. Kitty turned her back. I lifted her ragged dress and tried to go, but it was impossible.

'Have you been yet?' Kitty asked, her back still turned.

'I can't!' I said. 'I'll have to wait until we go somewhere with a proper closet.'

'Then you'll be waiting a long time, because we're going to be staying here all night long,' said Kitty.

I was already in agony. If I waited all night I'd likely blow up and burst. 'Well, could you please walk further away. Much further than that. So you can't possibly hear me,' I begged.

She sighed, but sauntered off. I waited until she'd gone far into the distance and then I crouched down and tried again, successfully. Then I straightened up and looked for her, so I could wave her back. But she wasn't there. I peered this way and that, shading my eyes from the evening sun, but I couldn't see her anywhere.

'Kitty!' I called. 'Kitty, you can come back now.'

Several birds flew out of the hedge, startled by my voice. Their flapping wings frightened me, and I ducked down, and then felt foolish, ready for Kitty's mocking laugh. But she was silent.

'*Kitty?*' I shouted. Then at the top of my voice, 'KITTY!'

Nothing.

'Come on, the joke's over!' I called. 'Now come back here this instant or—'

Or what? I couldn't do anything. I was stuck in this huge strange park that I'd never known existed. It was locked for the night, so I was clearly trespassing. I was going to have to stay here all night long. The sun was already low in the sky. It was getting late, past supper time. It would be bedtime soon. I looked round desperately but saw no lamps. It was going to be dark, pitch dark. I was so scared of the dark that I had to have a candlestick on my bedside table. If it went out in the middle of the night and I woke up I'd pull the blankets over my head and cower there. I didn't have a candle or any blankets here.

It looked as if I didn't even have Kitty. She'd run off and left me here, all alone. What was I going to do? Should I try to find the gap in the railings and somehow find my way back home? I could make one more attempt at persuading them that I was Lucy. Papa hadn't believed me, and that was like a knife in my heart – but Miss Groan knew me. Would she manage to persuade him that I was telling the truth? Would Papa let me in after all? I could bathe and dress in any of my outfits and then he would see for himself that I was his own Lucy Locket.

But did I want to go back to a father who cared so little for his daughter that he couldn't recognize her? To a New Mother who disliked me, and a nursery governess who had never once smiled at me and corrected me a hundred times a day? If only Nurse was still there.

I ached for her now. It was all I could do not to cry out her name, though I had just enough sense left to know that she couldn't possibly be within earshot. I shut my eyes and whispered over and over again to her inside my head.

Dearest Nurse, I miss you so terribly. Please, please, please come and find me and then we will live together and be happy again. Please, oh please . . .

Then someone suddenly flung their arms round me and I jumped violently and cried out.

'Hey! Don't tremble so! It's Kitty!' she said. 'Who did you think it was?'

'Oh, Kitty, where were you? Why did you run away? How could you leave me all alone?' I cried.

'You told me to go away while you tinkled!' she said indignantly.

'But not for so long! How could you tease me so?'

'I wasn't long at all,' said Kitty. 'And I wasn't teasing either. I was busy getting our supper. Look!' She knelt down beside an unwieldy parcel wrapped in crumpled newspaper. She opened it up with a proud flourish. 'See!'

I stared in astonishment at the bottle of ginger beer, the patties, the cake and the orange. 'Is there a refreshment room in this park? How did you get the money for all this?'

'There are free "refreshment rooms" all over the park and they don't cost a bean,' said Kitty. 'They've got a special name – litter baskets!'

I stared at her. Then I looked back at the food. I saw there was a bite or two out of the patties, the cake had a crust of earth as if it had been dropped in a flower bed, the orange was bruised, and when I held it to the light I realized that the bottle of ginger beer was only half full.

'This is food that has been thrown away!' I said. 'We can't eat that! It's dirty!'

'So are we,' said Kitty cheerfully. 'You don't have to eat it if you don't want, but I'm going to tuck in.'

She spread out the newspaper and arranged the food neatly, picking off any dirty bits and peeling the orange, throwing away the bruised segments. Each item was divided carefully in two, with the bottle of ginger beer in the middle. She sat down cross-legged and smiled at me invitingly.

'There! Would you care to join me, Lady Lucy?' she asked.

It would have been churlish to refuse. And besides, I'd missed my own supper at home. I realized I was starving hungry.

I sat down beside her and we ate up every crumb, politely taking it in turns to share the ginger beer. The meal was totally delicious. I was used to such bland food at home. The meat in the patties was wonderfully flavoursome and the pastry rich with butter. The fruitcake was heavy with cherries and sultanas, and when the earth was brushed away the white icing was a marvel, crunchy and very sweet. The orange was juicy and slaked my thirst, and the ginger beer was still fizzy and tasted marvellous straight from the bottle.

'Thank you so much, Lady Kitty,' I said when I'd finished at last. 'That was the most excellent feast.'

'You're very welcome, Lady Lucy. Would you care to use my table napkin?' she said, passing me a torn-off piece of newspaper.

I blotted my lips with it and then she did the same.

'My maid is having a day off so I'd better do the clearing up,' said Kitty, neatly parcelling up the newspaper and the bottle and orange peel, scooping out a patch of earth and giving them a shallow burial. She kept back one large sheet of newspaper.

'Are we going to read it, Lady Kitty?' I asked.

'You can, if you was feeling the need to show off,' said Kitty. 'I'm keeping a piece handy for any necessary bum wiping.'

I felt myself blushing to the roots of my hair – but I could see she was only being practical.

'So we're actually staying here?' I asked uncertainly.

'For tonight, certainly. Them traps might still be prowling about. You know – the constables.' Kitty paused. 'You was brilliant, Lucy, getting that one off of me. You act so niminy piminy and yet you can be really fierce if you want. I like that.'

I took that as a great compliment and squared my shoulders, chin up, to look as fierce as possible.

'We haven't actually got a bed though, have we?' I said. I kept thinking of the rats and stoats and weasels. I knew I would scream like a banshee if they ran across my face in the night.

'Yes we have,' said Kitty, and she pointed to the biggest oak tree.

It towered above us, reaching up to the sky.

'We're going to climb right up it?' I whispered, sounding anything but fierce.

'Not all the way to the top!' said Kitty.

'But I can't climb at all,' I said.

'Right then, we'll be birds and fly up,' said Kitty. It sounded as if she might be losing patience with me now. I decided to play her at her own game.

'Then I am Lucy Lark and I'm very good at singing, trill trill trill, but my wings don't work very well,' I said, flapping my arms pathetically.

'And I am Kitty . . . Swift, yes, that was always Gaffer's favourite bird. I'm Kitty Swift and I *am* swift, and the cleverest of all the birds because I can sleep with my eyes open,' said Kitty, whirling round and round the tree. 'So I can protect us if anyone creeps up on us, only they won't, because there's no one else here, just you and me, and we'll be cosily tucked up, you'll see.'

She sprang at the lowest branch, swung there kicking her legs in joy, and then hauled herself up onto it.

'Now you come up too,' she said.

'I can't!' I said, but she made me try, one jump, two jumps, and then on the third jump I got my hands on the bark and managed to hang there somehow, gasping.

'That's the ticket,' said Kitty. 'Now, cock one leg up, and tuck your foot over and pull up. It's easy!'

She might have found it easy. *I* found it almost impossible, but I tried and tried until I managed to climb onto the wretched branch. My heart was thudding, and my arms and legs were grazed by the bark.

'It's no use. I can't go any further,' I gasped.

'You don't have to,' said Kitty. 'Pull yourself along a bit. See that hole? Right there! It's bigger than you think.

You can drop right down and that's it, our room for the night, and it's already lined with leaves because I've slept here several times.'

It was still frightening, dangling my legs down into that dark hole. I imagined a giant squirrel lurking under me, ready to sink its teeth into my bare toes – but there were only soft leaves, as Kitty had said. There wasn't much room for one, so with two of us it was quite a squeeze. We had to curl up very close together, which was actually very comforting. I hadn't had a cuddle with anyone since Nurse left.

'You OK?' Kitty asked, her breath tickling my cheek.

'I think so,' I said.

It was tremendously dark, which I didn't like at all. I clung to Kitty, thinking I'd never sleep a wink – but I started dreaming almost immediately.

6

It was the same dream, over and over. I was standing on the steps and Papa was wagging his finger at me furiously, telling me I wasn't his daughter. I was trying to tell him that I *was*, of course I was, but although I moved my lips and strained my throat, no sound came out. I looked down at myself and the borrowed ragged dress was there, hanging limply, but there didn't seem to be any body inside it. I didn't have any arms, any legs; there seemed nothing of me at all, though I knew I was there. I knew I was Lucy, but I couldn't make myself heard; I couldn't even make myself seen.

I woke with a start and I couldn't see a thing in the dark, and just for a moment I thought I'd really disappeared – but then I felt Kitty's warm body beside me, heard her soft snores, and remembered.

'Kitty? Can you hear me?' I said into her ear, and she mumbled indistinctly.

I couldn't catch what she said, but she could hear me, she could feel my arm going round her, because she burrowed into me like a little animal, still asleep. I was lulled a little, but then I started remembering everything properly. I thought of Ermintrude's melted face, my days of disgrace, and then the sudden leap of my heart when I had thought I saw Nurse from the window.

I longed to hear her dear husky voice saying, 'There, there, Miss Lucy, you've just had a nasty dream. It's all right, my dearie. Nursie's here.'

But she wasn't here with me in the nursery – and *I* wasn't here. I was huddled in a tree with wildlife rustling all around me. The only friend I had in the world was Kitty, and I still wasn't certain she wouldn't run off and leave me.

Then I slept and woke again, and felt for Kitty – but she wasn't there. It was no longer pitch dark now and I could see I was crouched in the hollow by myself. I struggled to stand up, stiff and aching, but managed to haul myself out into the daylight. It was a beautiful day, the sun warm already, the sky a brilliant blue, and a light breeze gently rustled the leaves on the trees.

A bird with a forked tail flew high above me. Was it a swift? I watched it until my eyes blurred and it disappeared.

I hauled myself out onto the branch and sat there trying to pluck up the courage to jump down. I did it at last, and tumbled over, but didn't hurt myself.

'Kitty?' I called. 'Kitty, you haven't left me, have you?'

I waited, staring in every direction, but there was no sign of her. I hoped she might be looking for a litter basket breakfast for us, but I couldn't be sure. I relieved myself in the ferns again, and wished I could scrub myself clean and put on proper clothes. How could I go out of the park and show myself to people when I looked such a sight?

I wondered when the park keeper came along with his keys and opened the gate to the general public. I should make myself scarce before he came and caught me. But where would I go? How would I manage?

'Kitty!' I wailed. 'Kitty! Kitty!'

'Miaow!' someone replied.

'Oh, Kitty, where *are* you, you bad girl!' I called, limp with relief.

'Here I am!' she said, running out of the shadows under the trees. 'Sorry to worry you! You were sleeping so soundly I didn't like to wake you.' She was clutching something to her chest.

'Have you found us some breakfast?' I asked hopefully.

'I had to do a whole round of the litter baskets. I could have fed myself twenty times over, but I know how fussy you are, Lady Lucy, turning up your nose at a little bit of honest dirt. I found some ham that seemed promising, but it tasted a tad rancid, so I didn't think that would do either. So it's cake again, and it's gone a bit hard, but it was so well wrapped it hasn't got a speck of dust on it. Couldn't find any left-over pop in any of the bottles, but I've got a couple of tomatoes in this bag, they'll slake our thirst,' she declared, setting out our picnic.

'It's very good of you, Kitty, and I'm sure it will be delicious,' I said.

In actual fact I gobbled up the strange breakfast with relish. I would normally never dream of eating stale sponge cake and an over-ripe tomato – especially for a breakfast – but I had an extraordinary appetite now. When I was finished I had crumbs all round my mouth and tomato juice all over my hands. I wrung them uncomfortably.

'Just wipe them on your dress,' said Kitty.

'But they'll make it all dirty,' I said.

'I don't care, and it's my dress,' said Kitty.

I rubbed them on the grass instead, because the dress was already dreadfully stained. My hands still felt horribly sticky.

'I wish we had some way of washing,' I said, sighing.

'Ah! Let's see now – what time would you say it was?' said Kitty.

'I haven't got a pocket watch,' I said.

'Don't need one of them,' said Kitty. She squinted up at the sun. 'I reckon it'll be a good hour and a half before that keeper comes to open up the park. Time for us to take our bath, Lady Lucy.'

'You mean, *pretend* to take a bath?' I asked uncertainly.

'Well, that wouldn't get you very clean, would it, Lady Fussyguts?' said Kitty, her eyes sparkling. 'Come with me.'

She led me towards the flower beds and carefully mown lawns. I felt more self-conscious than ever about my appearance, and kept glancing round nervously in case anyone was peering at me in horror, although I knew we still had the park to ourselves. We seemed to be walking for quite a while, and I was worried that Kitty's time-keeping was simply guesswork. If the keeper unlocked the gates and did an early patrol of his park then he could easily spot us.

'Kitty, are you *sure* we've got plenty of time?' I asked anxiously.

'I've never known anyone who's such a worrit!' she said, clucking at me. 'We have oodles of time – and we're very nearly there.'

She took me down a long laburnum archway casting a golden yellow shade and there at the end of it was . . . a boating lake! It was a circle of clear blue-grey water gleaming in the sunshine. The small rowing boats were tied up neatly to a little jetty. There was a hut with a notice saying it cost sixpence per adult, children only a penny.

'Oh dear, we haven't got any pennies,' I said.

'There's nobody there to take any money! And anyway, we're not going to take one of them boats. We're going for a swim,' said Kitty. 'That's even better than a bath, isn't it?'

'But we haven't got any bathing costumes either,' I said.

'Oh, for goodness' sake!' said Kitty, exasperated. She pulled her shift over her head, took one leap, and landed in the water with a big splash. She frolicked about, the shallow water only coming up to her waist, shrieking with delight.

'Jump in, Lucy!' she called.

I stood at the water's edge, wavering. I couldn't possibly leap about naked like Kitty. Yet the water looked so inviting and I longed to get properly clean. Should I jump in wearing my dress? It certainly needed a good wash. But then how would I get it dry? It would drip all day long.

I couldn't get the dress wet. But skin would dry in this sunshine in no time. I suddenly tugged the frock off and jumped in too. It was far colder than I'd thought it would be, and I screamed in surprise, but I was soon leaping about and splashing like Kitty. I wondered what on earth Miss Groan would say if she could see me now. Her beady eyes would pop right out of her head. But Miss Groan wasn't here. I was free!

'Come in deeper, Lucy!' Kitty called.

I waded towards the middle of the pond, greatly daring, until the water came up to my shoulders.

'That's the ticket! Now, let's swim. I'll race you to the other side,' said Kitty, jumping up and down to keep warm.

'I don't really know how to swim,' I said.

'It's easy!' said Kitty. I thought she might be pretending again, but she glided over to me and then swam around me with strong even strokes, her legs splashing behind her.

'Oh, my goodness, you *can* swim!' I said, tremendously impressed.

'Gaffer showed me how,' said Kitty. 'I've been swimming right from when I could walk. Gaffer said I was like a little fish.'

'Can you show me then?' I asked.

Kitty did her best, but I was nervous and clumsy, and couldn't really get the hang of it. She tried to support me, but my legs drooped, and I didn't dare take them off the bottom.

'Never mind. You'll learn soon. But why don't you flip over onto your back and float for a little?' said Kitty. 'Look, like this.' She lay down and floated as easily as a leaf.

'I could never do that,' I said, but she insisted that I try.

So I flipped over and let my hair drift around my head. Kitty took hold of my legs and held them up.

'Don't let go!' I said anxiously.

'Stick out your stomach! That's it. Now you'll find your legs will float by themselves,' said Kitty.

'Do you promise?' I begged.

'Promise, promise, promise,' said Kitty, and she let my legs go.

I was ready to sink like a stone but I stayed floating! It was as easy as lying on my back in bed, and yet I had clear water instead of a mattress.

'Oh, I'm doing it, I'm doing it!' I said. 'I'm like a mermaid! It's wonderful!'

Kitty lay on her back beside me and we floated together, staring up at the blue sky, and all my worries and anxieties drifted away.

'I'm so happy!' I said.

'I am too,' said Kitty.

'Let's stay here floating for ever and ever,' I said.

'Maybe for ten minutes more but then we'll have to get out and scarper before the park opens,' said Kitty.

'It's not a park any more. I am Lady Lucy and you are Lady Kitty and we live here in our tree house and this is our very own lake and we won't allow anyone into our grounds. This is our magic place just for us,' I said.

I shut my eyes and wished it were true with all my heart, but now I was conscious of the minutes ticking by. I didn't protest when Kitty gave me a little tug and started wading out of the pond. I followed her, starting to shiver when we stepped onto the grass, and conscious again that I was totally bare.

'We have to run about now,' said Kitty.

So we ran as fast as we could round and round the boating lake, first one way and then the other when we started to get dizzy. The sun was already hot but I still stayed soaking wet.

'We'd better dress anyway,' said Kitty. 'I don't think we've got too much time left.'

She shrugged on her flimsy shift and ran her fingers through her wet curls. She looked so different now she was clean – younger and sweeter. I suddenly imagined her in a proper frock and stockings and shiny shoes and saw she could easily be taken for a gentleman's daughter if she only chose to speak properly. Whereas I looked anything but, even though I was moderately clean again. I tried to arrange my own hair, but the last vestige of ringlets had disappeared. My hair hung long and lank to my shoulders, and I couldn't untangle it without a brush. I knew I looked awful in Kitty's stained torn frock. I sighed miserably as I tugged it this way and that, hating the coarse feel of it on my body, missing my soft clean petticoats.

'What's the matter? Have you got a pain?' Kitty asked.

I couldn't really tell her that I hated wearing her filthy ugly frock because it would sound so rude and ungrateful.

'I was just wishing that hateful woman had left me some petticoats,' I said. 'It feels very odd without them. And my feet are so sore now without boots.'

I stood on one leg like a heron and examined one. It was scratched badly, with several deeper cuts where I'd trodden on sharp stones.

'Oh dear, look! Are yours scratched too, Kitty?'

She shook her head and showed me. Her soles seemed as tough as leather, without a mark on them.

'I'm used to going barefoot,' she said. 'But I think we're going to have to get you some footwear. Don't want those cuts getting worse or you'll be hobbling.'

'But who will get them for me?' I said. 'I haven't got any money.'

'Don't you worry. I'll buy them for you,' said Kitty. 'I'll fetch us some money.'

'You've got some money?' I asked, astonished.

'I told you, it just needs fetching,' said Kitty.

She spoke with such conviction that I believed her.

'Really? Oh, I'd love some proper boots, and stockings too so they don't rub my feet. And drawers and petticoats. And maybe – maybe a frock too, so I can give you yours back? Just a cheap plain frock, it needn't have a lace trim and I can do without a pinafore,' I said. 'Will there be enough money for a frock, do you think?'

'I daresay, given time,' said Kitty. She put her arm round me. 'Don't worry, Lucy. Stick with me. I'll get you anything you want. But we must scarper now.'

She led us all the way back to the broken railings. I hated having to crawl through the hedge, getting my hands and knees filthy all over again, but it couldn't be helped. I had learned the trick of sliding through sideways now and squeezed through the narrow gap without too much trouble.

'That's the ticket,' said Kitty.

We straightened up and walked down the pavement together hand in hand. We turned into a narrow side road where there were many men in caps hurrying to a big factory. I was still damp and dishevelled, but no one paid me any attention whatsoever. This seemed very strange. When I went out for my walk with Miss Groan I was used to working men doffing their caps to me and moving respectfully to the side of the pavement. These men brushed past me without a second glance.

There were women in coarse clothing and aprons, but none of them bobbed their heads either. One of them impatiently gave me a shove towards the gutter.

'Out my way, you dozy little kid! Some of us have work to go to,' she snapped.

'How dare you push me like that!' I said indignantly.

She stared at me, and I thought for a moment she was going to raise her great red arm and give me a blow about the head – but then she cackled with laughter.

'You're a rum one!' she said. 'That voice! You sound like a real toff, you do!'

For a moment I wondered whether to catch hold of her and tell her that I was truly a little lady, and had been set upon by thieves. But then she might call a policeman or try to take me home myself. Was that what I wanted? I had enough sense to see that if I went home I'd never ever be allowed to see Kitty again. She was my true friend now. I'd never had a friend before. She was so brave, so lively, so full of fun – and she looked after me. I loved her only second to Nurse.

Kitty was looking at me, her eyes narrowed. It was almost as if she were reading my mind. I gave her a little reassuring smile and marched past the rude woman.

We walked on, Kitty and me, keeping step in our bare feet. We went down a very narrow street of shabby tenement houses huddled together, some so old they were propped up with great posts. There were lines strung between them and one woman was already hanging her washing on one. The clothes were almost as ragged as ours, but the tattered sheets were scrubbed white, though already gathering smuts from the factory chimney.

The washerwoman gave Kitty a nod. 'Haven't seen you round here for a bit, little 'un,' she said.

'Been on my travels,' said Kitty.

'Lost your frock, I see!'

'Lent it to my friend here,' said Kitty.

'I could give you my old one. Even if I cut it short it'll still swamp you, but it's better than nothing. You look a sad little scrap in that wispy shift,' said the washerwoman.

'That's truly kind, but I reckon the sadder I look today the better,' said Kitty mysteriously.

'Oh well. Suit yourself,' she said. 'I've got the kettle boiling on the hob indoors. Do you want a cup of char, you and your friend?'

'Yes please!' said Kitty. She nudged me.

'Yes please,' I said, though I had no idea what char was, and wasn't at all sure I'd like it.

'Make it yourselves then, while I get this washing sorted,' said the washerwoman.

Char turned out to be tea, very strong, with no milk or sugar, served in a chipped mug. I couldn't help shuddering when I swallowed, but it proved strangely refreshing and I felt fortified when I'd finished my mugful. Kitty shared hers with a little child of about two, holding her mug out

89

and helping him sip from it. I could see all too clearly that he was a little boy, because he only wore a shirt. There was a baby lying on a pile of rags in a washing basket, kicking its legs and sucking on an empty bottle.

'Why is it in a basket?' I whispered to Kitty.

'It's her little cot,' said Kitty.

'Oh, poor thing!' I exclaimed.

'She's happy as a bird in a nest,' said Kitty. 'Here, baby, let me fill your bottle for you.'

The baby had char too, weakened with cold water. It seemed an unlikely brew for such a small person, but the baby sucked on its bottle greedily. When it had finished Kitty picked it up and rubbed its back expertly.

'You're very good with little children, like a little nurse,' I said.

'I like minding them,' said Kitty. 'Gaffer says I'll make a fine mother in the future. But I'm not bothered. He's the only one I want to look after.'

'So where exactly is he now?' I asked.

'Told you. He's gone away,' Kitty mumbled.

'Ah, Kitty,' said the washerwoman, coming through the door with her empty basket. 'You're a brave little kid.'

'Ain't got no choice, have I?' said Kitty.

'You could always stay here for a bit. You could come in useful, minding my kiddies,' she said.

'Nah. I like to be on the move,' said Kitty. 'But thanks all the same.'

The washerwoman looked at me. 'She's a stubborn girl, your friend,' she said.

'She's been very kind to me,' I said.

The woman raised her eyebrows at my voice. 'What are the likes of you doing hanging round with Kitty?' she said. 'Haven't you got no home to go to?'

I shook my head. 'I just go where Kitty goes,' I said.

'Then you'll do all right,' she said. 'She knows what's what, does Kitty.'

'Well, we'd better get going now. Thanks for the char,' said Kitty.

She bent over the drawer and kissed the baby, and then went to kiss the little boy too. He chuckled and ran away behind the battered chair.

'I can see you,' said Kitty, peering over the top. 'Oh, he's having a tinkle on the floor!'

'Albert! Use the pot! How many times do I have to tell you?' his mother shouted.

Albert wasn't the only one needing to relieve himself.

'Do you think I might possibly pay a visit?' I asked, embarrassed.

They stared at me blankly.

'You know.' I lowered my voice. 'Use the facilities?'

The washerwoman laughed. 'Funny way of putting it! Yes dear, out the back. Show her, Kitty.'

There was a little hut at the end of the yard. It reeked horribly. It was even worse inside. I felt quite ill when I came out, wondering if I might actually faint, but Kitty dashed in and out without flinching.

'There now,' she said. 'Right, let's get some money, girl.'

7

Kitty led me down the lane, along another, and then suddenly we were out in a wide road with newly built villas and neat gardens. I stared in surprise.

'Nearly there,' she said.

'Is *this* where you keep your money, Kitty?' I asked.

She gave me an incredulous look and then laughed. 'Yes, course it is. This is my own house, that one there with the roses in the garden and the green painted door. Ain't it grand? All I have to do is go knock knock on that there door and my manservant opens it and says, "Welcome home, Lady Kitty. I guess you've come for some money." He'll go to this great big trunk in the middle of the drawing-room floor and inside there are all these gold sovereigns and he'll give me a handful and then off we go, to buy the finest frocks you ever did see,' she said in a rush, eyes sparkling.

'I know you're making it all up,' I said, a little huffily. 'I'm not stupid, you know.'

'Aren't you?' said Kitty. 'I don't know about that!'

'I wish you wouldn't keep teasing me. How do *I* know where you keep the money?'

'I ain't got no money yet! I've got to earn it,' said Kitty.

I tried hard to think of a way a small girl like Kitty could earn money.

'By minding children?' I asked.

'Respectable rich folk who live round here wouldn't want the likes of me minding their little boys and girls,' said Kitty.

'Then . . . will you work as a kitchenmaid?' I wondered, because our own kitchenmaid at home was young and always looked a little down at heel.

'I'm not thinking of paid employment,' said Kitty. 'I work for myself. Gaffer always says that way happiness lies. No bowing and scraping to any bosses.'

'So what sort of work?' I asked.

'I sing for my supper,' said Kitty. 'And my dinner and my breakfast!'

'What do you mean?'

'You'll see,' she said. 'It's too quiet up this end of the road. We'll go right down the busy end where the shops and offices are.' She thumped herself on the chest and coughed several times. 'Just clearing my throat in preparation!' she said.

I didn't like it at the busy end, where there were ladies bustling in and out of the shops, little maids scurrying after them, and gentlemen in top hats were strolling at a leisurely pace into their banks and coffee shops. I felt so conspicuous in my ragged frock. Some of the ladies swished their skirts aside in case they brushed against me, and a very unpleasant gentleman barged between Kitty and me, nearly knocking us over.

'Out of my way, little rats, I'm in a hurry!' he said, brandishing his walking cane.

Little rats! 'Did you hear what he called us?' I hissed, my eyes stinging.

Kitty stuck out her tongue at his back. 'If Gaffer were here he'd grab his stupid cane and whack him on the head with it,' she said.

'Can't we go somewhere quieter? I don't like it here. People stare at us,' I said, blinking hard to stop the tears rolling down my face.

'We need lots of people, Lucy. Don't take on so.' She looked at my miserable face. 'Tears are good though! Yes, start crying, looking as sad as possible.'

'What?'

'Just cry! It's not too difficult, you've been doing it on and off ever since we met,' said Kitty, a little too sharply.

I did start crying then at her tone, and she nodded in approval.

'Good girl. How long can you keep it up?' she asked.

'I cried all day and all night when Nurse went,' I said. 'My eyes were just little peeps because I'd made them so sore.'

'Well, cry for a while, but maybe not *too* much,' said Kitty. 'We need you to stay looking pretty.'

'I'm not pretty!' I said, astonished.

No one had ever called me pretty before. Nurse had called me her lovely girl, and her little darling, but I was sure she'd never mentioned my looks. Papa had sometimes peered at me and sighed, even when I was in my best clothes with my ringlets newly teased into place, so I assumed I was very plain. The New Mother was pretty, with her sparkling blue eyes and smooth dark hair and her womanly curves. Baby Angelique had big blue eyes too and hair like duckling fluff and rosy cheeks. How could *I* possibly be pretty when I looked so pale and wan?

'Of course you're pretty,' said Kitty. 'You look so . . . delicate.'

I wasn't too sure I wanted to be delicate, not in this new hurly-burly world where people elbowed you out of the way and called you unpleasant names. Still, I was aware Kitty was paying me a compliment.

'You look delicate too,' I said politely, although it wasn't true. Kitty was a small scrap of a child, with arms and legs like matchsticks, but there was a tough wiriness about her, and a defiant lift of her chin that showed you'd have to be brave to cross her.

'*Me?*' said Kitty, and she made a rude blowing noise with her lips that was anything but delicate. But then she grinned, pleased. 'I think that spot over there looks a good pitch,' she said, pointing to a big draper's shop with a lot of ladies bustling in and out of the open door. 'Now all we need is a container of some kind.'

She bent her head, peering along the gutter.

'Aha!' she said, pouncing on a tattered blue cone that had once held a pound of sugar. 'This will do.' She handed it to me. 'Don't look so bewildered!' she said. 'When the crowd gathers and I finish a couple of verses then just start offering the cone to people, and ask them if they can spare a penny for our poor mother at home what has got a dreadful disease.'

'But that's begging!' I protested.

It was Kitty's turn to look bewildered. 'Of course it's begging,' she said. 'How else are we going to get any money?'

'But begging is wrong,' I said. 'Nurse always said beggars were up to no good and should do a decent day's work instead of hassling honest folk.'

'Then your nurse was a heartless fool,' said Kitty. 'How else can you get by if so-called honest folk won't give you work?'

'How dare you call Nurse a fool!' I said, shocked to the core. 'I won't have you saying she was heartless either. She had the biggest heart ever.'

'Don't get so angry! Your face has gone all red now, and you need to look sickly pale. And you've stopped crying. Get them tears rolling again,' Kitty commanded.

'You can be as nasty to me as you like, but you're not to be horrid about Nurse,' I said. 'You wouldn't like it if I said such nasty things about your Gaffer person.'

'He'd always help out a beggar in dire straits if he had enough tin,' said Kitty. 'And if we didn't have enough tin ourselves then he'd beg for us so we could go to bed with full bellies.'

I was so startled that Kitty could use such a vulgar word as belly that it was hard to take in what she was saying. Did she really mean that her great and glorious Gaffer was actually a beggar man? And why did they want this tin?'

'What *is* tin?' I asked.

'Money, stupid! Don't you know anything?' said Kitty. 'And it's you whining for money for fancy clothes, not me! I'm doing this for you so you might at least be grateful.'

'Are we quarrelling?' I asked anxiously. 'You will still be my friend?'

'Of course I'm still your friend, pudding head!' said Kitty.

I swallowed this further insult. I decided there were new rules in this new life of mine, and if I stayed with Kitty I had to go along with them.

'So I just look sadder and ask people for a penny and hold out the cone?' I said.

'That's it,' said Kitty, looking relieved.

'But what if they say no?' I persisted.

'Then you look even sadder and move on to the next person. It couldn't be easier,' said Kitty. 'Just think about the new dress you'll get. What colour do you like best?'

'Blue.'

'Then we'll get you the finest blue dress ever, all frills and lace,' said Kitty.

'And one for you too!' I said. 'What's *your* favourite colour, Kitty?'

'Red!'

'I'm not quite sure you can get red dresses, not for little girls, but maybe we'll be lucky,' I said.

'Then we'll really look like Lady Kitty and Lady Lucy. But right now we're poor little beggar girls and our ma's dying of some dreadful disease – maybe folk will think you're ill too, because you've gone so pale and look so anxious. Let's start, eh?'

Kitty stood in the centre of the pavement, threw back her head and started singing. She had a high clear voice, surprisingly powerful for such a small girl. People stared in surprise. By the time she'd started the second verse of some old folk song about a lover and his lass a little crowd had gathered round her.

She caught my eye and nodded at the cone. So I swallowed hard and addressed the person nearest to me.

'I'm sorry to trouble you, madam, but I wonder if you could possibly give me a penny for my poor mamma?' I asked, and then realized I was using my usual voice.

I switched to Kitty-speak. 'Ma's got this dreadful disease, see, and we need to get the tin for the doctor,' I said.

'Oh, you sweet dear lasses – bless your little sister, singing her heart out for your poor mother!' said the woman, and she fumbled in her reticule and brought out *threepence*.

Nearly everyone put a coin in the cone. One gentleman donated sixpence – although another tossed in an old button, which I thought very underhand. Kitty went on singing. There were many verses, but she didn't pause when she got to the end. She started another song straightaway, and then another. I went on circulating round the growing crowd until an irate gentleman with a tape measure round his neck came stomping out of his shop.

'You girls stop this singing business at once and clear off!' he shouted. 'My customers can't get in and out my own premises. Be off with you!'

'Shame!' said the threepenny lady, who was still loitering. 'The poor little things are doing their best to get medical help for their sick mother.'

'You expect me to believe that old story!' said the draper. 'They're artful little liars, that's what they are. Maybe they're singing for their mother, but I'll bet it's for her gin, not medicine.'

The crowd started murmuring uneasily. Kitty went on singing but they weren't paying her any attention now.

'Oh, sir, how can you say such a thing!' I said, letting the tears pour down my face. 'If you could only see our dear ma, you'd understand. She's fading away before our very eyes. She can barely lift her head off the pillow. She needs a doctor so bad.'

The threepenny lady looked near tears herself. She patted me on the shoulder. 'I shall send for my own doctor, my dear, and we'll go to see your poor mother and do what we can,' she said firmly.

'Oh, thank you kindly, but you mustn't trouble yourself,' I said, looking round desperately for Kitty.

'No, I insist,' she said, taking hold of my arm. 'Does she live near here?'

'She lives far away. Please. You mustn't try to see her,' I gabbled.

'Ma would hate it if she knew we were begging,' said Kitty, coming to my rescue. 'It would upset her – it might even make her have another fit. Come along, Lucy, we must be getting back to her.'

She pulled me away violently, and a few coins spilled out of the cone. There wasn't time to try to pick them up. Kitty grabbed the cone from me, put one hand protectively over the top, and pulled at me with the other.

'Run!'

She didn't need to tell me twice. We both ran like the wind, elbowing our way through the crowd, rushing down the wide pavement, dodging here and there, crossing the road to get further away. Coach drivers shouted at us and horses whinnied, but Kitty was equal to them all, and steered me through the crowded traffic. Then we darted down an alleyway, and then another, through a maze of humble backstreets, until we had to lean against a greasy wall in an old tunnel to get our breath back.

'Do you think they're still following us?' I gasped.

'Nah, we've lost them good and proper. And we've still got our tin – well, most of it! Butterfingers!' said Kitty, clasping the cone to her chest.

'It wasn't my fault some spilled out. That lady grabbed hold of me,' I said.

'I know. You were clever with her too. Anyone would think you'd been on the streets all your life!' said Kitty. 'There, I told you begging was easy, didn't I?'

'But that shopkeeper shouted at us, and there was such a commotion, with everyone staring!' I said. 'It was so embarrassing!'

'Well, we got away, didn't we? And we got a lot of tin,' said Kitty, cautiously shaking the cone. 'We'll have a slap-up dinner.'

'I thought we were going to buy clothes?' I said.

'Well, we are. But we haven't got enough money *yet*, not if you want truly fancy togs,' said Kitty.

'I just want to look decent,' I said. 'And you badly need a frock too, Kitty. You can practically see through that shift.'

'It's a good look for begging,' said Kitty.

'But we can't go back there! The shopkeeper will get so angry. And what if that lady comes back and wants to see our mother?'

'Poor dear ma what has got a dreadful disease?' said Kitty, play-acting.

'Who hasn't long for this world, poor soul, and in such pain. A little medicine would help her so,' I said, joining in the game.

'And some fine grub too,' said Kitty. 'Fruit and buns and sugar plums!'

'And proper bedding with soft pillows and a clean coverlet,' I said, still stiff from my cramped night in the tree.

'How about a whole cottage where she can live in peace till the end of her days,' said Kitty. 'And then when she's gone, poor blessed soul, you and me can live there so cosy like, eh, Lucy?'

'Where *do* you live, Kitty?' I asked, stopping the game. 'You can't live in that park all the time?'

'I live here and there. Wherever I fancy. I can kip in any corner,' she said.

'What about when it rains?'

'I've got friends who'll let me sleep under their roofs. Though I like it best outside. Gaffer always says there's no finer bed than a haystack on a moonlit night,' she said, her voice wistful.

'But there aren't any haystacks round here,' I said. 'You only get haystacks in the country.'

'I know,' said Kitty, and she sighed.

The tunnel was so dark it was hard to make out her face but she sounded unhappy.

'Kitty . . .' I began. 'Is Gaffer living in the country now?'

'Nope.'

'So where *is* he then?' I asked.

'Somewhere in town,' she mumbled.

'Yes, but *where*?' I persisted.

'Not telling,' said Kitty. 'Now, let's count the money.'

She shook it carefully onto the ground, so that not a single coin rolled away. She might not have had any schooling but she was far quicker than me at adding up all the pennies and the odd threepence and sixpence and converting them into shillings.

'Two shillings and a penny ha'penny!' she said. 'That's not bad for half an hour's work! Well done, Lucy! It's your sad little face what's bringing in the tin. Hey, it's like a song, isn't it? *Bringing in the tin, Bringing in the tin, Let's both sing, We're bringing in the tin!*'

Kitty's silly song reminded me of all those little ditties Nurse used to make up.

Let's get little Miss Lucy washed
And then let's dress her too
Then we'll brush her pretty hair
Cock-a-doodle doo!

Nurse would throw her head back and crow like a cockerel, and I'd crow back even louder, and we'd create a rumpus in the nursery. I imagined crowing with Miss Groan but it was impossible. The New Mother would slap me for making such a racket. It was a joy to be rid of both of them! I didn't even think I missed Papa. He was away on business so often that he'd never really become part of my daily life. I never felt free to climb on his knee and kiss his cheek the way I did with Nurse.

I'd thought I loved him very much even so – but did he really love me back? Surely he should have recognized me in Kitty's ragged dress? Maybe I'd never ever go back home again, even when I had proper clothes.

'Is two shillings and a penny ha'penny enough for us to buy an outfit each?' I asked Kitty.

'Na, not if you want all your fancy *undergarments*. Not to mention boots. We've got to do a full week's begging to get enough tin for that, especially if I'm to get a frock too,' said Kitty.

'A whole week!' I said. 'But how can we? If you sing outside that draper's shop again he'll be so angry. He might even fetch a policeman!'

'We won't go back there, stupid. We'll find another place. And another and another. Keep moving on, that's Gaffer's motto.' She gave a sudden sniff. 'Though he can't do that now,' she muttered.

I suddenly understood. It seemed obvious now. Gaffer was dead. He was lying in his coffin in some lonely churchyard and Kitty was on her own now. She loved him so much she couldn't bear to admit that he was no longer alive. I knew I'd do that if I found out Nurse had died. The very idea was enough to make my heart beat faster.

'I'm sorry, Kitty,' I said softly, to show her that I understood. 'Yes, we'll find another place. We make a good team, you and I.'

8

I began to get used to begging. We wandered from one shopping street to another, right across town. We tried begging at omnibus stops too, but people were in too much of a hurry. Markets were the best place of all, because women had their purses out already to buy their bags of fruit and vegetables, but we had to take care not to obstruct any of the stalls.

One of the stall holders took a shine to us and gave us a rosy apple each, and then a wonderful bag of strawberries at the end of the day as a special thank you, because we'd attracted folk to his stall. If no one gave us food, we were free to help ourselves to the fruit that had tumbled into the gutter. We also bought half a dozen ha'penny currant buns from a baker's, and the shop lady there gave us seven instead of six. We ate three each and then broke the last bun in half and shared it.

I thought this new diet wonderfully exciting after endless bland nursery meals. I didn't even mind so much about not being able to bathe properly. I couldn't like wearing Kitty's dreadful frock, but I kept myself entertained imagining the outfit I'd choose when we had enough tin for proper clothing. Meanwhile, as Kitty said, our skimpy outfits were perfect for begging.

Kitty found a purse with a long silver chain lying by one of the rubbish bins.

'Aha!' she said, opening it eagerly, but it was empty.

'Why would someone throw a purse away? It looks quite new,' I said, fingering the soft leather.

'It was probably snatched off of some lady doing her shopping,' said Kitty. 'They took all her money and then tossed the purse.'

'Oh dear, the poor woman!' I said.

'But lucky us! Now we've got somewhere safe to store all our money,' said Kitty, tipping into it the contents of our makeshift cone. She pulled the silver chain over her head so that the bulging purse hung down her front like an unwieldy necklace. 'No one can snatch it off me!' she said.

'But you'll have to give it to me when you start singing,' I said.

'Yes, of course. Though you could take a turn singing for a change,' Kitty suggested.

'Me?'

'You've got a sweet voice. You're Lucy Lark, remember?'

'But I don't know any proper songs like you,' I said. 'I only know hymns.'

'What are they?' Kitty asked.

'You don't know what hymns are?' I said, astonished. 'They're songs about God that you sing on Sundays. Have you never been to church?'

'Na, Gaffer didn't think much of church folk – though we both liked the bells ringing. You try singing some of them hymns then, Lucy. We'll see if they're popular,' said Kitty.

'I'd much rather not,' I said, but she insisted I had a go.

'Fair's fair. I've been doing most of the work. My voice is going husky from all that warbling. Take a turn, girl,' she said.

So I tried, though I was so nervous I could hardly get the words out and sang so softly folk could scarcely hear.

'Sing up!' said Kitty, giving me a nudge.

So I sang louder, and once I'd got through a couple of hymns, I found I was quite enjoying myself. Kitty went round the crowd with the purse, telling them about our poor dear mother, and I chose the most mournful hymns I could think of. *Abide With Me* was the best of all for drawing a crowd. I deliberately made myself think of Nurse, and found the tears rolled down my cheeks.

'Oh, poor little mite!' people exclaimed, and handed Kitty so many coins she could scarcely fit them in the bulging purse.

'You've been brilliant, Lucy!' Kitty said at the end of the day. 'I think we've almost got enough tin now. Let's treat ourselves to a hot meal tonight, and then we'll go shopping tomorrow.'

We went to a fried fish shop and had a portion of cod each, and a newspaper full of chipped potatoes, all washed down with a bottle of lemonade. We ate our fill and then looked for a handy sleeping place. The park was some distance away, so this time Kitty led us up and down little streets until she spotted a derelict house at one end of a terrace, with broken windows and a door chalked with rude words.

'It's not exactly a mansion house, Lady Lucy, but I think we might be comfortable in here for the night,' Kitty said.

I wasn't so sure, but I wanted to show willing, so I tried to turn the door handle.

'Oh dear, I think it's locked,' I said.

'We'll try round the back,' said Kitty.

The back door was locked too, but someone had been there before us and smashed all the glass out of the window.

'So we'll go in this special little door,' said Kitty, standing on a couple of bricks and climbing up to the windowsill.

'But what if someone else is already in there?' I whispered. 'It could be some terrible old tramp.'

'Tramps are not terrible,' Kitty said sharply. 'Not true country tramps. I very much hope there *is* a tramp here, because he'll likely share his supper with us and be a good friend.'

I very much hoped there *wouldn't* be a tramp waiting there in the dank little house – and thank goodness, there didn't seem to be anyone there at all, though someone had left a few newspapers scattered on the floor and several empty bottles.

Then I heard rustling and clutched Kitty's hand, starting to tremble.

'Listen! Quick, let's climb out the window again! It *might* be a tramp!' I hissed.

'Well, it would have to be a very tiny tramp because there's no one here. Look around you!' said Kitty.

I could see the logic of what she was saying – but then the rustling came again.

'Aha!' said Kitty. She lifted one of the newspapers and there was a little brown mouse nibbling at the newsprint.

'A mouse!' I shrieked, standing on one leg.

'A very very little mouse who's trying to make herself a soft bed for the night. Don't scream like that, you'll frighten her!' Kitty scolded.

All the maids at home screamed their heads off if they ever saw a mouse scamper across the kitchen floor. Cook climbed onto her own scrubbed wooden table, gathering her long skirts up to her plump knees. She always yelled for Mr Barnaby the butler, and he'd come running with the broom as if going into battle.

But Kitty knelt down and spoke soothingly to the mouse, even stroking it very lightly. It twitched its nose, seeming to like the attention.

'There now,' she whispered to the mouse, as if it were her own little pet.

I calmed down, peering at it warily. It was starting to seem ridiculous to be scared of such a small creature.

'Do you think it's got any friends here?' I asked. I felt I could cope with just one mouse, but a whole tribe of them would be more than I could manage.

'I think she's all on her ownio,' said Kitty. 'Poor Trampy mousie. It's best to have a friend, isn't it, Lucy?'

'Yes it is,' I said.

I was especially glad to have a friend that night, because I was still scared someone would come climbing in the window after us. I clutched Kitty all night long for comfort. The bare floorboards were appallingly hard and the newspapers were inadequate bedcovers. I dozed fitfully and was wide awake at dawn.

I sat up and stared at Kitty. She looked so much younger when she was asleep, especially now, sucking her thumb. The little mouse was nestled up in the crook of her neck, fast asleep too.

I felt much less nervous now in the daylight. I plucked at the coarse material of my dress. It would be such a joy to change it for some new clothes today! I tried on different outfits in my head, experimenting with colours, but still favoured blue, with perhaps a little white lace at the neck, and white undersleeves too. But was white really practical for this new life of mine? It would get so grubby in a day or two. And *I* was dirty too. How could I go to a dressmaker and be measured for a new frock in such a state?

I breathed in sharply and Kitty opened her eyes instantly.

'What's the matter now?' she mumbled.

'I've just thought, Kitty. We have to have a bath before we visit the dressmaker!' I said urgently.

'What?' Kitty stretched and the mouse ran over her neck, making her laugh. 'Hey, little Trampy, you're tickling me!'

'We can't go and get measured for our clothes without clean undergarments. Without *any* undergarments!' I said.

'You and your blooming undergarments!' said Kitty. 'We're not going to no fancy dressmaker, noodle! We don't want to hang around for days waiting for our outfits. We can fit ourselves from top to toe down Monmouth Street. Best clothes in the whole of London town.'

'Well, I daresay, but I'd still so love to bathe properly!' I said. I held out my hands in front of me. They were filthy, with black rims under my nails.

Poor Nurse would have had a fit to see me in such a state. She insisted I had a proper steaming hot scrub once a week, the maids pouring jug after jug of boiling water into the tin bath. I turned as red as a lobster when I got in, and I hated being scrubbed with carbolic soap because it stung my eyes so – but it was heavenly lying back afterwards and daydreaming in the warm water while Nurse made up a story for me.

'I'd be so happy if only I could have a proper bath,' I muttered wistfully.

'You'll be the death of me, Lady Lucy, wanting this and wanting that,' said Kitty, but she sat up and cradled Trampy in her own dirty hands. 'I expect there'll be a pump in the back yard.'

'A pump?' I said doubtfully.

'I'll show you,' said Kitty, sighing. She set Trampy down on a piece of newspaper. 'Stay here, you. You're my little mousie now, all right?'

She managed to unbolt the back door so we didn't have to climb through the window again. There was a communal yard that stretched the whole length of the terrace. There was a reeking hut every five houses. Kitty didn't have to explain what they were used for because the smell made it obvious. There was just one pump for the row of thirty dwellings.

'There you are. Water for your bath, my lady,' said Kitty. She raised the arm of the pump and demonstrated how to make the gush of water.

'But how do we make it hot?' I asked.

'We don't,' said Kitty. 'Look, it's a summer's day – you don't need hot water! Heavens, some kind soul has even left you some soap!'

There was a greasy sliver of harsh yellow scrubbing soap balanced on a brick. I picked it up gingerly and managed to work up a lather. I washed my hands, my face, my neck, and my poor sore blistered feet. I wanted to wash the rest of me too, but I didn't dare take my frock off in case someone from the other houses came into the yard and saw me.

'Happy now? How about you work the pump for me so I can wash too?' Kitty suggested.

I couldn't pump as energetically as she did so the water came in trickles, but she didn't complain.

'There, I'm fresh as a daisy now,' she said, dancing round the yard.

She was still pretty dirty, but somehow in her little shift she really did look like a daisy, even though it was no longer white.

'If only we could wash our clothes too,' I said.

'They'll get washed when it rains,' said Kitty. 'Gaffer always said it was nature's way of giving us a bath.'

I was getting a little tired of hearing what Gaffer said, but I knew how much he meant to Kitty so I simply nodded politely.

'Now we'll fetch Trampy, go and have some breakfast, and then buy our new togs,' said Kitty.

I was sure Trampy would have run away, but she was still there, nibbling on the newspaper.

'She's hungry, poor little mite,' said Kitty. 'Don't you worry, we'll make sure you get breakfast too,' she whispered to the little mouse.

She tried to find a comfortable way of carrying Trampy, but she wasn't very good at balancing her on her shoulder. The reticule round her neck would make a perfect pouch, but it was too full of money. Kitty tried looping one end of her shift up to make a little hammock for her, but it came undone whenever she scrabbled.

'My dress has got a pocket,' she said. 'You'll have to carry her for now, Lucy.'

I wasn't at all keen. I didn't mind when Trampy was on Kitty, but I didn't want her scurrying all over me. Still, I didn't want to seem churlish, so I let Kitty put her in the pocket. It felt very weird at first when she darted this way and that, but thank goodness she soon settled down and went to sleep.

We stopped at a street stall for a mug of coffee and a buttered roll. I felt very grown up taking coffee, even though I disliked the taste intensely and had to put several spoonfuls of sugar in it to take away some of the bitterness. But it was warming too as the morning was quite fresh, and I still wasn't used to managing in such skimpy clothing. The buttered roll tasted wonderful however. I was only ever allowed a scraping of butter at home and a thin slice of bread with the crusts cut off. It was a joy to bite hard into the roll and taste the rich salty butter on the soft inside. I could have eaten two rolls, three, even four but knew we'd probably need every penny of our takings for these new clothes.

I made a list in my head of what I'd need on the very long walk to Monmouth Street. A shift was important, a soft muslin one with lace edging, and a liberty bodice acting as a junior corset. I needed drawers of course, preferably broderie anglaise, and two petticoats, a plain one to go underneath a fancy one to match my pantelettes. Then white stockings with a black stripe and kid boots as soft as possible so they wouldn't rub on my sore feet.

The dress was the most important item, of course. I settled on blue silk, with puffed sleeves and a lace trimmed collar, and a very full skirt that swished as I walked, and a pinafore over the top to keep it clean. I'd need a bonnet too, and a light pelisse to keep my shoulders warm on a cool day.

It would only be fair if Kitty had exactly the same, but in a different colour. She surely couldn't be serious about a red frock? She would look fetching in lilac, or a pretty pink, or maybe a pale green. And we must make sure her frock had a pocket for Trampy.

We seemed to be taking a positive age to reach this Monmouth Street.

'Perhaps we should take a ride on the omnibus?' I suggested, rubbing my poor feet. I had never been on one before because my family considered it a vulgar way to travel, cramming into such a small space with a lot of total strangers – but I thought it looked tremendous fun. 'It surely wouldn't cost too much, and your purse is brimful with coins,' I added.

'They wouldn't let us on, even if we brandished gold sovereigns,' said Kitty.

115

I thought she was talking nonsense, but when I tried to board one the driver flicked his hand at me dismissively and told me to clear off.

'But I have the money for the fare, and so does my friend,' I insisted.

'I'm not having little ragamuffins on my bus, you'll upset all my other customers. They'll fear they'll catch something off of you. So get off that step or I'll push you off,' he threatened.

Kitty pulled me away. My face was burning.

'How dare that man talk to me like that!' I said.

'I told you,' said Kitty. 'Don't take on so. It's not too far now, I'm sure.'

'What do you mean? *Aren't* you sure?' I asked.

'Well, it's Seven Dials way, and I've been there before. There's a bird market and it made me sad because birds should all be free to fly.' Kitty put her arms out and swooped about the pavement, pretending to be a bird.

'Don't you fly away, Kitty Swift,' I said. 'Else I might have to keep you in a cage.'

'You're the one who might fly away,' said Kitty. She was dancing lopsidedly now, one foot on the pavement, one in the gutter, stepping on stones without wincing because her hard blackened soles were as tough as boots.

'What do you mean?'

She looked suddenly serious. 'I'm no fool. Once you get proper togs again, fancy frock and bonnet and boots, you'll fly straight back home, won't you?' she said. 'Your wretched papa will recognize you this time and welcome his little lost daughter back with open arms. There will be such celebrations! It will be "Hello Lucy, Goodbye Kitty".'

'I'm not going back,' I said firmly. 'I don't think Papa has ever cared for me, not properly. The New Mother certainly doesn't. Miss Groan openly admitted I was the trial of her life. Why would I want to go back? I want to go forward, with you. Once I get some proper clothes and some shoes we can set off together, you and me. We're going to go to Sussex and find Nurse.'

'Oh, Lucy! I do hope you do stay with me! It's like we're sisters now, though you're rich and I'm poor. But I can't go to the country, Lucy. I have to stay somewheres in London all the time,' said Kitty. 'So's I can be near Gaffer.'

'About Gaffer . . .' I started delicately. 'I take it you can't actually *be* with him?'

Kitty pressed her lips together. She shook her head.

'Is it because . . . ?' I couldn't quite say the words.

'I don't want to talk about it,' Kitty muttered.

We walked on together, neither of us saying anything. I thought I understood. She wanted to stay near his grave. I wondered if she'd ever show me where it was. Perhaps one day she'd feel able to leave him. And *then* we could go to Sussex and search for Nurse.

9

Monmouth Street wasn't at all how I'd expected. I'd imagined a couple of drapers' with neat window displays and smart staff in black dresses and white aprons. *Every* shop here sold clothes, the windows crammed full, with stalls in front of the stores with further clothes laid out like whiting on a fish stall. They were mostly garish colours and designs, the kind that would make Miss Groan wince. Some were grubby with hanging hems. Some had obvious stains down the front. A few were almost as ragged as the frock I was wearing.

'But these aren't new!' I wailed.

'Yes, but you can find some fine stuff in amongst the rags,' said Kitty.

'But it's all second-hand. Or third- or fourth-hand, judging by the condition! I could never wear another person's clothes!' I declared.

'For pity's sake, ain't you wearing *my* frock?' Kitty asked impatiently.

I blushed at my lack of tact. 'I'm sorry, Kitty. I didn't think. I just meant I couldn't wear a *stranger's* clothes.'

'Well, make out you know them then.' She picked up a limp checked garment with a split seam. 'Hello, little frock. Who used to wear you? Oh my, a Miss Proud-Girl with pots of money, is that right? Only she ran away and didn't have a kind friend to look after her, so she had to sell you for sixpence to stop herself starving!'

'All right, you don't have to carry on like that. I get your point,' I said, shame-faced.

'Anyway, they don't keep their best clothes out on the stalls, in case they get stolen. They have all the fancy stuff inside, where they can keep an eye on them. Hey, you might even find your *own* clothes, Lucy, and then we can buy them back!' said Kitty.

'So you think that horrible old woman stole them from me in that alley and then sold them to someone else?' I said.

'Well, what else would she do with them? She couldn't squeeze into them herself, could she?' said Kitty.

119

'I know that – but I thought she might want them for her granddaughter,' I said.

'Oh, Lucy, you're a comic, you are!' said Kitty. She took my hand. 'Come on, let's size up all the shops, see if there's one that takes your ladyship's fancy.'

We found a better one right at the end of the street, with a display of children's clothing in the window. There were several small jackets with full sets of brass buttons, some nankeen trousers, and an assortment of frocks in checks and floral patterns, a little washed-out but in reasonable condition. A row of button boots were lined up two by two as if about to set off on a march. In pride of place there was a beautiful lace christening robe with a matching soft little bonnet tied with long ribbons. It looked brand-new.

'Oh my goodness, do you suppose the baby died before it could even be christened?' I said. 'How terrible!' I imagined little Angelique sickening and dying in her cot, and felt a surprising pang of sisterly grief.

'Buck up, Lucy! Let's go inside and see what they've got tucked away,' said Kitty.

There was an old crone sitting in a rocking chair inside the shop. She appeared to be sound asleep, her bonnet pushed sideways so that she seemed to have only half a face. But at the sound of our footsteps her one visible eye opened, her shaky old hands adjusted her bonnet, and she sat up straight, scowling at us.

'Shoo, you little varmints!' she said.

'That's a fine way to treat your customers!' said Kitty, tossing her head.

'You ain't got enough money to buy the scrapings from under my fingernails!' the old woman snapped, rocking her chair vigorously. 'Out! And woe betide you if you try to snatch anything!' She reached for a stout stick nearby and tapped it hard on the floor, making me jump and take two steps backwards.

Kitty was undeterred. 'What's this then,' she said, tapping the reticule round her neck so that the coins jingled together. 'Tinny tinny tin! So could you please stir yourself and show me and my companion your finest frocks because we was robbed of our own clothing, see.'

'A likely story,' said the crone. 'Show us that tin then. How do I know it's genuine?'

Kitty unhooked the reticule from her neck and brought out a handful of pennies and a silver sixpence. The old woman took the sixpence and put it in her mouth. I stared in astonishment, thinking she was *eating* it, but she was biting it to see if it was real.

'Hmm,' she said, nodding her head, and then went to slip it in her apron pocket.

'Hey, we haven't made a purchase yet! Give that back, if you please,' said Kitty.

'No flies on you,' said the old woman and gave the sixpence back, glistening with her saliva.

Kitty popped it back with the rest of our funds without grimacing. 'So are *these* the finest togs you can offer?' she said, running her fingers along the limp frocks hanging from a clothes rail. 'Don't think much of them, do we, Lady Lucy?'

It was hard to see them properly in the shadowy shop, but they certainly didn't look very promising.

'I don't suppose you have any silk dresses, preferably in blue?' I asked.

'And red? Scarlet or crimson, I'm not fussy,' Kitty added.

'Silk, eh? You're a pair of droll little madams,' said the crone, huffing and puffing as she eased herself out of her rocking chair. She shuffled to a large wardrobe right at the back of the shop and opened it up.

I peered at the frocks hanging inside, feeling the materials. Several did seem to be silk, but they were ladies' frocks, far too big for me, and rather too fancy too. There *was* a blue one, but it was very immodest, tremendously low cut at the front. I didn't possess a bosom to fill it out, so it would show me all the way down to my belly.

'Could you maybe cut it down to your size and sew it so it fitted?' Kitty asked.

'I'm afraid I've always been a total duffer at needlework,' I said truthfully.

'Gaffer was always very nimble with his fingers. He could sew a treat – but he never learned me how,' said Kitty. She turned to the old woman. 'Could *you* alter the frock so it fits my friend?'

'With these hands?' she replied, waving her crooked fingers in the air. 'I sells frocks, I don't sew them. Can't sew on a blooming button nowadays. Now, let me see. It was blue you was wanting, wasn't it?'

'And red,' said Kitty.

'Well, I've got blue,' said the old woman, rummaging in another closet. 'Here, girlie, the prettiest little frock in the whole shop, and I reckon it'll fit you perfectly. Not silk, but it's the finest cotton, and a lot more practical.'

I stared at the frock, shivers running up and down my arms. I knew that material. It was a soft sky blue, patterned with small sprigs of white flowers. I had lain my head against that sweet cotton countless times. I had sometimes pretended my fingers were fairies dancing round and round each flower. Nurse had a dress made of that exact material.

I held the frock to my face, breathing in deeply. It didn't smell like Nurse's wonderful warm toastiness, because it wasn't her *actual* frock, just a tiny replica made for a little girl, but it was still greatly comforting. It looked just about the right size for me too. It wasn't silk, it wasn't grand, it was a simple summer dress without a single frill or scrap of lace. The New Mother and Miss Groan would think it a frock far below my station, but I wanted it more than anything in the world.

'I absolutely love this dress!' I declared. 'I must have it!'

I looked at Kitty hopefully. She was frowning at me.

'Oh dear, do you think it's too expensive?' I asked.

'It will be now, as you've shown her how much you want it!' Kitty hissed.

The old woman was smiling and rubbing her hands together. 'Of course your little friend wants it! She has taste. She's fallen for the most special frock in my establishment, and who can blame her,' she said. 'Ten bob and she can have it – with a petticoat thrown in. An absolute bargain!'

'*Ten bob?*' said Kitty. 'Are you crazed in the head? Come on, Lucy, we'll go somewhere else.' She took my hand and pulled me towards the door.

'What *is* ten bob?' I said, confused by the term. 'Ten pennies?'

'Ten whole shillings,' said Kitty. 'It would use up practically all our money – and it's just a cheap country dress not worth a single bob.'

She had us outside the door by now, though I was looking back longingly.

'I do like it so, though. Can't we ask her to save it until we have enough of these bobs?' I said.

'You can have it now, you noodle, if you act like you don't want it,' Kitty muttered. 'Come on, quick march, look like you're disgusted. Then she'll come running after us.'

I tried to do as she said, bewildered. We went out of the shop and walked back down the road.

'She's not coming!' I said, peering round.

'You wait. And don't look back!'

So I went on walking – and sure enough, we heard tottering footsteps behind us.

'Oy, you two. Don't go so fast – I can't keep up! I'm only a poor old woman, not too steady on her pins. Come back and I'll see if I can make some kind of reduction, seeing as you're two sad kiddies with scarcely a stitch on your backs. I bore eight children and I've still got a mother's heart,' she said.

'No, my friend's just spotted something better in this shop here,' said Kitty, winking at me.

We played this charade for a while, but eventually let the mother's heart beat faster by accompanying her back to her shop. She held the blue frock against me and my own heart swelled at the sight of myself in her cracked looking glass.

Kitty beat her down to half a crown, two shillings and sixpence, and that was with the offered petticoat and a pair of drawers too.

'Because my friend needs undergarments, don't she?' she said.

I needed stockings and boots too, because my feet were so sore now they stabbed me at every step. I wanted fancy stripes and kid boots, but I could see they were an extra expense, and realized that kid boots wouldn't last long if Kitty and I went walking so much. I settled for rather ugly black boots that were a little too big for me, but very stout with good soles scarcely worn down. I chose a thick pair of grey socks that filled up the space in the boots.

Kitty bargained hard for these too, knocking the old woman down to a shilling for the boots and tuppence for the socks – and there I was, kitted out for three shillings eight pennies, which really did seem a bargain.

'Try them all on first,' said Kitty. 'Make sure they all fit proper and aren't falling apart.'

'You cheeky madam, my clothes are all the finest quality,' said the old woman, but she seemed to have grudging respect for Kitty now. 'You've got an old head on those skinny little shoulders.'

I stepped out of Kitty's ragged dress, peeping inside the pocket. Trampy was curled up, nose twitching, wondering what was going on. I put the dress on the floor, folding it over so that she couldn't climb out. Kitty nodded at me approvingly. She nodded even more when I'd put on all my new clothes and tied the laces on my boots.

'There now! You look a picture, Lucy,' she said.

I peered in the old looking glass. I didn't really look like me any more, prim little Lady Lucy in all my many fine garments. I didn't look like a street urchin either in poor Kitty's wretched frock. I looked a whole new person, cherished and respectable, like a little granddaughter for Nurse.

Kitty handed over the money, counting it out carefully penny by penny. There seemed quite a lot left in the reticule.

'Now it's your turn, Kitty,' I said.

'Na, let's save the rest of the tin. I'll just have my own frock back,' she said.

'But it's all dirty and torn,' I said. 'And it's such a dull colour.'

'I like it,' said Kitty, her chin up.

Perhaps it was because Gaffer had bought it for her. 'Well, I'm sure it was a lovely rich colour once upon a time.' I thought of my paint box at home. 'Burnt umber!'

'I've never burnt it,' said Kitty, who clearly wasn't familiar with paint colours. 'And I don't mind that it's a bit faded now.'

'But I thought you said you'd like something red?' I said.

'Red!' said the old woman, folding her arms. 'I could find you a saucy scarlet number easy as winking, but it's not for the likes of you, little girl. Shame you're not a boy – I've got a trunkful of clothes from a theatre troupe what went bust, and there was a fetching crimson number from a boy acrobat.'

'An acrobat's outfit?' said Kitty, suddenly eager. 'Oh, I've seen tumblers performing! They were wonderful. Can I see it?'

'But it's for a *boy*, with little trousers,' said the old woman.

'Let me see them, please!' said Kitty, clasping her hands pleadingly, forgetting all her advice to me not to sound too eager.

The old woman went to a big trunk in a corner and undid the clasps with much huffing and puffing. Then she drew out the most marvellous garments in rich scarlet and gold and Prussian blue, and several white muslin frocks with very short flimsy skirts.

'Oh, they're like fairy dresses!' I said, but Kitty wasn't interested.

She waited, watching intently, until the old woman found a small crimson velvet number. There was a little jacket edged with gold braid, and matching trousers, very short and puffy, rather like bloomers. And there was a cap too, with a gold tassel.

'Oh!' Kitty said softly. And then again, 'Oh!'

'But they're boys' clothes, Kitty,' I said.

'I don't care,' said Kitty. 'How much are they?'

'Well, this is quality velvet, scarcely worn. And the outfit is beautifully cut, smart but so soft,' the old woman crooned, rubbing the jacket against her cheek. 'And fancy having the little cap to set it all off! Look, it's even got a silk lining! Finest theatrical clothes always fetch a high price because of their quality. Made to last years, they are. I reckon I could get fifteen bob for this little number.'

'You're out of your mind,' said Kitty, regaining her common sense. 'Fifteen bob for used theatricals! Na, come on, Lucy, let's go. I wouldn't pay fifteen bob if they was sewn with gold thread and studded with rubies.'

'Do you think I'm falling for that trick again? You can prance out of here if you like, but I'm not following you this time. Twelve bob – and that's my final offer. Take it or leave it,' said the old woman.

They faced each other, both of them breathing heavily.

'We ain't got twelve bob,' said Kitty. 'You know that.'

'Then clear off and come back when you've got it,' the old woman replied. 'I daresay you've got ways and means. Steal another couple of purses.'

'I'm not a thief!' Kitty said angrily. 'We earn our tin honestly, don't we, Lucy?'

'Yes, of course we do,' I said, anxiously thinking of the sad stories we'd told about our dead mother when we were begging. Were they lies? Both our mothers *were* dead, after all. I tried to remember all ten of the Commandments in the Bible, checking whether lying was amongst them. I didn't think so. But I remembered the strange command not to covet my neighbour's ox or ass. Kitty didn't have any neighbours – but was coveting a shopkeeper's acrobat outfit vaguely similar?

Perhaps we were both destined to go to Hell? Why on earth did Kitty want the acrobat clothes so much anyway? Why wouldn't she settle for a nice plain frock like mine? Then we'd pay another three shillings and eight pence for undergarments and boots, and we'd both be fully kitted out and a matching pair.

I looked at her face, sharp with longing. I couldn't bear it. I went up to the old woman and took her hand. 'Couldn't you find it in your heart to reduce your price a little?' I said. 'My poor little sister used to have a red velvet cloak that could have been cut out of the very same cloth as this acrobatic outfit. Our mother sewed it specially for her because she loved the Little Red Riding Hood story so much. It was her dearest possession. When our dear mother died of a fever Kitty wore her cloak all the time, even when we went to bed. Then we had to run away from home because our father took to drink in his grief, and a wicked woman stole all our clothes from us. We have had to beg on the streets and eat scraps and now we have earned just enough money to clothe ourselves decently. You can guess why Kitty wants something red. Please, dearest madam, take pity on us.'

She had remained stony-faced inside her bonnet until the last sentence of my speech – but she softened in surprise when I addressed her as 'madam'.

'Five bob,' she said huskily.

'Thank you so so so much,' I said. I reached into the reticule and scooped out nearly all the cash. I had to squat on the floor to count it out in five rows of twelve pennies, trying to be quick before she changed her mind. Kitty looked stunned. Then she opened her mouth. I guessed she might argue and try to get the price down further – and I could see that the old woman had reached her limit.

'Hush now, dear,' I said warningly. 'Put your little outfit on.'

Kitty stuck her skinny arms into the jacket. It fitted her perfectly. She pulled the bloomers up her legs, tucking her shift neatly inside. She looked like a real acrobat – and when she put the cap on top of her curls I couldn't help clapping.

'Oh, Kitty, you look splendid!' I said.

Kitty peered at herself in the looking glass, and grinned from ear to ear. 'I do, don't I!' she declared.

The old woman folded her arms and looked at Kitty, her head on one side. 'Well, it ain't an outfit you could wear in church of a Sunday, but I must admit it suits you down to the ground,' said the old woman.

'But don't you need coverings on your legs, Kitty?' I asked.

'Nah, I've got brown skin, that's covering enough,' she said.

'And boots, for when it gets colder?' I suggested.

'I hate boots, they just rubs my toes and heels,' said Kitty.

The old woman was rummaging in a box of black kid slippers. 'Try these,' she said, selecting the smallest pair.

They were an exact fit and so light that Kitty danced around the room. 'They're perfick!' she declared.

She unclasped the reticule for the last of the money, but the old woman shook her head.

'You'll think I've gone soft as butter, but have them on me, kiddy,' she said. 'Now scram!'

We thanked her and scrammed obediently. We got to the other end of Monmouth Street when Kitty stopped dead.

'My old frock!' she said.

We rushed back and dived into the shop again. The old woman was back in her rocking chair, her bonnet askew. Her eye opened.

'Not you two again! You ain't having any more out of me!'

'No, no, madam, and we're extremely sorry to trouble you all over again, but my friend just wants her old frock back, that one I was wearing,' I said.

'What?' she said impatiently. 'Oh, for pity's sake! Look, it's over there!' She gestured to a big box labelled *Penny rags*.

'The cheek of it! My dress ain't a *rag*!'

'Shush, Kitty,' I hissed, worried the old woman might change her mind and demand more money for her outfit. 'Just take your dress and we'll be off.'

Kitty rummaged in the box, up to her elbows in old rags.

'What's the matter? It's there, right at the top, can't you see?' I said.

'I can see my frock – but the pocket's empty!' said Kitty, burrowing further.

'Oh!' I gasped, getting her meaning.

'What do you mean, the pocket's empty?' said the old woman. 'What was in it then? More tin? Are you accusing me of stealing off of you?'

'No, of course not, madam. There was no money in the pocket, I promise you,' I said.

'So what *was* in it, might I ask?' she said, squinting at me.

I had a very strong feeling she wouldn't like it if I told her the truth.

'Just her pocket handkerchief. Very ragged, and not even worth a penny, but she needs it because her nose keeps running,' I blurted out.

Kitty looked furious. 'No it don't!' she protested, but then she made a sudden pounce. 'Got you!' she said.

'What's she got?' the old woman asked, heaving herself out of her rocking chair suspiciously.

Kitty had her hand on the waistband of her red velvet bloomers. Then she wriggled.

'My handkin,' she said. 'Right, we'll be off now.' She clutched her brown frock and hurried to the shop doorway, adjusting her bloomers, giggling as if she were being tickled.

'Once again, thank you for your kindness, madam,' I said, and hurried after her.

We made it all the way down Monmouth Street this time, and then dodged down an alleyway so Kitty could rescue Trampy from inside her bloomers.

'There now!' she said, stroking her. 'I think you need a little treat after all your adventures.'

She popped her in the pocket of her brown frock, folded it carefully into an envelope shape and then wore it on her hands like a muff. It slightly spoilt the effect of her outfit but she still cut a very dashing figure. People turned and stared at her, smiling. Kitty walked a little stiffly at first, not used to wearing slippers, but she soon got used to them.

We went to a baker's shop around the corner and spent our last coins on a big bacon pie and an apple turnover for dessert. I carried them carefully in a paper bag until we found a little park. We sat on a seat in our new finery and shared our picnic, feeding Trampy little titbits. There was a drinking fountain nearby so we could quench our thirst. Kitty held Trampy so that she could drink too.

'That's what I call a good meal!' said Kitty, rubbing her tummy.

'But we've spent all our money,' I said.

'We'll earn heaps more!' said Kitty. 'We can both sing – and *I* can work up a little tumbling act. Watch!'

She gave me Trampy and demonstrated on the grass, turning several somersaults and then standing on her head, waggling her legs. She'd have looked indecent if she'd chosen a dress from the old woman, but she looked just like a little circus boy in her red velvet outfit. Several strolling couples smiled appreciatively and one gentleman actually threw a penny into the rolled-up dress, thinking it was a begging bowl. I had a quick peep at Trampy, but luckily it hadn't stunned her.

'Shall we try begging properly now?' I suggested. 'I could try singing something jolly while you tumble.'

I thought hard, going over words in my head.

'See the little tumbling boy
Round and round he goes
Like a little spinning toy
Till he falls on his nose!'

'Is that a proper song?' Kitty asked, looking astonished.

'No, I just made it up,' I said.

'How do you do that?' Kitty frowned, her face screwed up with effort. She thought for a couple of minutes and then gave up. '*I* can't do it.'

I couldn't help smirking.

'Still, I don't like that bit when I fall on my nose. I never fall over,' said Kitty, trying to put me in my place.

'Yes, but that's just the first verse,' I assured her.

'There's *more*?'

I knew there had to be now. I thought quickly.

'He blows his nose without a care
And wipes his velvet vest
Then does a handstand in the air
To give his feet a rest!'

'You're really making this up, just like that?' Kitty asked.

'There's a bit more coming,' I said. 'Aha!

'Throw a coin for the tumbling boy
And he'll waggle and wave his feet
It will give our boy the greatest joy
And also a bite to eat.'

'Oh, Lucy, you're a magician!' said Kitty. 'Sing it again, so I can practise.'

'I'm not sure I can remember it all!' I said, but I did my best.

Kitty circled me, tumbling over and over, pretending to fall, and then walking round on her hands, waggling and waving for all she was worth. By the fourth run-through we had the whole little item off by heart and a crowd had gathered round us, clapping and cheering and throwing coins.

'Looks like we're going to make our fortune, Lucy!' said Kitty.

10

We refreshed ourselves with hokey-pokey bought from a stall in the park. I'd always longed to try this iced cream, but Miss Groan had paled at the thought of my eating out of doors, and even Nurse said it was only for common children. Well, I was common now, and when I took the first delicious milky mouthful I was very glad of it.

'Oh, Kitty, that was so wonderful,' I said, when I'd finished. 'I could eat it all over again!'

'Then let's,' said Kitty, and she bought two more scoops. It was strawberry flavour this time, and even tastier.

Miss Groan and Nurse would both say I'd get a stomach ache for being so greedy, but it didn't hurt at all, it just felt blissful. We did ten turns of the tumbling boy until the reticule jangled with tin and then we went for further refreshments at the park cafeteria.

We knew we could scavenge in the wastepaper bins and find discarded sandwiches and pies and cakes for nothing, but it felt very grand to go right into the cafeteria and order for ourselves. We had two freshly cut sandwiches, ham and cheese, and a plum tart and a ginger parkin, and a drink of lemonade each, served in a proper glass. The woman behind the counter had been watching us earlier and seemed almost in awe of us.

'Are you theatre folk or from a circus, girls?' she asked as she served us.

'We are professional performers and prefer doing our show in the open air,' said Kitty grandly.

'Well, you're both very talented little girls. So where are your parents, then? They must be very proud of you,' she said.

'Oh, they are, madam. They call us their own dear little sugar plums and make such a fuss of us,' I said.

'And quite right too,' she said. 'Well, eat up your meal quickly, girls, because the park will be closing in ten minutes.'

We had no trouble wolfing everything down, surreptitiously sharing our feast with Trampy whenever the cafeteria woman turned her back on us.

When we went outside it had started to rain. It was only a light drizzle, but it came as a shock. We had had such glorious fine weather all week that we had forgotten the possibility of rain.

'Oh lordie, do you think it will spoil my velvet?' said Kitty, and she seized a discarded newspaper from a bench and wrapped it round herself like a cloak. She gazed into the distance, peering at every clump of trees. 'I can't see any big oaks. These trees are all too little and spindly to offer any protection.'

'Can't we go indoors somewhere again?' I said, clutching my clean blue dress. 'I don't want to get my frock dirty.'

'Aha!' said Kitty, staring at something on the horizon. 'I know where we can go!'

I stared at the silhouetted dark buildings, the tall chimneys of a factory, the fancy domes of the gin palaces and a solitary church spire. I couldn't see anywhere that promised safety and shelter, but Kitty was smiling now.

'You'll see!'

We went out of the park and walked along with the crowds hurrying home. Kitty stopped outside one of the taverns, which was already crowded.

'Oh, Kitty, we can't go in there!' I said, seeing the red-faced men and the rude women shrieking with laughter.

'We're not going to,' said Kitty. 'I'm simply taking my slippers off, as they're stopping me wiggling my toes.

'That's a relief. Only bad people go in gin palaces,' I said primly.

'We're *good* people,' said Kitty. 'We're going to church.'

I stared at her.

'Church? You mean, *pray* to find a place to stay?'

'No, you noodle! We'll stay in the church itself,' said Kitty.

'But we can't! It's not allowed! You only go to church if there's a service,' I said. 'We'll get into so much trouble. Churches are holy places.'

'Well, we'll *be* holy. You can sing one of them hymns,' said Kitty. 'Come on, my newspaper's getting soggy.'

We ran through the streets, Kitty clutching her old frock to her chest. Poor Trampy must have been bounced head over heels inside the pocket, but we didn't hear a squeak from her.

We slowed down when we got to the church and opened the old-fashioned gate. We sidled up the path, peering left and right at the gravestones. Kitty looked very solemn. I wondered if she was thinking of Gaffer. Perhaps this was the very graveyard where Gaffer was buried? I put my arm round her and she stared in surprise, but smiled at me.

She didn't stop short at any of the graves and start weeping. She simply patted all the ones she passed, as if she were greeting them, so I copied her.

The church door was closed. I tried the large iron door handle but it wouldn't move.

'Oh dear! It must be locked. We can't go in after all!' I said.

But Kitty gave me her frock to hold, took the large iron handle with both hands, twisted it round with all her strength, and pushed hard. The door creaked open.

'Aha!' she whispered triumphantly. She put her finger to her lips and then crept inside.

I followed her cautiously into the dark silent church. The fading light cast red and yellow and blue patterns on the stone floor but the rows of wooden pews were very shadowy. I peered hard, trying to see if anyone was still sitting there. I was very conscious of my boots squeaking as I advanced up the aisle. There was a large statue of Mary holding baby Jesus beside a marble pillar. Her head was on one side, as if she were looking at me.

I bobbed a little curtsy to her and then scuttled further up the church to the altar. I bowed my head to the cross and mumbled, 'Hello, Our Father which art in Heaven, I do hope you don't mind us being in your House.'

'What?' Kitty asked.

'I'm being polite,' I hissed. 'And keep your voice down. The vicar might still be here.'

'Where?'

'Maybe round the corner, in the little private bit where he puts his robes on,' I said.

We tiptoed cautiously forward. There was no sign of the vicar, but his special cape and long dress were hanging up neatly on two pegs, and his copy of the Bible was lying on top of a small cabinet. Kitty stroked the fine black leather and the ornate silver clasp and opened it up carefully. She squinted at the words at the beginning of Genesis.

'In the beg-ging God creted the haven and the eth,' she said, wrinkling her nose with effort. Then she went on more fluently, 'And he said I've creted this church for

140

any little girls who want to stay there. And Kitty and Lucy are especially welcome.'

'That's good!' I said.

Kitty was poking in a cupboard now. 'Oh my!' she said, bringing out a bottle of wine. 'The vicar is a secret drinker, naughty man.'

'No, I think that's special communion wine, Kitty,' I corrected her.

'Shall we have some?' said Kitty, fingering the cork.

'No! We absolutely must not! We're not allowed to drink any kind of wine, *especially* church wine. I daresay we'd be struck down dead if we took so much as a sip,' I declared.

'Nonsense,' said Kitty. 'It's already opened. Watch!'

She eased the cork out and tilted the bottle. I thought she was just teasing me, but she put her lips to the end of the bottle and drank.

'*Kitty!*'

She spluttered, wine dribbling down her chin. 'Now look what you made me do! My stars, I haven't splashed my jacket, have I?' She checked to make sure.

'It would be God's punishment if you had!' I said, shocked. 'You mustn't drink any more!'

'It didn't taste nice anyway,' said Kitty, shuddering. She recorked the bottle and thrust it back in the cupboard.

She wandered back into the church and tried lying on a pew.

'They're not very comfy,' she said. 'But I like these little cushion things – they'll be good for pillows.'

'They're for when you pray. You kneel on them,' I said. 'Only Nurse used to say her swollen old knees needed a cushion each.' I suddenly bent over, clutching myself.

'What's the matter?' Kitty asked. 'Have you got a stomach ache?'

'No, I just miss Nurse so much,' I mumbled.

'I know that feeling,' said Kitty, and she came and put her arms round me. 'I miss Gaffer that way.'

We held each other tightly for a moment.

'But now we have each other,' I said.

'That's right,' said Kitty. 'And we look after each other, don't we? You've even written me my very own song.'

I started singing it to cheer us up, and Kitty turned somersaults all the way up the aisle and back. I hoped God wouldn't mind too much.

Then we wandered up and down the pews, wondering which one to sleep on.

'Look!' Kitty shouted suddenly, making me jump.

'You mustn't shout in church! What is it?'

'Someone's left their shawl behind! It's slipped down in the shadow under the pew. Oh, it's so soft and lovely, look!'

It was the finest quality paisley cashmere, the sort of shawl the New Mother would wear. Kitty wound it round her shoulders. It looked a little strange over her red acrobat outfit, her skinny bare legs sticking out below, but Kitty seemed very pleased with herself.

'I'm Lady Kitty wearing my best shawl!' she said, stepping out grandly. 'You can be my little servant girl

Lucy, and must do everything I say. Oh, this will be a good game!'

I wasn't so sure about that, but I let her boss me about for five minutes or so. Then she let me have a turn at being Lady Lucy while she grovelled and scraped – and then we were *two* ladies, and I rocked the shawl in my arms, pretending I was showing my new baby to my friend.

'I have a real baby sister at home. She's called Angelique,' I told Kitty.

'Do you miss her?' Kitty asked.

'Not very much,' I said truthfully. 'They didn't let me play with her because she was so small. I wonder if they'll tell her she has a half-sister when she's a little older? Or maybe they'll forget all about me. Nobody will know I ever existed.' My voice wavered.

'Your Nurse will know,' said Kitty firmly.

'Do you think I will ever see her again?' I asked.

'Yes, I'm sure of it. If you want to enough,' said Kitty. She paused. 'Do you think I'll ever see Gaffer again?' she asked in a tiny voice, so I could barely hear her.

I didn't know what to say. If Gaffer was dead, how could she possibly see him? Did she mean in Heaven? Kitty didn't seem at all a religious person, but perhaps she still had faith.

'Yes, I think you will. But not for a long long time,' I said, because obviously I didn't want her to die in the near future.

She seemed satisfied with the answer, nodding thoughtfully.

It was getting darker now and we had had a long and tiring day, so we decided to settle down to sleep. We tried out the pews, but they were so narrow there was a danger we'd fall with a clunk if we turned over in the night. We settled on the floor itself, with the shawl wrapped round both of us, and the hassocks for pillows.

They were a little too high and made our necks ache, so we took Trampy out of her pocket and rolled up Kitty's dress for a shared pillow instead.

'Trampy can stretch her legs and have a little run around,' said Kitty, kissing the mouse on the end of her nose. 'But you have to come back, promise me, little Trampy.'

Trampy squeaked, which Kitty took for a yes. She let her go and the mouse darted away. We cuddled up together – and we were still clinging to each other when we woke at dawn.

I felt someone very tiny scrabbling at my ankle.

'Trampy's trying to get into my boot!' I murmured.

'She can't be – she's curled up by my neck,' said Kitty.

I sat up stiffly, and saw Trampy by my toes, Trampy at Kitty's head – then Trampy running across the stone flags, Trampy twitching on top of a pile of hymn books, Trampy, Trampy, Trampy everywhere.

'Oh my lord!' I said.

'Are you praying?' Kitty asked sleepily.

'No, I'm exclaiming. There are masses of mice all over everywhere!'

Kitty sat up too and exclaimed.

'How will we know which one's Trampy?' I asked.

'That's easy! This one's Trampy because she's nestled up against me,' said Kitty.

But that Trampy suddenly ran off – and another took her place, running up Kitty's leg, and yet another jumped into her hand.

'Oh dear,' said Kitty. 'I think they all want to be Trampy.'

'Well, we can't keep them all,' I said, not at all sure I liked so many mice playing together at one time.

Then we heard the sudden creak of the door, and a shaft of early sunlight illuminated the church. I saw the dark silhouette of a man with a significant high collar. The vicar!

The mice dashed for cover, disappearing in the darkness under the pews. Kitty pulled me underneath too. We lay there, trembling, while the vicar strode down the aisle, his boots ringing on the flagged floor. We hoped he'd disappear into his little room so we could run like the mice – but he stopped by the front pew, bent his knee in front of the altar, and then started murmuring to himself.

'What's he doing?' Kitty whispered into my ear.

'I think he's saying his prayers,' I whispered back.

'Well, I wish he'd be quick about it,' said Kitty. 'I've got cramp in my leg from lying tucked up like this.'

The vicar was very slow. He must have prayed for a full ten minutes, maybe longer. I wished he wasn't quite so devout. But then at long last he murmured Amen, straightened up, and walked off to his room, humming a hymn to himself.

'Quick!' said Kitty.

We scrambled to our feet.

'Trampy? Trampy!' Kitty whispered, but her little mouse didn't seem to hear.

'Who's there?' the vicar called, sounding alarmed. 'I will not have any tramps desecrating this holy church, especially on the Lord's day!'

'We must run for it,' I said, gathering up the shawl, and we charged for the open door.

We were good runners and the vicar was elderly and encumbered by his robe, so he didn't have much chance of catching us. We ran down to the lychgate and out along the road, and didn't stop until we were streets away. Then Kitty leaned against the wall, clutching her chest.

'We've left Trampy!' she said.

'Oh no!' I said. 'But we didn't know which one she was.'

'*I* did,' Kitty insisted, though I think she was fibbing. 'And I've left my brown frock too!'

'But it was very old and ragged – and rather dirty,' I said. 'But look, I've still got the shawl. I'm sure it's cashmere because it's so soft. You can have it if you like, to make up for losing Trampy.'

'She will think I've deserted her,' said Kitty, still sounding heartbroken.

'No she won't. She's got lots of little friends now. She's going to *love* being a church mouse,' I said.

'Not as much as she loved being with me,' said Kitty. 'And I want my frock back! Gaffer bought it for me. I *have* to get it back.' She turned and started running in the direction of the church.

'You can't! Not now! That vicar will catch you,' I warned her, clutching her by the shoulder.

'I'll wait till he's gone,' said Kitty.

'But he'll be there all day if it's Sunday,' I said.

'How do you know it's Sunday?' Kitty asked, stopping still.

'The vicar said. It's the Lord's day. People go to church on a Sunday to say their prayers,' I explained.

'I know,' said Kitty. 'And chapel. Stop keeping on telling me stuff as if I'm stupid. I know far more than you do. So just hold your tongue, will you?'

I stared at her in shock. 'Why are you being so mean all of a sudden?' I asked.

'Because . . . oh, because,' said Kitty, and she had tears in her eyes. She turned her face away and wiped her face fiercely, but I could hear her sniffling.

'I suppose we could sneak back to the church after the morning service, when the vicar goes to have his dinner,' I said. 'If you're really missing Trampy that much. I expect your frock will still be tucked under the pew. We'll get it back for you, Kitty.'

She sniffed hard. 'It would be silly to go back, I know. The vicar might be on the lookout for us. I don't imagine I'd ever find Trampy. Anyway, you're right, she seemed very happy to be with all the other mice. And I wish I still had my old frock but I know it was all ragged. I've got my red velvet now.'

'You look very nice in it,' I said. 'It really suits you. And you can be the tumbling boy when you wear it.'

'*You're* being very nice. Even though I was mean. I'm sorry, Lucy,' Kitty said, turning to me. She had tears running down her cheeks now.

'Oh, poor Kitty!' I put my arms round her and hugged her. 'Don't be so sad. We're going to have a lovely day today. We've still got plenty of tin so we'll have a good breakfast and then we'll walk around and try to find the perfect place to do our performance. We need somewhere with lots and lots of people but no shops. Can you think of anywhere? Kitty?'

She wiped her face with the back of her hand and took a last big sniff. 'I can't do the tumbling boy this morning,' she said.

'Why not? Have you got tired of it? Don't worry, I'll make up something else. Maybe you could be . . . a little red elf? A little red elf who looked after himself, but then he got lonely all on his owny, and – and wanted a friend so who shall we send? Yes! Then you choose someone from the crowd and dance with them and then you give them your elf cap to go round the audience asking for a penny, if you have any! Oh, it'll be perfect!' I said, very pleased with my idea.

I hoped Kitty would cheer up and be suitably impressed, but she didn't seem to be listening.

'Don't you want to be an elf?' I asked. 'You don't have to be, if you think it's too babyish.'

'No, I can't be anything this morning. I have to go and do something. I always go on Sundays,' she said.

'Well, all right then. What is it?' I asked.

'It's a secret,' said Kitty. 'You can't come.'

'But I'm your friend! You can't have secrets from me!' I protested.

'It's just one secret, that's all. I'll buy us breakfast first and then you can go back to that park and wait for me there. All right?' said Kitty.

It wasn't all right at all. My heart was thudding hard beneath my blue cotton bodice.

'Please don't leave me all by myself!' I begged.

'Don't be silly. There will be lots of people in the park later on. You'll find some other children easily and then you can play with them until I come back,' said Kitty.

'You *will* come back? You absolutely promise?'

'I absolutely promise,' Kitty echoed.

I had to do my best to believe her.

11

It was the longest morning ever. Kitty set off straight after we'd eaten our rolls, hot from the baker's and spread with butter and jam. She bought an extra one for me to eat during the morning, which worried me even more, because it meant she was going to be a really long time.

I was so anxious that after she'd said goodbye I waited until she'd taken twenty paces or so and then set off after her. I decided I'd follow her so that she couldn't run away from me. But Kitty glanced quickly over her shoulder and then dodged down an alleyway. By the time I'd caught up she had disappeared, and I had no idea whether she'd gone left or right at the end of the alley, or even if she'd climbed over a wall.

I took the opportunity to use the darkest corner as a public convenience, and then rushed out towards the daylight, terrified that another hateful old woman would pounce on me and rob me of all my clothes. I loved my new blue cotton dress painfully. When I was still hidden in the alleyway I actually put my arms tight round myself, pretending with all my might that Nurse was holding me.

'There there, little angel,' she murmured. 'Nurse's brave darling. Cheer up, chicken. We'll be together one day, just as your little friend Kitty promised.'

'She *is* going to come back, isn't she, Nurse?' I whispered.

'For goodness' sake, my baby, stop this fretting! She came back last time, didn't she? She'll come back this time too, because she's your little friend, and you look after each other through thick and thin,' said Nurse.

I was a little comforted, even though I knew I was making Nurse up.

It took me quite a while to find the park where we'd performed the tumbling boy. I set off in entirely the wrong direction first, and started to panic when I couldn't find the entrance anywhere, or see even a glimpse of green. I had to ask several folk out early, but this time they were polite, even reassuring. I didn't look quite the young lady, but decent enough in my frock, and the paisley shawl was good quality.

One gentleman even offered to take me to the park himself, but I was a little doubtful. He seemed very kind, and he had a fresh pink face and white whiskers, but Kitty had given me serious warnings about bad men who might want to hurt me, so I ran away.

It was a great relief when I got to the park eventually. I found the spot we were in yesterday and sat on a bench, eating my second roll almost without thinking. In fact, I was so hungry I put my hand in the bag for any spare crumbs or smears of jam. Then I wadded the bag into a ball and played a listless game of catch with myself.

I was quite good at catching, because I'd had a shuttledore at home and had played for endless hours after Nurse was sent away. It was only a few days since I ran out of the house, yet it seemed as if years had gone by. I didn't just look different now. I had grown into another person altogether. I was so much happier now – as long as I had Kitty.

If I had more paper bags I could try throwing three balls in the air to see if I could teach myself to juggle. I rather fancied the idea. Then Kitty could sing and I could be the Little Juggling Girl.

Oh, there's the Little Juggling Girl
Throwing three balls in the air
See them flying, see them whirl
Show her that you care!

Yes, it was a great start. I sang it softly under my breath, making up a new tune as I went, and after several false starts it sounded very jolly. I walked to a wastepaper basket and found a discarded newspaper. I fashioned two more balls out of the front page and then did my best to juggle them. It was far harder than I'd imagined. I couldn't seem to get the hang of it and dropped all three balls repeatedly.

Two little boys rushed past bowling their hoops and jeered at me for my poor performance. I sat back on the bench, blushing, and straightened out the newspaper balls, pretending I was simply interested in having a read. I applied myself to the columns of print until the little boys lost interest and went on their way.

Then my eyes focused on the newspaper advertisement.

THE GREAT EXHIBITION!

Opened by Her Majesty the Queen!
The magnificent Crystal Palace in Hyde Park!
The eighth Wonder of the World!
OVER 100,000 EXHIBITS!
Apply for tickets now.

I knew about this exhibition. I had overheard Papa talking about it with the New Mother. They were planning to be season ticket holders and visit it whenever they pleased. Miss Groan was hoping to go later in the summer, when the cheaper shilling daily tickets were available. She had a brochure showing the huge glass building containing large living trees, the Majolica fountain, the Koh-i-Noor diamond, the lace-making machine, the blue steel church bells, the ivory throne and marble statues, and the immense stuffed elephant from India.

I wasn't especially interested in diamonds or lace or bells or statues but I *longed* to see the stuffed elephant. I imagined this immense creature towering above me and wondered if it would be possible to stroke its long trunk or even climb a ladder to sit upon its massive back. Miss Groan saw my shining eyes and clasped hands. She mentioned the possibility of taking me with her, because it would be so good for my education.

'But of course you would have to do your lessons very diligently every day and behave impeccably,' she said.

Well, she certainly wouldn't be taking me now! But I wasn't thinking of going *into* the Exhibition (though perhaps children were half price? It would be so splendid to see the elephant!). I was thinking of the great park itself, thronged with hundreds and thousands of visitors. I imagined there would have to be great queues for such an attraction. I thought of all the folk waiting there, needing distraction. Perhaps they might enjoy the antics of the Tiny Tumbling Boy and the Little Juggling Girl!

I was thoroughly distracted for the next half hour, planning ways of refining our act. Perhaps I could even make up a topical song, though words like Koh-i-Noor, Majolica and Exhibition were a nightmare for rhyming.

But then as the morning wore on I became more and more worried. Where had Kitty gone and why was it so important to her? Why couldn't she take me with her, wherever it was? Was she ever coming back?

I tried to console myself that I had been agitated before, convinced that Kitty had abandoned me, and yet she had scurried back with breakfast, all smiles. But now I'd eaten my mid-morning roll and already families were sitting down on rugs beneath the trees and opening picnic hampers, ready for their lunch.

I watched them miserably, especially the little girls with fond papas who made sure they had the choicest slice of tart and sugar bun and then wiped their sticky hands with their own large pocket handkerchiefs. I thought of my own papa at home and wondered if he might be missing me. Did he think of that little ragged girl at his front door and wonder if she might have been his own daughter after all? If I went back in my respectable blue frock would he recognize me and weep with joy?

That world at home with Papa and the New Mother and Miss Groan seemed unreal now, like something I'd once read in a book. Miss Groan took pains to make sure most of my books were instructional nowadays, but she did allow storybooks occasionally too, but only if they were chock full of morals, like sultanas in a pudding. *The History of the Fairchild Family* was a gripping tale, but whenever the children were mildly naughty they were taught a dreadful lesson. The chapter where they quarrelled with each other and were taken to a hangman's gibbet to see what happened to bad children had given me nightmares for weeks.

The History of Lucy Browning would contain the most dreadful scenes, especially when she ran away from home. The direst things would happen to her and when she eventually found her way back home, ready to beg for forgiveness and be punished with bread and water meals for the rest of her life, she would find her house shut up and empty. A neighbour would tell her that her poor papa had died of grief, and then Lucy would cast herself down on the stone steps and sob, repenting bitterly.

I started shivering in the warm sunshine, wrapping the paisley shawl tighter round myself. And then I suddenly spotted a flash of crimson in the distance, and I leaped up and waved frantically. It was Kitty, it had to be, because no one else would be wearing a red acrobatic costume – and yet this small person didn't walk like Kitty at all. She didn't have her springing step, with her head held high. She trudged slowly, with a strange jerky gait.

'Kitty!' I ran towards her – and as I got nearer I saw she had the beginnings of a bruise on her face and a badly grazed knee.

'Oh, Kitty, what happened to you?' I gasped, rushing to put my arms round her.

'Nothing, nothing,' Kitty mumbled ridiculously.

'Did you fall over? Oh, you poor thing, you're hurt all over – and you're limping!'

'It's nothing, I tell you. Just a twisted ankle. Yes, I took a tumble – but aren't I the tumbling boy?' said Kitty, trying to be jaunty.

'Don't tell such fibs! I think someone set upon you!' I said, horrified.

'All right, yes they did. Not one person, but two, boys bigger and stronger than me – but I fought back and bloodied both their noses,' Kitty boasted, sounding more herself.

'But that's terrible! Didn't you call a policeman?' I said without thinking.

Kitty looked at me with wide eyes. 'Are you mad, Lucy? The police are out to catch us! Besides, you don't get traps in the district I was in – they'd be too fearful, even walking in pairs.'

'So what were you *doing*, walking in this dreadful district?' I demanded.

Kitty sank down on the grass and leaned against a tree, her head bent. 'I go there every Sunday,' she muttered. 'And I've never been picked on before, when I was wearing my old frock. But I suppose I stood out in my velvet outfit, and these big lads started mocking me, calling me names, telling me lies. So I hit them and they hit me back and knocked me to the ground. But like I said, I gave as good as I got. I'm willing to bet they're cut all over with great swollen noses and serve them right! They tried to snatch the bag of tin around my neck but I wriggled away in time. And look, my velvet hasn't got a mark on it, it's still beautiful – though I'm afraid I won't be able to be the tumbling boy for a day or two, because I've hurt my wrist too, and I doubt I could do a single handstand. But don't look so worried, Lucy, I swear I'll be better soon and able to earn us some tin.'

'Don't fret about it, Kitty. I'll sing for us until you recover. There now!' I put my arm round her and held her close.

She gave a little sigh and huddled against me. 'Don't be so kind to me, Lucy. You'll make me cry,' she said.

'Can't you tell me *why* you were in this dreadful district?' I asked.

Kitty shook her head.

'Well, at least promise me that you will never ever go there again!' I insisted.

'I have to go there,' said Kitty. 'But I will be more careful next Sunday, I promise. Oh dear, I'm starting to hurt all over.'

She tucked her sore wrist into her armpit while I gently stroked her poor ankle which was already swelling visibly. I wanted to run to an apothecary for bandages and ointment, but they would be closed on a Sunday, and I wasn't sure we had enough money left anyway.

'Gaffer used to make up a poultice from different herbs,' said Kitty. 'But I don't remember which they were. Oh dear goodness, what use to you am I now?'

'Well, it's time *I* was of use to you,' I said. 'I know just the thing for your poor wrist and ankle. Dock leaves!'

Nurse had rubbed me with dock leaves when I once fell over into a patch of stinging nettles. I wasn't sure if they worked for any other ailment, but they were better than nothing and easy enough to recognize. I sat Kitty down, wrapped the shawl round her and looked for dock leaves under the trees.

I found a big clump, pulled out a handful and applied them gently to Kitty's throbbing limbs.

'Now then, I think you might feel better if you had a little lunch,' I said.

Kitty offered me the reticule but I shook my head.

'No, we'll keep that for the moment. I'm getting us a free lunch – you've shown me how,' I said.

It was easy enough to forage in the remnants of other people's picnics. I returned with cheese sandwiches, several tomatoes, and a whole pork pie that had rolled away in the grass. Someone had stood on it, but it still seemed clean enough. I ran backwards and forwards with my findings, and collected a variety of glass bottles which still contained liquid, though I had a rival here, a little boy intent on gathering them too.

I snatched a couple from the waste bin before he could get his small hands on them. He looked so devastated I felt guilty. He was clean enough, and his blue shirt was freshly laundered, though he had a patch on both sleeves, and his trousers were far too big for him, so that they were kept up by braces. Perhaps he was as poor as us.

159

'Are you very thirsty?' I asked, ready to hand one over.

'I don't want to drink from them!' he said. 'I'm collecting them to take to the grocer's shop. He'll pay me a penny a half-dozen and then I can buy a liquorice stick.'

'Well, let my friend and me drink and then you can take every single one from us,' I said. 'What's your name?'

'I'm Tommy Magpie,' he said. He was only about six, with a peaky face and big brown eyes and a thatch of thick hair. It had recently been severely barbered, so that it stood up all over, making him look startled. He had black lips and black teeth and a black tongue, so he'd either purchased some liquorice already today, or hadn't done a very thorough job of cleaning his teeth last night.

'Is your mamma with you, Tommy Magpie?' I asked.

'No, Ma's at home with a new baby,' he said. 'It bawls a lot. It fair makes my head ring sometimes.'

'Well, I expect you bawled too when you were little,' I said. 'So are you with your papa today?'

'No, Pa drives a cab, see, so he works of a Sunday. I'll be meeting him at the end of his shift. I get to feed the horse!' said Tommy.

'Well, you're very welcome to join my friend and me for a picnic lunch,' I said. 'We haven't any liquorice but we can offer you a fine pork pie.'

'Don't mind if I do,' said Tommy Magpie.

We went to join Kitty. I introduced her proudly, but Tommy Magpie wrinkled his nose.

'Kitty? What sort of name is that for a boy?' he said scornfully.

'I'm a girl, booby,' said Kitty wearily.

'Well, why are you wearing that boy's outfit then?' Tommy Magpie asked, reasonably enough.

'I can wear whatever I want,' said Kitty. 'This is velvet, I'll have you know. And not a stain on it. It's an acrobat's costume. And *I* am an acrobat, with a crowd-pleasing routine of tumbling, see.'

'Well, looks like you've *taken* a tumble,' said Tommy Magpie, unimpressed.

'*You'll* be the one taking a tumble if you don't watch your lip, little mutt,' Kitty snapped.

'Shush now, you two,' I said, clucking like Nurse. 'Let's eat up nicely.'

We ate and drank, and then I practised my juggling, hoping I might have miraculously improved. I was even worse, if anything.

'You keep dropping them,' Tommy Magpie pointed out unnecessarily.

'She's doing her best,' said Kitty. But then she murmured, 'Only her best ain't good enough.'

'Then I'll just have to sing,' I said. I looked at Tommy Magpie. 'Can *you* sing? Would you like to beg for some tin? We can earn much more than a penny. I reckon you could earn enough for six liquorice sticks in an hour or so.'

'Cor!' said Tommy Magpie, his eyes shining. 'I'll sing my head off for you then!'

He tried to demonstrate.

'Tom, Tom, the Piper's Son,
Stole a pig and away he ran
The pig got eat
And Tom got beat
And Tom went howling down the street.'

He knew the words, but he was hopeless at keeping in tune. He croaked like a frog, wavering up and down the scale, though he looked quite sweet standing there, hands clasped, in his blue shirt and braces.

'You'll drive the crowds away if you sing like that,' said Kitty bluntly, with her hands over her ears.

'Perhaps *I* could sing the rhyme and you could do a little jig,' I suggested.

Tommy Magpie tried to oblige, jumping about violently, but with no grace or rhythm whatsoever.

'Never mind. I could sing this song about a tumbling boy, and you could do a cartwheel or two, Tommy Magpie,' I said.

'Yes, I can do cartwheels like a good 'un,' said Tommy Magpie.

He showed us. Perhaps he *thought* he was turning splendid cartwheels, but his feet barely left the floor.

'Haven't you got any talents whatsoever?' Kitty asked.

'Yes, I collect bottles and jars and get pennies for them,' said Tommy Magpie.

'Perhaps you could collect the pennies from the crowd while I sing,' I suggested. 'You'd be good at that because you look so sweet.'

'I don't look *sweet*,' said Tommy Magpie, offended, but he agreed to be the money collector.

I decided it was simplest to sing hymns as it was Sunday, and there was no way of demonstrating our novelty songs while Kitty was hunched up in pain. She watched from under the trees while I sang solo and Tommy Magpie collected the tin, stuffing it in the deep pockets of his wide trousers. I was very nervous at first, and sang the first verse of *Praise my soul the King of Heaven, to his feet they tribute bring* in a timid quaver, but I grew in confidence after that. People seemed to appreciate the hymns and most gave us coins with a smile.

I encouraged Tommy to bow and say thank you kindly as he pocketed the pennies, which went down well. I sang until my voice went husky and Tommy's pockets were so heavy that his trousers were in danger of falling down, even with his braces on.

'Look, Kitty!' I said excitedly, when we had a rest at last. 'Let's count how much money we've got! I reckon we should give Tommy Magpie half, don't you? The crowd seem to take a shine to him.'

Kitty shrugged. 'Any fool can collect the tin,' she sniffed. 'Still, do what you like. He's your little pal, not mine.'

'You don't have to be so grumpy,' I said. 'What's the matter with you?'

'I *hurt*,' said Kitty.

I was hurt that she wasn't pleased with me. I'd thought I'd done so well. I'd earned us lots of money and I must have sung well, because people smiled so. I heard one lady call me a little darling. The only person who had ever called me that before was dear Nurse.

'I know you hurt, and your wrist and ankle look horribly sore, but there's no need to be so nasty to me. It's not *my* fault you got set upon. You didn't *have* to go off on this mysterious errand,' I said.

'Yes I did,' said Kitty, and she put her head on her knees.

She wouldn't say anything more to me, even when I pleaded with her. So I simply left her there and went off for a walk with Tommy Magpie. He jingled as he walked, pink with pride. He even managed to ignore empty ginger beer and lemonade bottles.

'Don't need any more pennies! Wait till I show my ma and pa! They'll be so pleased with me!' he crowed.

'Half of it's for Kitty and me, remember,' I said.

'Yes, of course. But I earned my share fair and square, didn't I? I did all the bows and said thank you over and over.'

'You did it all beautifully, Tommy Magpie,' I told him.

He grinned – and bowed and thanked *me*. We sauntered along enjoying the sunshine. When we saw a hokey-pokey man I said we should treat ourselves.

'We deserve it, because we've worked so hard,' I said, delving into his pocket for three pennies.

'What you getting three for? There's only two of us,' he said.

'I'm getting one for Kitty too,' I explained.

'But she hasn't done no work!'

'Yes, but we can't leave her out. She's not very well, poor thing,' I said.

I bought Kitty her lump of hokey-pokey too, but by the time we'd got back to the trees our own iced cream was finished and Kitty's was melting all the way up my arm.

'Kitty! Look what I've got you! Some hokey-pokey to make you feel better,' I called out.

But she wasn't sitting under the tree where we'd left her. I ran round all the trees. I looked in the bushes. I hurried up and down the grass. I looked everywhere, but there was no sign of her.

Kitty had gone.

I searched and searched.

'But we've just looked in that clump of trees. She's not there, else we'd have seen her,' said Tommy Magpie. 'Can I have her hokey-pokey?'

'No you cannot! It's Kitty's!'

'But it's all melted. Can I lick your arm?' Tommy Magpie asked.

'*No!*' I said, pushing him away.

'All right, all right, no need to get into such a tizz. I'll go and buy another one then,' he said.

'For goodness' sake, how can you fuss about iced cream when Kitty's gone missing!' I said, nearly in tears.

'She'll turn up like a bad penny,' said Tommy Magpie. 'That's what my ma always says. Only she says he, because we're all boys, though she was hoping like anything the new baby would be a girl. He can't go missing yet, because he can't even crawl. He's pretty useless if you ask me.'

'I'm not asking you! Do hold your tongue and help me look for Kitty. Do you think she might have gone out of the park altogether?' I wondered.

Tommy Magpie shrugged. 'I don't know. Maybe. Yes, I think she's just gone home,' he said.

'But she hasn't *got* a home. And how am I ever going to find her again if she's walked off?' I said, the tears starting to roll down my cheeks.

'Well, she can't walk far, can she, not with a poorly ankle. Don't get so upset. I'll do the collecting for you now. You don't need her,' said Tommy Magpie heartlessly.

'I do need her! She's my best friend in all the world and I can't manage without her,' I shouted.

'Really?' The voice came from right up above me. I craned my neck – and there was Kitty, sitting high up in the tree like a monkey.

'What are you *doing* up there? Come right down this instant!' I commanded.

Kitty scrambled down expertly, even with all her injuries, and landed cleverly on one leg so she didn't jar her ankle.

'How dare you hide like that? I was so worried! You must have seen me looking for you and heard me shouting! You were hiding there just to plague me, weren't you! You're a wicked girl!' I took hold of her by the shoulders and gave her a good shaking.

'Ow! Stop it! Leave go of me! I was hiding up in the tree to get away from this interfering old biddy who wanted to take me to that hospital for sick children. Catch me going there! I'd catch a fever and be dead as a doornail within a week, that's what Gaffer always says,' said Kitty.

'Stop talking nonsense! You were doing it to worry me. You got jealous because we managed to make a lot of tin without you, me and Tommy Magpie,' I said. 'You don't like it that I've made another friend.'

'As if I care,' said Kitty – but I saw that her cheeks were tear-stained too.

I suddenly stopped being angry with her. 'Oh, Kitty, I was so scared you'd really walked off and left me this time,' I said, and I gave her a big hug.

'You noodle,' said Kitty, but she hugged me back hard. 'We stick together, you and me.'

'Yes, we do,' I said.

'And me,' said Tommy Magpie. 'I do the collecting.'

'Any fool can do that,' said Kitty. 'You give us the tin and then buzz off.'

'I said he could have half of it,' I said. 'He did try hard.'

'Yes, I did,' said Tommy Magpie indignantly.

'He didn't sing or dance or tumble,' said Kitty. 'He just collected.'

'I did it beautifully!' said Tommy Magpie. 'I asked nicely and looked at them like this.' He rearranged his round face into a grotesque caricature of wistfulness, his eyes wide, his mouth sucked into an O.

Kitty burst out laughing. 'All right, he can have a quarter,' she said. 'Turn your pockets out, Tommy, and we'll give you back your share.'

She sat down and counted out the money and then gave him back some pennies.

'My share's more than that,' said Tommy Magpie, watching her beadily.

'Just testing your arithmetic,' said Kitty. She stood up to give him a further handful, momentarily forgetting her ankle. She winced with pain, and said a very, very rude word.

'Oh my, my ma would give me a royal beating if I said that,' said Tommy Magpie, giggling.

'Well, it blooming well hurt,' said Kitty.

'You need some of my ma's yellow ointment,' said Tommy Magpie. 'She rubs us with it when we've gone and hurt ourselves and it makes us better in no time, truly.'

'Can you get us some?' Kitty asked.

'Course I can,' said Tommy Magpie, seemingly bearing her no grudge, though she'd not been very kind to him.

'We'll pay her, of course,' said Kitty.

'You can try, but she won't take your money,' said Tommy Magpie. 'She's like that, my ma. Soft. But you know what mothers are like.'

Kitty and I were silent. We didn't know what mothers were like, though we wished we did.

'Come on then, girls,' said Tommy Magpie, taking both our hands.

After just a few wincing steps we realized we'd have to give Kitty more help than that. I put my arm round her and clutched her tightly so she could keep her balance and hop, which didn't work terribly well because I was taller than her. So Tommy Magpie took a turn and didn't complain at all.

'This is my street,' he announced finally, as we turned down a terraced row of red brick houses.

They were humble homes, the sort that have two rooms up and two rooms down, but they nearly all had clean windows and freshly painted doors, and little gardens at the front. Some grew red geraniums and blue lobelia and white alyssum in patriotic patterns; others let roses and honeysuckle ramble where they wanted; some grew vegetables too, mixing their marrows with their marigolds.

Tommy Magpie's garden was high with hollyhocks, pink and red and yellow, all of them towering over his head, and his front door was painted a shining green to set them off.

We stood by his gate, peering.

'Come in!' he said, beckoning. 'The door's on the latch.'

'Your ma will wonder who we are,' said Kitty.

'No she won't. She'll just say, "Come in, chickies, and have some bread and dripping," you'll see,' said Tommy Magpie.

Kitty would never have agreed normally, but she was pale and pinched with pain, so she simply nodded wearily. We trooped up the crazy paving and went in the door. There was no hall at all, so we found ourselves in the living room straightaway.

It was crammed full of children. I stared in astonishment, wondering whether they could possibly all be Tommy's siblings. There were so many boys joshing each other, wrestling on the rug, playing marbles over the bare floorboards, pulling hideous faces at each other, but there were also a few little girls in pinafores, swapping glass beads and playing with a family of Dutch dolls. A plump woman with a pink face lay on the sofa with her blouse open, feeding a baby.

I couldn't help staring, because I'd never seen such a thing before, and felt my own face going pink with embarrassment – but the lady seemed perfectly at ease. She gave Kitty and me a big smile.

'Come in, chickies, and have some bread and dripping,' she said.

Tommy Magpie gave a whoop and punched the air. 'Told you she'd say that, didn't I? The exact words!' he said triumphantly.

I didn't even know what bread and dripping was. Well, bread was familiar enough, but the coarse brown loaf on the board on a table looked very different from the dainty slices of white bread I'd eaten at home. There was also a blue-and-white striped pudding basin containing some strange beige substance.

'What is it?' I whispered to Kitty, who was cutting the bread expertly in spite of her sore wrist.

'Dripping. It's all the juices and fat from the Sunday roast. Farmers' wives used to give it to Gaffer and me. It's good, very good,' said Kitty.

I wasn't at all sure. It looked perfectly revolting, and the slice of bread was too large and still had its crust on – but when I took a tentative bite I was surprised. It really did taste good, meaty and satisfying, and the bread was nutty and wonderfully filling. Kitty and I ate our slices with relish.

'Is that nice?' the woman asked. 'You two look as if you haven't eaten for weeks!'

'It's positively delicious. Thank you so much, Mrs Magpie,' I said.

'Oh, what a lovely little way of speaking you have, dear! I wish my kiddies talked like you. But it's not Mrs Magpie, bless you, it's Mrs Chubb. We nicknamed our Tommy a magpie because he's just like one, ever after sparkly gewgaws and hiding them away. Aha, he's been at it up the park! See, his trousers are all slipping down one side. I reckon it will be full of shiny stones and bottle tops and even an odd bottle itself, because you save them up to swop for liquorice, don't you, darling? And judging by the black all round your mouth you've already had one!'

'Well, you're wrong, Ma, because I've got a pocketful of real money, look!' said Tommy Magpie, sticking his hand in his bulging pocket and bringing out a fistful of pennies.

'Oh my lord, Tommy Magpie, what you gone and done!' said Mrs Chubb, sitting upright. The baby protested furiously, momentarily dislodged from his supper.

'I've been collecting, Ma, and I'm ever so good at it, ain't I, Lucy?' said Tommy Magpie.

'Ssh now!' Kitty said sharply, moving to give him a nudge.

Mrs Chubb looked at her properly now. 'Oh dear, have you taken a tumble, little Curlyknob? Tommy Magpie, run and fetch a bowl of cold water and some clean rags and Ma's special golden ointment, there's a good lad. Why didn't you tell me this little missy has been in the wars?' said Mrs Chubb, sitting the angry baby up and rubbing its back vigorously.

It gave such a loud belch that the roomful of children all rocked with laughter. Tommy ran his errand well and brought back everything Mrs Chubb had asked for. She handed him the baby in exchange.

'I don't want him, Ma! Ugh, he's all soggy!' Tommy Magpie protested, holding him at arm's length.

'Well, get on and change him then, son. You're the eldest,' said Mrs Chubb, sitting Kitty beside her and tutting over all her injuries.

I realized *I* was actually the eldest child in the room. And I knew how to change a baby because I'd watched the new nurse dealing with Angelique.

'I will change him. I have a baby sister, Mrs Chubb,' I said, to reassure her. 'I'm very experienced.' This last sentence was a downright lie, but I'd often longed to have a go at tending Angelique. Babies were so much more interesting than dolls.

'Well, thank you kindly, little sweetheart,' said Mrs Chubb. 'Pop him upstairs to the bedroom.'

I took hold of the baby carefully, making sure his head was supported, and carried him up the rickety stairs. I was immensely curious to see what the Chubb bedrooms were like. They proved much poorer and plainer than the bedrooms at my own home, but I thought they were beautiful. One room had five truckle beds, each with a gay knitted coverlet in a different wool: red, yellow, blue, green and purple. The walls were stuck all over with pictures from magazines and papers. I thought how comforting it would be to wake up in one of these little beds and look at all these pictures of chubby children and cats and dogs and horses and country cottages and carriages and cabs.

The second bedroom had one large bed with a crocheted coverlet all the colours of the rainbow. There was a washstand with a flower-patterned china jug and basin, and a chest of drawers, with the bottom biggest drawer taken out and put beside their bed. It had been turned into a little cot, with a pillow for a soft mattress, and a snowy white coverlet. There were only two pictures on the whitewashed walls: one of a couple holding hands and gazing at each other lovingly above the big bed, and the other of little cherubs stuck right above the makeshift baby cot.

'You're a very lucky little baby,' I told her, as I laid him gently on the rug and gingerly took off his wet napkin. I found his bare bottom very alarming but I washed him and dabbed him dry and then tucked a clean napkin into place, wishing he wouldn't wriggle so, particularly when I was trying to fasten the safety pin. It took me several goes, but at last it was on, and when I held him up the napkin stayed securely attached.

I felt so triumphant I kissed the baby and he stopped whimpering and gave me a smile.

'You're rather a dear little baby. My own little sister never smiled at me like that,' I said. 'Oh, I wish Kitty and I could live here and be your proper big sisters! Wouldn't that be lovely?'

But when I took him downstairs I found Mrs Chubb speaking sternly to Tommy Magpie and Kitty scowling ferociously.

'Oh dear, what's the matter?' I said.

'Well might you ask, little sweetheart!' said Mrs Chubb, and she shook her head at me. 'Were you involved in this begging lark too?'

I nodded, shame-faced.

'I can't believe it!' she said. 'You with your lovely voice and pretty manners, begging in the street!'

'It wasn't in the street, Mrs Chubb, it was in the park, and it wasn't truly begging. I was singing,' I said.

'Singing so that good folks would give you money? Well, I calls that begging, plain and simple. And that's an abomination and I won't have it, do you hear? Especially when it involves my Tommy Magpie. He's a good lad, even though he can be led astray at times.'

'He pleaded with us to let him have a go!' said Kitty angrily. She glared at Tommy Magpie. 'Why did you have to blab it all out? Now look what's happened.' She stood up, though Mrs Chubb was only half finished with her bandaging. 'Come on, Lucy, we don't need to listen to this lecture. Let's scarper.'

'Now you hold still a minute, Miss Hoity-Toity. You can't go anywhere, not with a sore ankle like that. Let me tend it for you – and then when my other half comes home he'll carry you back to your ma and pa. You're only a little scrap of a thing and he's strong as an ox.'

'I ain't *got* no ma and ma,' Kitty muttered.

'Now, now, don't start telling me stories,' said Mrs Chubb.

'It's true!' I said, determined to defend Kitty. 'We haven't got any proper parents.' I knew this was a downright lie, because I still had Papa, but I felt he wasn't really a proper parent if he'd not recognized me and turned me away from my own doorstep. 'That's why we're forced to beg – though it's honestly more like entertaining. I know it's a little shameful, but I can't think of anywhere in the Bible where it says thou shalt not beg. I sang hymns today too, because it's Sunday.'

'That's true, Ma, she was singing loads of hymns – word perfect she is,' said Tommy Magpie.

'Then I'm truly sorry, my poor dears. I've judged you far too hasty like. My lord, what a world we live in when little tots like you have to beg for their bread. Well, you're welcome to come here any time and have a slice and a bit of loving care, like all the little ones here,' she said.

It turned out that they were mostly neighbours' children whose mothers were out working the Sunday shift at the local factory. Mrs Chubb acted like an unofficial childminder for all of them. When they were collected at half past five I worked out the five owners of the little beds upstairs. Tommy Magpie was the eldest, then there were rumbustious twins called Johnny Rowdy and Frankie Rumpus, a quiet boy called Arthur Thumb who always had that digit in his mouth, and a very little boy called Mikey Totter who could barely walk.

The baby was called Little Albert Angel.

'He nearly joined the angels too. We were both very poorly, weren't we, little Albert? I can't have any more children, so he's my last little baby. I've lost my chance of having a little girl. I'd have loved one too, especially a dear little thing like you, so kind and helpful. Little Albert Angel has fair taken to you!'

I glowed with pride. It was wonderful to be trusted with such a precious baby when I hadn't been allowed near my own little sister. I knew Kitty was impatient to be off as soon as she was bandaged, but I wanted to stay with this lovely family as long as possible.

Tommy Magpie put on a very large cap much too big for his shorn head and announced that he was off to meet his pa and help him stable the horse.

'We'll come too!' said Kitty eagerly. I knew she thought it would give us a chance to run for it, but when she stood up she could see that running was impossible – she had stiffened up and could barely stand.

'You need to rest that ankle, my dear. It needs time to heal,' said Mrs Chubb. 'You walk on it now, then it might never mend.'

'I can hop, can't I?' said Kitty, but she was grey with pain and looked in a poorly state.

'I think you need to come here on the sofa with me and take the weight off that poor little leg,' said Mrs Chubb.

She gently pulled Kitty up on the sofa and put her arm round her. I'd have found that heavenly, but Kitty stiffened and edged as far away as possible.

Tommy Magpie took my hand. '*You* come and meet Pa with me,' he said.

I looked at Kitty, silently asking for permission. She shrugged sulkily. I felt a little cross with her. She was behaving very rudely when Mrs Chubb was being so kind to us. I knew Kitty was in a lot of pain but it wasn't *my* fault she'd been attacked by those savage boys.

'Lucy's a real little lady, Tommy Magpie. She don't want to go to a mucky stable and have the hoss breathing all over her,' said Mrs Chubb.

'It would scare her silly,' Kitty muttered.

'I'd *like* to,' I said. 'Come on, Tommy, show me the way.'

The stables weren't too far away. Tommy Magpie kept hold of my hand, skipping beside me. He chattered non-stop about his pa, telling me he was big and tall and so powerful he could pick a child right up in the air with just one hand. He told me about Nelson too, the horse that drew the hackney cab, a giant of a creature and as strong as six oxen even though he was ageing, but he still had all his teeth, top and bottom set.

'He won't bite, will he?' I asked.

'Nah! Nelson's got the gentlest nature of any hoss in the world. Pa lets me feed him slices of apple for a treat and his lips tickle my hand, as soft as feathers,' Tommy Magpie declared. 'Look, I'll show you. Hold out your hand.'

I did so, and Tommy bent and snuffled at it, pretending to eat.

'I tried him with liquorice, but he don't care for the taste so he blew out his nostrils like this.' Tommy Magpie demonstrated, laughing.

I was expecting a giant man and a mammoth horse, but when we got to the stables I saw a small shrunken man who clearly went to the same barber as Tommy Magpie and an old grey nag with a weary expression and long yellow teeth.

'Dad! Nelson!' Tommy Magpie cried, as if they'd been parted for months. Mr Chubb swung Tommy round and round in the air, and Nelson cocked his head up and snuffled hopefully.

'Who's your little lady friend, young Tom?' asked Mr Chubb, nodding at me.

'That's Lucy. We was playing in the park together all day long,' said Tommy Magpie, sensibly not mentioning his collecting role in case his pa grew as stern as his ma over the begging issue. 'She's got another friend too, a fierce girl, but she's at home cos she's hurt herself.'

Mr Chubb nodded, clearly used to Tommy Magpie collecting up waifs and strays the way he collected bottles.

'She wants to have a go at giving Nelson a treat, Pa,' Tommy Magpie said. 'She can, can't she?'

'Surely. We'll just give him a nice rub-down first and get him comfortable,' said Mr Chubb.

Tommy Magpie attended to Nelson's flanks while his father rubbed the rest of him. Then Mr Chubb produced an apple from his pocket and cut it in half with his penknife. Tommy went first to show me exactly how to hold my hand out. Then I went second and shivered with excitement when Nelson's lips snuffled my hand. They were as gentle as Tommy Magpie had promised, and I patted his head very fondly.

'There now, Nelson,' I murmured. 'Good boy. It must be lovely to get that horrid bit and bridle off and be free of that heavy cab.'

'He don't mind it, miss. He's got used to it, see. Knows it's his job. But it's nice that you're such a thoughtful little lass. Would you like a go on riding the old boy before I settle him down for the night?' Mr Chubb asked.

I could hardly believe my luck. 'Oh, please! I would love that more than anything,' I breathed.

Mr Chubb might be small and rather wizened, but he proved as strong as Tommy had boasted. He picked me up easily, and gently pushed me right onto Nelson's back. I tried to hitch both legs to one side but he frowned at me.

'You'll tie your legs in a knot if you're not careful. I could never be doing with that side-saddle nonsense. You can't be in control of a hoss like that,' he declared.

So I rode Nelson round the stable yard sitting bareback, with a leg at either side. I tensed up for a few seconds because it seemed so extraordinarily high but I soon got my balance and sat very upright, jogging up and down to Nelson's stride. I clutched a few strands of his long silvery mane but took care not to pull on them.

'That's it, miss! Why, you're a natural! Look at her, Tommy Magpie! She looks like them toffs what ride in Rotten Row,' said Mr Chubb, slapping his side.

I wondered if he was simply being kind, but gloried in his praise all the same. I wanted to stay riding Nelson all evening, but I could only stay on his back a few minutes.

'He'll be feeling a bit tired, miss, after a full working day – and we have to get home anyways, because it's supper time,' he said.

He helped me down again and I cradled Nelson's head and gave him a kiss. We left him standing in fresh straw in his stable, munching hay contentedly.

I seemed to be invited in the supper invitation. I certainly hoped so. When we got back Mrs Chubb was bustling around in the back kitchen, the little boys were jumping up and down, the baby was kicking his bare legs on a cushion, and Kitty was still lying on the sofa, her face pinched.

I went to give her a kiss. 'Does it hurt very much?' I whispered.

She shook her head but I felt the wet tears on her cheeks.

'You smell very horsey,' she said irritably, but she clung to me all the same. She pulled my head nearer and started whispering. 'She hates us being beggars. We have to make a move. She'll report us to the traps and take us to the workhouse!'

'No she won't!' I said. 'She's kind. She'll let us stay for a while. Oh, Kitty, please don't spoil it. It's lovely here.'

Kitty wrinkled her nose dismissively. 'No, it's not. It's . . . stifling. You get told what to do all the time and there are too many children and it's all too cosy.'

'I *like* it being cosy,' I said. 'And supper smells delicious. Let's wait till after supper if we really have to go.'

The supper was superb: a vast steak and kidney pie, with potatoes and carrots and greens in the richest gravy. Mr Chubb had the biggest slice. Mrs Chubb cut herself a modest portion and then gave Kitty and me and Tommy Magpie and Johnny Rowdy and Frankie Rumpus a fair serving. Arthur Thumb got a little bit of steak mashed up with potato, and Mikey Totter got a bowl of meaty gravy. Little Albert Angel had already had his supper and dozed on Mrs Chubb's lap.

I'd seen steak pies at home but never tasted one. I was told steak was too rich for a little girl, and it would make me ill. I didn't feel ill at all now, just deliciously full and rather sleepy. I hated the idea of having to go now, and search for a derelict house or an open church, but I didn't want to upset Kitty too much.

She was looking terribly tired herself now, and after she'd finished her pie she put her head down on the scrubbed table and fell instantly asleep.

'Poor little mite,' said Mrs Chubb. 'Here, Mr C, carry the little lass up to bed. The twins can double up and the girls sleep in their bed.'

Kitty didn't protest when Mr Chubb lifted her. She laid her head on his shoulder, nestling in, murmuring affectionately.

'Ah, bless the little mite. I think she's dreaming I'm her pa,' said Mr Chubb.

I knew she was more likely dreaming of her mysterious Gaffer. I was so glad she wasn't making any protest about staying.

'It's tremendously kind of you to let us sleep here, Mrs Chubb,' I said gratefully.

'You can stay as long as you like, little sweetheart. It's a pleasure to have you, especially as you're so good with little Albert. You're a grand example to my boys. I love your dainty manners and your pretty accent. I wish they'd talk pure and proper like you,' she said.

I joined the queue at the privy in the back yard. It was very basic, but scrubbed clean, so it wasn't too much of an ordeal. Then I went upstairs to the children's bedroom. I worried that I didn't have a nightgown, and I didn't want the boys staring at me, but they just jumped into their beds in their underwear without making any fuss, so I did too. Kitty was very hot, perhaps because she was still wearing her velvet tumbling outfit. I helped her take it off and then cuddled up beside her. She was still burning and I was scared she might have a fever.

'Please get better soon, Kitty,' I murmured into her damp curls.

'I want Gaffer,' she mumbled.

'I know. He's not here – but I am. Everything's all right, just as long as we're together. You and me, Kitty and Lucy.'

'Kitty and Lucy,' she repeated under her breath, and then slept again.

13

The bed was small for one child, let alone two, but I still had the most wonderful night's sleep. I'd never really slept properly at home since Nurse left, even though I had a spacious bed with fine cotton sheets. I think it was because it was *too* spacious. It made me feel so little and lonely. I'd lie wide awake in the dark, dreading the dawn, because then the eerie grey light turned my wardrobe into a looming monster all set to lurch across the room.

I felt safe in this cosy room with Kitty beside me, and all the small boys snuffling in their sleep. I didn't wake up properly until Mrs Chubb bustled into the bedroom with two china mugs of milk. She had Albert Angel tied neatly to her chest with a shawl so she had both hands free. There was no sign of a single boy.

'Where's everybody gone?' I asked in surprise, sitting up.

'They were up for their breakfast a good hour ago, and now they're playing out in the street. I thought you two could do with a proper rest. How are you feeling?' Mrs Chubb asked.

'I feel very well!' I said.

'How about you, little Kitty Crosspatch?' Mrs Chubb pulled up the coverlet and examined Kitty's ankle. 'That's good, the swelling's gone down a bit. My golden ointment works a treat. Drink up your milk now, it will do you good.'

Mrs Chubb pressed the mug in her hand. Kitty took it reluctantly and didn't say thank you, even when I nudged her. I scolded her as I helped her dress, which made her even more surly.

'Do try to cheer up, Kitty. Mrs Chubb is being so kind to us. Something smells delicious downstairs. I think she's cooking us breakfast!' I said.

'Don't want no breakfast,' Kitty muttered, as she hobbled downstairs.

But she couldn't resist bacon, wedged between two slices of toast. The little boys left their street games and came indoors, begging for bacon too. Mrs Chubb gave them more bread and dripping, but wouldn't let them have any bacon.

'It's a special treat for these two poorly waifs. They need building up, see,' she said.

'You're too kind, Mrs Chubb,' I said happily.

'That's right, she's *too* kind,' Kitty mumbled, when she'd gone to see to the washing steeping in her sink. 'I can't stand her fussing about us all the time.'

'I like it,' I said.

'You're just a soft little rich girl,' Kitty jeered.

'And you're a hard little poor girl,' I retorted.

'Anyways, it's time we were off,' said Kitty. But when she tried to walk properly she went white and she had to bite her lip to stop herself crying.

'You can't go, not before your ankle gets properly better,' I said, with secret glee. 'We'll have to stay here another day at least. If Mrs Chubb lets us.'

'Oh, she'll be delighted,' said Kitty. 'Well, about you. She thinks you're wonderful, with your pretty voice and fancy manners. She doesn't like me at all.'

'Don't be silly. She likes us both equally,' I said, though I knew Kitty was right. I felt bad about it. 'I can't see why you can't be more polite to Mrs Chubb. She's been immensely kind to us. I wish you'd act a little more grateful.'

'But I'm not,' said Kitty.

'Well, *I* am,' I said, and I went to help Mrs Chubb with the washing.

I watched, fascinated, as she scrubbed the sheets on a dolly board and then boiled them up in a copper. Then there were several rinsings, the last with a sprinkling of

Reckitt's blue, because Mrs Chubb said it brought out the white. Then each sheet had to be put through a mangle and heaped in a huge basket ready to be hung on a line. Our sheets were sent out weekly at home and returned a day later folded crisp and clean.

I'd never given much thought to how this happened. I was amazed that it was such hard work. My arms ached trying out two minutes of scrubbing, and I couldn't even lift a sopping sheet, though Mrs Chubb picked them up as easily as if they were dusters.

I was a little more help when it came to pegging them on the line. It stretched from the Chubbs' house across the road to the lamppost opposite. Most of the women in the street were hanging out their own washing. Children dodged in and out the flapping sails. The twins took a stick and started poking the sheets until Mrs Chubb picked them up, squealing, and said she'd beat them with the stick if they carried on plaguing her. But it was clear she was only joking. She even stopped to have a little game with them, giving each a piggyback while they cried, 'Gee up, horsey!'

Little Albert Angel was wailing hard when we got back inside the house. Arthur Thumb and Mikey Totter were shaking his drawer, trying to soothe him. Kitty was lying on the sofa with her hands over her ears.

'You could have tried to pick him up!' I said. 'Little Albert Angel probably needs changing.'

'Little Albert Angel!' Kitty repeated mockingly. 'They have such daft names in this family.'

Mrs Chubb said nothing, though she looked vexed. Later on, when we were in the kitchen together, and Kitty was having a nap, she asked me if Kitty and I were related.

'We're sisters,' I said quickly, but she looked at me doubtfully.

'You never are!' she said. 'You're like chalk and cheese, the way you speak, the way you act, the way you look.'

'Well, we're as good as sisters,' I said. 'Better, in fact. We're the best of friends.'

'Kitty's very lucky to have you as a best friend, Lucy Sweetheart. But I'm not so sure you're lucky to have *her* as a friend. I think she's been a bad influence. I'm sure *she* was the one who started up this shameful begging nonsense,' she said.

'No, I sang too, and made up all the rhymes,' I said, but she didn't act as if she believed me. 'Kitty was a tumbling boy, doing handstands and cartwheels so cleverly.'

'I daresay,' said Mrs Chubb. 'She certainly looks like one of them heathen acrobats in that fancy costume. Don't she have any other clothes to wear? She can't go out like that, not showing all that bare leg!'

'She loves her velvet costume. I think it suits her,' I said, determined to stick up for Kitty, though I wanted to stay in Mrs Chubb's best books.

'It's not right or fitting for a little girl to dress like that. Perhaps I can cut down one of my own frocks for her,' she said.

'It's very kind of you, but I think Kitty would much prefer her red velvet even so,' I said.

'I think it would do young Kitty good to be *told* what to do,' Mrs Chubb said firmly.

She did her best to do that over the next few days, while Kitty was still confined to the sofa or the bed. She told Kitty to stop slurping when she drank and to use her knife and fork properly when she ate. She told Kitty to have a proper wash every day. She told Kitty to brush her unruly curls. She told Kitty to say please and thank you. She told Kitty that she shouldn't argue or protest.

Kitty argued and protested bitterly that first day. And the next day too. On the third day she insisted she was completely better and marched around the house, but her ankle started swelling again, and she was hobbling badly by the afternoon. Mrs Chubb picked her up as easily as if she were Little Albert Angel, and put her back to bed.

'Why won't you do as you're told, you silly little girl?' she said sternly.

'Nobody tells me what to do. I do what I like,' Kitty insisted.

When I went up to bed myself that evening I could tell Kitty had been crying.

'Oh, Kitty,' I said, trying to cuddle her.

She went rigid. 'I hate it here. I hate all these silly boys. I hate that wailing baby. And I especially hate *her*,' she muttered.

'She's only trying to look after you,' I said.

'I don't need looking after. I can look after myself,' said Kitty. 'My ankle's *nearly* better. And my wrist. And all these stupid scratches. We're getting out of here. We're leaving tomorrow, right?'

I hesitated. I didn't *want* to leave. I loved living in this cosy house with all the Chubb family. I loved helping Mrs Chubb with all the household chores. I loved tending Little Albert Angel. I loved playing silly games with all the little boys. I loved going to greet Mr Chubb with Tommy Magpie. I loved Nelson, who whinnied when he saw me now, and gave me a ride on his back.

I wanted to stay part of this safe kind family for ever, and eat their tasty food every day and sleep in the bed with the knitted coverlet every night. Why, oh why, couldn't Kitty want that too? She knew how to be sweet and charming when she liked. If she would only hold her tongue and smile then I was sure she'd be petted like me. She just had to give way a little.

Kitty seemed incapable of giving an inch. She stayed as rigid as iron.

'So you want to stay here?' she said, when I still hadn't answered.

'Perhaps – perhaps just for a little while – until you're completely better?' I suggested tentatively.

'I *am* better. You just don't want to come with me!' said Kitty, grinding the words out.

'Oh, I do, I do, just not quite yet,' I said.

'Well, *I'm* going tomorrow, whether you come too or not,' said Kitty, and she turned her back on me and seemed to go to sleep straightaway.

I lay wide awake and fretting, wondering what to do.

Kitty seemed in a softer mood the next morning, to my great relief. She even thanked Mrs Chubb for her breakfast and drank her milk without slurping once.

'Good girl!' said Mrs Chubb. 'Now, see what I've got for you, dear! I stayed up late last night, getting it finished.' She produced a pink cotton dress, similar to the one she wore under her apron, but cut down to a tiny size – a Kitty size.

'Oh!' said Kitty. It was the wrong sort of *oh* – one of horror.

Mrs Chubb misunderstood. 'Don't worry, Kitty, I've got two other dresses – and I don't have any little girls to use them up.'

'Yes, but I didn't *ask* you to make it for me,' said Kitty. 'You see, I don't really wear dresses, not pink ones like that.'

'I know, dear, but you'll look just like a little lady in it, just you wait and see. Slip it on now.'

Kitty backed away from her, but Mrs Chubb was used to capturing children and getting them dressed. She held Kitty tight with one hand, slipped the dress over her head with the other, and then pulled her arms through the sleeves.

'There now!' she said triumphantly. 'Come and see how sweet you look!'

She took hold of Kitty by the shoulders, steered her into her own bedroom and brought her up short in front of the looking glass.

Kitty stared, eyes open wide. 'That's not me!' she mumbled.

'Doesn't it make a difference, dear! You look quite pretty! And we'll see if we can buy you a decent pair of stockings too. You'll have to wear those strange little slippers for now, but that can't be helped.'

Kitty wasn't listening. She was looking agonized. I could see why. The dress was well-stitched and in proportion, but pale and limp from many scrubbings in the washtub. It made Kitty look pale and limp too, and the pastel pink turned her tanned skin sallow. She didn't look brave and bold and bizarre any more. She looked like any wishy-washy little London girl from the back streets.

'I'm not wearing it,' she said, desperately trying to pull it up over her head.

'Don't be silly, Kitty,' said Mrs Chubb.

'I'm not being silly. I don't want to *look* silly! I *won't* wear it and you can't make me.' She must have seen me looking horrified and bit her lip. 'I'm sorry. It was very kind of you to make it for me. I just don't want it. Give it to Lucy or save it till you have a baby girl. But I absolutely won't wear it myself, thank you very much.'

She was trying to be polite now but somehow she was making it worse, as if she were mocking Mrs Chubb's insistence on good manners. Mrs Chubb herself went very red in the face. She said nothing further – she just took the dress and marched off with it.

'Oh, Kitty! Now you've done it,' I said despairingly. 'You've hurt her feelings terribly. And you've upset her, because she can't have any more babies.'

'I didn't know, did I? I didn't ask her to make me that dreadful dress. You saw what it looked like, Lucy,' said Kitty, hurriedly putting her acrobat outfit on and stroking the velvet for comfort.

'Yes, but she meant well. She must have spent hours on it, sewing it by candlelight. She was just trying to be kind to you,' I said. 'She wants you to fit in to her family.'

'Yes, but I don't fit. I don't want to fit. I'm not this sort of family girl,' said Kitty.

'Don't you *like* having a family?' I asked. 'Don't you feel lonely without one?'

'I just want to have a family of two. I had Gaffer. Now I've got you. That's all I need. I don't see why you want all this lot,' said Kitty reproachfully.

'They make me feel safe,' I said. 'And loved and cared for. It's almost like having Nurse back.'

'You're soft, you are. Silly little rich girl wanting her Nursie,' said Kitty.

'Stop being so mean to me!' I said, and I gave her a push.

She pushed me back, quite hard. I stumbled, and landed on my bottom.

Mrs Chubb came rushing back. 'What's all this noise! Oh my goodness, are you two *fighting*?'

'No,' I said quickly.

'Yes!' said Kitty.

'Oh, Lucy Sweetheart, you poor little thing,' said Mrs Chubb, helping me up. 'Did Kitty knock you to the floor?'

'We were just playing. She didn't mean to knock me right over. And I'm not the slightest bit hurt, truly,' I said.

Mrs Chubb didn't believe me. 'I've had enough of you and your tantrums today, Kitty,' she said sternly. 'You can stay in this bedroom today as a punishment. I'm not having you near all the other children if you can't be trusted to behave yourself.'

'You can't make me stay in this blooming bedroom!' Kitty declared defiantly.

'Oh yes I can,' said Mrs Chubb. She took hold of my hand, whisked me out of the room with her, and then turned the key in the lock of the door. 'There!' she said, putting the key in her apron pocket.

'Let me *out*!' Kitty called, and she started yelling a string of strange words in a language I didn't understand. Even so, their meaning was quite clear. She was unmistakably cursing Mrs Chubb.

She looked immensely shocked. 'Oh my lord, hark at her! Come with me at once, Lucy,' she said, and walked me down the stairs with her.

Kitty heard our footsteps and started screaming.

'Oh, poor Kitty! Listen, she's crying so!'

'That's just temper,' said Mrs Chubb. 'She'll stop when her throat gets sore.'

'You are just joking, aren't you, Mrs Chubb?' I asked. 'I mean, you're not really going to keep Kitty locked in the bedroom?'

'She has to learn. I can't be doing with her wild ways. I can't have any roustabouts in my household, not with so many little ones running around. I daresay the twins can look after themselves, but what if she pushed poor little Arthur Thumb or Mikey Trotter? What if she was rough with Little Albert Angel?' said Mrs Chubb.

'But she wouldn't! Not ever! Kitty's not like that. She's really kind. She's looked after me so. She's only being so surly because she hates feeling helpless. She's just not used to this sort of life,' I said.

'Oh, you're such a dear forgiving child, Lucy Sweetheart. But I do know best, you know. I'm rearing six splendid boys, and the whole street compliments me on my fine family. All the other mothers want me to mind their children. It's how I earn my tuppenny worth so we can have good food on the table and a roaring fire in winter. But if I let young Kitty rule the roost and answer back and hit the other children then some of the little ones will copy her. Then where will we be?'

'I know Kitty must seem very rude and naughty and ungrateful – but she's truly a dear sweet girl too,' I insisted.

Kitty's screams were still piercing, even though we were downstairs now. Mrs Chubb took no notice, and folded the new dress in soft paper and tucked it in a drawer. Her hands were trembling.

'I'll save it for one of the other little girls that I mind,' she said. 'Seeing as I can't ever hope for a daughter myself now.'

'Kitty sounds so upset,' I said, nearly in tears myself. 'I'm sure she's learned her lesson. Can't we let her out?'

'She needs to rest that ankle of hers,' said Mrs Chubb. 'It will do her good to have a quiet day.'

'You can't keep her locked up *all day*!' I said. 'What about when she has to pay a visit?'

'There's a chamber pot under the bed. And I'll take her something to eat at lunch time. Don't look so tragic, Lucy. I'd act the same with any of my own children if they were as wilful and wild. Now, I thought I'd bake another pie today. I'd better get busy.'

I didn't know what to do. I felt I should stamp my foot and start screaming too so I could be locked up with Kitty, but I badly wanted Mrs Chubb to keep liking me. I was a little bit scared of her now too. Miss Groan had punished me often enough, but she had never actually locked me away.

I could still hear Kitty's screams in the kitchen, even with the little ones playing a noisy game of marching soldiers. Tommy Magpie was the captain of the little army, and drilled them vigorously.

'You can be a soldier too if you want, Lucy,' he offered.

'I don't really feel like being a soldier right this minute, Tommy Magpie,' I said. 'I just feel so sorry for Kitty.'

'But she's been bad,' he said. 'Hasn't she, Ma?'

'Yes, she has, dear. Lucy, come and watch me make the pastry. Let's see if you can rub the fat into the flour.

You've got neat little hands. I think you'll make a light pastry.'

I felt I was being a traitor to Kitty, but I let Mrs Chubb teach me how to make a pie, even though the screaming upstairs continued relentlessly.

'Kitty sounds really unhappy, Ma,' said Tommy Magpie, nibbling on a shred of raw pastry from the tabletop.

'I daresay,' said Mrs Chubb. 'But she'll quieten down soon. Don't you eat raw pastry, Tommy Magpie, or you'll get worms.'

Mrs Chubb rolled the pastry out to make the pie and then gave me a leftover strip to make jam tarts. I made ten tiny ones, and decided that I'd keep the best for Kitty. Maybe I'd give her two when she was released at last. Her screams were getting hoarser now, making my own throat ache.

'She sounds as if she's really in pain, Mrs Chubb,' I said.

'There's nothing up in that there bedroom that could possibly hurt her,' she said.

'Perhaps she's stamped her foot and hurt her poor ankle all over again?' I suggested.

'My, you've got a vivid imagination, Lucy Sweetheart!' said Mrs Chubb, unmoved.

We put the pie and the tarts in the oven and cleared up the table. Then Little Albert Angel woke for his mid-morning feed, and Mrs Chubb lay on the sofa to do this.

The room filled with the sweet smell of baking pastry.

'It's a shame to disturb the little pet,' said Mrs Chubb. 'Do you think you could have a peep and see if they're ready to come out of the oven, Lucy? Wind a thick cloth round both your hands to make sure you don't get burnt.'

I did as I was told, proud that she'd trust me to do this. The jam tarts were shining red with raspberry jam and Little Albert Angel was changed and nodding back to sleep again when I suddenly realized something. My heart started thudding with a new fear.

'Kitty's stopped screaming!' I said.

'Yes, I know. She stopped a good ten minutes ago,' said Mrs Chubb. 'I knew she'd get tired of it eventually.'

'Can I go and see if she's all right?' I asked.

'Of course she's all right. She's simply tired herself out and gone to sleep. Don't you go disturbing her or she'll start all over again and my ears are ringing as it is. What a temper that child has!' said Mrs Chubb.

'It's just that she hates being locked up,' I said. I was getting terribly worried now. What if Kitty had tried to escape? She couldn't get out of the door. What if she tried to get out of the window? If she jumped she wouldn't just hurt her ankle again. She could easily break her neck.

My chest was so tight I could hardly get the words out.

'She could have jumped out of the window,' I said in a rush.

'No she couldn't. It's nailed shut, because I needed to make sure none of my boys tried any silly tricks like that,' said Mrs Chubb. She came over to me and put her

199

arms round me. 'There now. Stop worriting that pretty little head of yours.'

It worrited until I thought it would explode. I begged Mrs Chubb to let me take a jam tart up to Kitty, but she made me wait until dinner time, and even then frowned at the idea of giving her a treat.

'By rights she should have plain bread and water as she's being punished, but I don't hold with a child going without proper nourishment, and she looks half-starved already. We'll give her a bowl of my tomato soup and she can even have a dab of butter on her bread – but no jam tarts,' she said firmly.

She wouldn't let me take the meal up to Kitty, no matter how hard I begged. She took it herself. I waited, holding my breath, wondering if Kitty would start screaming again. She might even take it into her head to throw the soup at Mrs Chubb. I looked for scarlet splashes on her apron when she came down, but it remained pristine.

'How is she?' I asked breathlessly.

'Well enough. At least she's quiet now. She's in a bit of a sulk and wouldn't say a word, but that's better than all that screaming,' said Mrs Chubb.

I blinked, thinking this over. 'She did sit up though, and start eating?' I asked.

'I'm sure she did, the moment I was gone,' she said.

'But you're certain she was all right? Was she asleep? Did you listen to make sure she was breathing?' I said, the questions tumbling out of my mouth.

'For goodness' sake, Little Missy Worrypot, your tiresome friend is perfectly well. Now stop this nonsense and eat your own soup,' she said.

I was even more worried when she sent Tommy Magpie to fetch Kitty's tray an hour later and he brought her food back untouched.

'Her spoon's shining clean so she hasn't had even a lick of soup. And her bread hasn't got a single bite,' he said, in wonder that any child could leave her lunch. 'Can I eat it up, Ma?'

'You may have the bread, son, but eat it quick before the other kiddies see.' She looked at me. 'Perhaps you'd like to share it with Lucy Sweetheart?'

'I don't want it,' I said.

'Now don't you go into a sulk too,' said Mrs Chubb. 'You're my good girl!' She settled herself on the couch with the baby and then patted the space by her side. 'Come and have a cuddle, dearie.'

I couldn't resist. I walked over to her and she pulled me close to her.

'There now! My two new babies,' she said.

I closed my eyes and nestled into her. It felt so good to be held in her warm strong arms. I still worried desperately about Kitty, but even so I found I was lulled to sleep. Little Albert Angel slept too, snuffling happily. But then Tommy Magpie came to report that the twins were having a fight over a toy top and Mikey Totter had tried to climb the stairs and tumbled down again. Mrs Chubb sighed and got to her feet.

'Can you hold Little Albert, sweetheart?' she asked.

He started wailing, wanting his mother back, but I held him against my chest and walked him round the room, showing him things to distract him, and he soon perked up. I jogged up and down and he liked this a lot, chuckling away, one of his little starfish hands clutching my finger.

Mrs Chubb smiled when she came back into the room. 'You two look such a picture! You're like a real big sister to him, Lucy Sweetheart,' she said, her head on one side.

I tried to be sisterly to all the Chubb children. Tommy Magpie showed me his secret stash of liquorice and insisted I have a nibble at the end of a stick. I realized this was a great favour and tried to act grateful.

'It's the best taste in the world. I'd have liquorice for breakfast, liquorice for dinner, and liquorice for supper,' Tommy Magpie declared.

'Liquorice porridge, liquorice soup, liquorice pie – all washed down with a jolly glass of liquorice cordial,' I said, which made him laugh.

It was harder talking to the twins because they were such fidgety little boys who couldn't keep still. I wished Kitty was free to teach them how to tumble. They knew how to do forward rolls already so I sang the Tumbling Boy song while they performed the actions. I could see they had the makings of a good comedy act that would maybe bring in the crowds, but I knew Mrs Chubb would faint at such an idea.

It was easy enough to entertain Arthur Thumb. I simply told him a story, pulling him onto my lap. The Chubbs didn't have any proper books, only a big Bible, so I told him the story of Tom Thumb instead, and he loved this, though the giant ogres made him squirm a lot. I hoped he wouldn't have bad dreams about them.

Mikey Totter couldn't concentrate on a complicated story. His favourite game was Peep-bo. I hid my face in my paisley shawl and then bobbed out at him, going *Peep-bo*! Mikey squealed with laughter every time, wanting me to play this game again and again and again.

'Give poor Lucy Sweetheart a rest, Mikey!' said Mrs Chubb. 'You wouldn't like to peel the potatoes with me, dear? It would be such a help when there's so many of us.'

I tied the shawl round my waist like an apron, but Mrs Chubb tutted and took it from me, wrapping it up carefully and putting it on a high shelf out of reach from the little ones with their sticky fingers.

'Such a beautiful shawl,' she said, rubbing it against her cheek. She hesitated, and then spoke in a lowered tone. 'Did it belong to your dear mother?'

'Yes, it did,' I said sadly, wanting her to feel sorry for me. I couldn't tell her I'd stolen it from a church pew. It didn't seem a total lie. I was sure my mother must have owned shawls, maybe even a paisley one.

'Well, it's very precious, I can see that. It suits you beautifully, the blue background bringing out the blue of your eyes,' said Mrs Chubb. 'I've got blue eyes too, but all my boys have brown eyes, taking after their father. If I'd been blessed with a little daughter I'm sure she'd have had blue eyes.'

She smiled at me wistfully, and I stood on a stool beside her at the sink while we peeled all the potatoes. It was cold dirty work, nowhere near as much fun as making the pie. It was heating up in the oven now and smelling delicious all over again.

When the potatoes were all peeled at last Mrs Chubb put them into a huge saucepan and set them on the range to boil. Tommy Magpie set off to meet his pa, and I wrapped the shawl round my shoulders and tagged along with him again, eager for another ride on Nelson. I wondered how I could enjoy myself when poor Kitty was still locked up in the bedroom but I tried to stop feeling guilty by telling myself that it was her own fault after all. If she'd only accepted her dress politely and acted grateful then she'd have been able to have a lovely day too. Her ankle might be strong enough now for her to walk to the stables. I was sure she'd like Nelson and love to ride on him too.

When we got home Mrs Chubb was trying to mash the potatoes while Mikey Trotter clung to her skirts and the twins tormented Arthur Thumb. I begged her to let me take Kitty her supper, with a little jam tart for pudding.

'Where *is* little Miss Kitty?' Mr Chubb asked, cuffing both twins, though they simply laughed at him.

'She's been in bed all day as a punishment for acting so wild,' said Mrs Chubb, mashing away fiercely. She looked as if she'd like to mash Kitty too.

'All day!' said Mr Chubb. 'That's a bit steep, isn't it, Mrs C?'

'She wasn't just incredibly rude to me, she knocked little Lucy to the floor!' said Mrs Chubb, red in the face.

'Yes, but she didn't mean to. And I pushed her first,' I said.

'There you are! Kiddies have their little scraps. Look at the twins!' said Mr Chubb.

'You don't understand, Mr C,' said Mrs Chubb. She lowered her voice. 'I'll explain later when the children are all in bed.'

'But don't you think it's time we let little Kitty *out* of bed,' said Mr Chubb.

'Well, she needed to rest that ankle to get it properly better. It's for her own good,' said Mrs Chubb. 'She can get up tomorrow.'

'So can I take her supper up to her now?' I asked again. I opened my eyes wide. 'Please, dear kind Mrs Chubb?'

She laughed at me. 'You might look like an angel, Lucy Sweetheart, but you're an artful little monkey. Very well.'

She cut Kitty a generous portion of pie and mash, with a glass of milk and my jam tart on a pretty little saucer, and set it all out nicely on a tray. Then she took the bedroom door key out of her pocket and handed it to me.

'Carry the tray up carefully now. Try not to spill. There's a good girl.'

I went up the stairs slowly and then set the tray down while I fumbled with the key in the lock until it turned. I picked up the tray and opened the door – and gasped.

Kitty was standing right in front of me, holding a full chamber pot up high.

'*What are you doing?*' I cried.

'Oh, for goodness' sake, it's you, Lucy!' said Kitty, setting the pot down on the floor, to my huge relief. 'I thought it would be old Ma Chubbychops! I was going to chuck it at her, and then barge past. I reckoned I had a good chance of getting out the front door before anyone caught me.'

'You were going to run away without me?'

'I said I would, didn't I?' said Kitty, but then she added, 'I hoped you'd come too. Would you have?'

'Ugh, put that pot back under the bed. I don't like looking at it. And I don't think we'd have a chance of getting away, not with Mr Chubb there, and all those little boys. They'd grab hold of us. We'll have to find another way.'

'So you *will* run away with me?' Kitty asked urgently.

'I want to stay here! But if you won't stay too, I suppose I'll have to go with you,' I said, sighing.

'Oh, Lucy!' Kitty flung her arms round my neck and gave me a fierce hug.

'But we'll have to make a proper plan. We don't both want to end up locked in here all the time, do we?' I said. 'Meanwhile, why don't you eat your supper before it gets cold? And see that jam tart – *I* made it!'

'I vowed I wouldn't eat anything at all while she kept me a prisoner,' said Kitty, but I could tell by the way she was looking at the tray that she was starving.

'Eat it. You'll need all your strength if we run away tomorrow,' I said.

'Well, maybe I'll just eat the jam tart then, seeing as you made it specially for me,' said Kitty.

She crammed it into her mouth whole and then set upon the pie and mash, washing it down with great slurps of milk. I didn't have the heart to comment on her manners.

'I haven't had *my* supper yet, so I'd better go and eat it before one of the boys does,' I said, picking up her tray. The plate and saucer were so clean they looked as if they'd been washed already.

'That was good, especially the jam tart. I don't suppose I could have any more, could I, seeing as I didn't have anything at dinner time?' Kitty asked.

'That was your own fault! But I'll see. I think Mrs Chubb is feeling a bit worried about locking you up for so long,' I said.

I went downstairs. The boys had all finished their suppers and were playing a violent game of Noah's Ark on the living-room floor, making the lions and tigers eat all the smaller animals. I sat down in the kitchen by myself and ate my own meal, which had been keeping warm between two plates on top of the range. Mr Chubb was out in the back yard smoking his pipe, and Mrs Chubb was keeping him company. I could hear them murmuring to each other outside the window.

I wasn't concentrating on what they were saying until I heard Mrs Chubb say the name Kitty. I swallowed my last mouthful and crept right up to the window, careful to keep behind the curtain so they wouldn't look round and see me. I pressed my ear to the glass and heard more distinctly.

'She's got to go,' said Mrs Chubb. 'I can't abide the child. She's such a bad influence on Lucy Sweetheart. She'll stick up for that wild little thing no matter what.'

'But what are you going to do? You surely can't turn her out onto the streets to fend for herself?' said Mr Chubb.

'It's where she came from, isn't it? You can tell she's never lived in a proper house with a decent family. She actually cursed me today, pointing her finger and talking some strange heathen language. I think she's a gypsy child, with those big dark eyes and wild hair and savage temper. There's a gypsy camp over at the common. I reckon we should take her there, so she can be among her own sort,' said Mrs Chubb.

'But what about Lucy? She'll never forgive you if you take her little pal away,' said Mr Chubb.

'We'll tell her she's run away of her own accord. She's such a trusting little soul I reckon she'll believe us,' said Mrs Chubb.

I was shaken to the core. How could my own dear Mrs Chubb betray me so utterly? To think I wanted her as my mother! I didn't want to be her little girl any more. I'd never let her take Kitty away from me, never ever ever.

14

I had to make a plan. My head ached with all kinds of outlandish and impossible ideas. I even wondered if Kitty's chamber pot might have to be used. But in the end it was simple. Mrs Chubb thought I was sweet and innocent. She trusted me utterly.

When the Chubbs came back indoors I'd washed up all the dishes and made the kitchen spick and span. I solemnly handed the key back to Mrs Chubb.

'Kitty ate up all her supper this time – and she said she was very sorry for being so naughty,' I said. 'She's wondering if she could possibly have another jam tart? She liked it so much.'

'For goodness' sake!' said Mrs Chubb. 'She's in disgrace! You don't punish a child by giving her another treat!'

'I reckon the little kiddy has been punished enough for one day,' said Mr Chubb. He lowered his voice. 'And we might as well make a bit of a fuss of her if . . . you know what.'

I knew what – but I kept my face smooth and bland.

'Then may I go and let her out, please, dear Mr Chubb?' I begged softly.

'You're an artful little miss, you are!' he said, chuckling. He looked at his wife. 'Let's let young Kitty have a bit of freedom now.'

'Oh, very well!' said Mrs Chubb. 'But if she starts any nonsense she'll get locked up again. It won't be in the bedroom this time – it'll be in the coal hole!'

I hoped she was joking – but I couldn't trust her now. She gave me the key and I ran upstairs two at a time.

'Have you got another jam tart?' Kitty asked hopefully.

'You might get one if you mind your manners,' I said. 'Oh, Kitty, I heard them talking, Mr and Mrs Chubb. They think you're a gypsy child because you cursed Mrs Chubb in a funny language!'

'That's comic!' said Kitty. 'I was just making up the words to make it sound more scary!'

'It's not comic at all. They're going to take you off to a gypsy camp and leave you there.'

The gypsies in my storybooks were always stealing children and doing very bad things. I thought Kitty would be horrified – but she was actually smiling!

'I like gypsies,' she said. 'Gaffer had a lot of gypsy friends. We travelled with them once. I love their bonfire stew! You'd like it too, Lucy – and they have horses, so you could ride them instead of that old nag Nelson.'

'Nelson's not an old nag! And *I'm* not being taken to the gypsies. They want me to stay here and be their little girl!' I said, anguished.

'Isn't that what you want?' Kitty asked sharply.

'No, not without you! We have to run away quick!'

'Well, that's what I've been saying all along!' said Kitty. She swung her legs out of bed and stood up. 'There, my ankle hardly hurts at all now.'

'But pretend it does when we go downstairs. And be very meek and sorry,' I told her.

'But I'm not!'

'*Act* it, you noodle,' I said, as she pulled on her beloved acrobat outfit. 'Then they won't be suspicious. So when we get a chance we can run for it.'

I wasn't sure Kitty could control herself, but she surprised me. She hung her head and tried to hide behind me when we went into the living room.

'What are you doing, lurking there?' Mrs Chubb said suspiciously.

'I'm so ashamed,' said Kitty in a tiny voice. She rubbed her eyes and managed to look tearful. 'I'm very, very sorry for behaving so badly, Mrs Chubb.'

'Ah, poor little mite!' said Mr Chubb. 'See, she's sorry now, Mrs C. Let her have that jam tart now.'

'She's already had one. And there's only one left. We should give it to someone else,' said Mrs Chubb.

'Well, I reckon the only one of us who hasn't had one is our Little Albert, and he ain't got teeth in his head to deal with it,' said Mr Chubb. 'So *I'll* have it, seeing as I'm head of this family.'

He took the remaining tart and acted like he was eating it – but when Mrs Chubb turned her back to lift Albert out of his drawer Mr Chubb pressed it into Kitty's hand. She stuffed it into her mouth and had swallowed it down by the time Mrs Chubb glanced up. She looked suspicious, but said nothing.

Little Albert Angel was wailing miserably and wouldn't settle, even when Mrs Chubb carried him round the room, patting his back.

'Oh, Albert, why do you always start fretting now, when I'm longing for a bit of peace and quiet?' Mrs Chubb said wearily, rubbing her cheek against his fluffy head.

'Perhaps he needs feeding?' Mr Chubb suggested.

'I fed him an hour ago. He's full to the brim,' said Mrs Chubb.

'I'll take him for a little while. You sit down and have a rest,' I offered.

'Thank you kindly, Lucy Sweetheart,' she said. 'Better take off that beautiful shawl though, just in case he's sick on it.'

'You wear it for a little while,' I said, and I wrapped it right round her.

'Oh my, it's so soft and warm,' she said, stroking it with a roughened hand.

'You can have it if you like,' I said.

'Bless you, dear, I couldn't possibly take your pretty shawl, especially as it was your mother's!' said Mrs Chubb. She handed me Little Albert Angel, who cried like a little devil at first, but then his wails slowed and his eyelids drooped. I thought he was nearly asleep so I tried easing him into his drawer but he screeched indignantly. I sighed and started walking him again.

'He's so little and yet he can really make your arms ache,' I said.

'I'll take him for a bit,' Kitty offered.

'No! No, let Lucy keep on nursing him!' Mrs Chubb said urgently, as if she thought Kitty might dash the baby's head on the hearthstone.

Kitty reddened and I tensed, waiting for an outburst that would surely get her locked up all over again – but she managed to bite her lip and stay silent. Little Albert Angel gradually calmed down and fell so soundly asleep that he didn't murmur when I tucked him into his makeshift cot.

Mrs Chubb was having a little doze on the sofa, worn out.

'I'll just nip to the outhouse,' I murmured to Mr Chubb. I looked at Kitty meaningfully.

'I will too,' she said quickly.

'Yes, I'll help you. Your poor ankle isn't any better, is it?' I said, as Kitty gave an exaggerated hobble.

I took her arm, and we went out of the living room, through the kitchen and out of the back door. Then we looked at each other, hardly able to believe it was so simple. There was a fence behind the outhouse, but not too high, and I'd learned how to climb now. We were both up and over it in a trice, and then we ran along the alleyway, faster and faster, out into the main road.

We didn't stop running until we were many streets away and then leaned against a wall, gasping for breath.

'We . . . did . . . it!' Kitty spluttered.

'And your ankle . . . you were running . . . really fast!' I panted.

'Well, no point . . . hanging around! But it's . . . much much better. And we're free, we're free!' said Kitty, flinging her arms in the air.

'Free as a bird!' I said, and whirled around.

'But you've had to leave your shawl behind!' said Kitty.

'I don't mind,' I said. I wanted Mrs Chubb to keep it. She had been so very kind to me, after all. And I couldn't help feeling guilty for deceiving her.

'Truly?' said Kitty. 'I know you didn't really want to run away.'

'I want to be with you most of all,' I said. 'Oh bother, I'll tell you another thing we've left behind – the reticule with all our money in it!'

'We've left it in the bedroom – but I've got the tin!' said Kitty, jingling coins in her pockets.

'Clever you!' I cried, and hugged her.

She hugged me back hard. 'Clever *you!*' she said. 'I couldn't have escaped without you.'

But we didn't feel quite so clever after we'd wandered around for an hour or more, trying to find a safe place to stay the night. Kitty started limping quite badly. She insisted her ankle didn't hurt at all, though we both knew she needed to rest. We couldn't risk going to the park in case Tommy Magpie led his parents there. We couldn't see a church. We couldn't find any derelict houses anywhere.

It was colder than usual and we shivered in our light clothing, but the only warm places were the ale houses, and we were chased away when we tried to go inside. We ended up taking shelter in a shop doorway, huddled together on the step.

'I wish I hadn't left that shawl behind now,' I said. 'I could have spread it over both of us.'

'I'm sure you're wishing you'd left yourself behind too,' said Kitty mournfully.

I *was* partly wishing that, but I denied it vehemently. 'I don't even like Mrs Chubb any more, even though she made such a fuss of me,' I insisted.

'*Mr* Chubb wasn't so bad,' said Kitty. 'We'll have to get right away from this district tomorrow. We don't want him driving past on his hackney cab and spotting us!'

'Where can we go?' I asked – and then I suddenly remembered my former plan! 'Mr Chubb won't see us because we won't be anywhere near here. We'll be at a palace in a great big park,' I said.

'And you'll be Princess Lucy and I'll be Princess Kitty,' she said. 'Go on with the story then!'

'It isn't a story,' I said. 'I'm being serious. We're going to the Great Exhibition!'

'What's that?' Kitty asked.

'It's a special show just opened in Hyde Park. They've built a crystal palace full of wondrous treasures. My governess told me all about it. Thousands of people go there every day. I'm sure they have to queue to get in. I think they might appreciate a little entertainment – like a girl singing and another girl tumbling!'

'Oh, Lucy!' Kitty exclaimed, hugging me tightly. 'Anyone would think you were born for this kind of life!'

It somehow didn't seem so cold any more. Even the stone step seemed softer. We curled up together and started to discuss our performance, but were both asleep in moments.

I woke at dawn, with a stiff neck and aching back, but I was still excited by my plan. The sky was glowing rosy pink with the sunrise and it seemed like a good omen. Kitty felt me stirring and stood up and stretched, wincing a little.

'How's your ankle?' I asked anxiously.

'It's completely better,' she said, probably lying.

'And your wrist?'

'As good as new,' she said, flapping her hand. 'Come on then, Lucy, let's get some breakfast and be on our way. We have to find somewhere quiet to practise our routine.

Perhaps it needs to be a little longer to make a good impression at such a grand venue. We'd better make up several more verses.'

She was acting as if *she* wrote the verses, and had planned the whole enterprise – but I was just happy she was in good spirits again. We found a bakehouse a few streets away where the woman let us sit inside in the warm and share a small loaf still hot from the oven, washed down with a mug of milk with a dash of coffee in it. She even let us use her own outhouse. Kitty tried to pay her a little extra for her kindness but she wouldn't take even a penny tip.

'You keep your money, dears. It would be a hard-hearted soul to try to make a profit from two little girls. Where are you off to so early?' she asked.

'We're going to the Great Exhibition,' I said proudly, though Kitty frowned at me.

'Oh my!' said the kindly lady. 'How exciting! I hear they've got a diamond there as big as a fist.'

'*We* want to see the elephant,' I said.

The lady chuckled. 'Then I'd better give you a bun to feed him,' she said, and she popped *two* into a paper bag and gave it to me.

I thanked her very much and Kitty did too, determined to show that she could have good manners when she wanted – but she shook her head at me outside the shop.

'You shouldn't have told her where we're going! What if Mr Chubb comes in here for a loaf of bread!' she remonstrated.

'Oh, for goodness' sake, Kitty, he lives miles and miles away, and I'm sure he won't come driving his cab round here,' I said.

'It's still a risk,' Kitty insisted. 'And what were you doing, making up such stories about elephants!'

'There truly *is* an elephant there! I know all about it,' I said.

'Can you ride on it?' Kitty asked.

'It's not a real live elephant, it's a stuffed one,' I said.

'So why did she give you the buns for it?'

'It was a *joke* because she wanted to be kind to us,' I said. 'Shall we save them or eat them up now?'

'Better save them,' said Kitty – which was sensible, because we were still a very long way from Hyde Park.

She never once complained about her ankle but she was limping again, and her lips were pressed tightly together with the effort to keep going.

'I think we should take an omnibus,' I said. 'We're better dressed now.'

'Do you think it's very expensive?' Kitty asked, jingling the coins in her pockets.

The driver only charged tuppence each, which seemed a considerable bargain. We sat up on top, and watched the world go by, munching our sugar buns. After quite a while the streets grew very congested and by the time we got to the West End the bus was crawling.

'Everyone out at Piccadilly Circus,' the driver shouted. 'We can't go no further. All the thoroughfares are blocked with folk going to the Exhibition. Out you get!'

Piccadilly Circus was the most extraordinary place. I'd never seen so many people crammed together in my life. There were rich people – the men in top hats and the ladies in crinolines – and poor people in ragged clothes, and lots of ordinary families wearing caps and bonnets and carrying picnic baskets for sustenance on their journey. There were folk talking in Scotch and Welsh and Irish accents, and foreign languages I didn't understand. There were African people in bright robes, and Indian people with turbans, and Chinamen with brocade jackets and pigtails hanging down their backs.

Kitty might stand out in most places wearing her crimson velvet, but now no one gave her a second glance. We held hands so we wouldn't get lost in the vast crowd. We didn't need to ask the way. The crowd was surging in one direction only.

There was an immense department store called Swan and Edgar decked out in red, white and blue ribbons, with a model waxen family displayed in the window supposedly going to the Great Exhibition too. It was getting very hot now and I hoped the family's faces wouldn't start melting in the strong sunlight. It seemed so strange to think that if Ermintrude's face hadn't melted I wouldn't be here with Kitty leading this odd new exciting life.

It was still quite a way along Piccadilly to Hyde Park and we had to go at a snail's pace in the jostling crowd, but everyone was in a happy mood, laughing and calling, some even singing merry songs. There weren't just people on the pavement and spread out all over the wide thoroughfare. Office folk hung out of the windows in the buildings above us, some clerks boldly sitting on the windowsills themselves, waving Union Jacks. Ragged boys shinned up lampposts for a better view, and there was a huge banner strung over us proclaiming:

**PEACE AND GOODWILL
TO ALL THE WORLD
GOD SAVE THE QUEEN
AND PRINCE ALBERT**

When we got to the park gates at last we still couldn't catch so much as a glimpse of the Crystal Palace, even though we scrambled up onto tables and chairs for a proper view of it. We seemed in the midst of a vast feast. There were big trucks selling baskets of gingerbread and lardy cake and sweets galore and ginger beer, while women carried great baskets piled high with oranges. One tumbled off onto the grass and Kitty grabbed it quickly and put it in her pocket.

There were men with trays selling silver medals of the Crystal Palace. I badly wanted one because they were only sixpence each, but Kitty took one look and said they were just cheap tin and not worth it.

We fought our way forward, most folk towering above us, every now and then conscious of a strange dazzle ahead of us, like the strongest sunlight reflecting on water, and then we suddenly had a clear view through the tall elm trees. We clutched hands, overwhelmed. There was the vast glass palace, a great rainbow gleam, wide enough to house ten thousand princesses and all the elephants in Africa.

As we got nearer, the colours settled to blue and yellow and red, with a multitude of flags flying from the glass rooftop, and a vast queue scarcely moving, all desperate to get inside the wondrous palace. Many wily folk had had the same idea as me: there were singers carolling anything from opera to bawdy ditties; flautists and violinists and hurdy-gurdy men with chattering monkeys; dancers and acrobats and strongmen; and simple beggars, some blind, some with missing limbs, some so small they only came up to my waist. They all had purses or caps half-full of pennies.

'Oh, Kitty, just look! How will we ever get the attention that we need when we have so many rivals?' I asked.

'We have a unique act,' said Kitty. 'And we're little children. The crowds will love us. Now, we have to work out the best vantage point! Perhaps we ought not to do our act too close to the palace itself. Folk will be so keen to get in they won't want to be distracted. Shall we try that little space over there, between that man with the big drum and the juggler? They are both so big they will make us look even smaller.'

'Yes, I see what you mean. But if we get much nearer then we'll be able to peer through the glass walls, and maybe, just maybe, we'll see the elephant,' I said.

Kitty sighed – but she let us be swept along by the crowds, and as we got nearer and nearer the Crystal Palace she couldn't help getting excited too.

It was impossible to get the view I wanted with so many other people blocking our way. We were all being channelled forward towards the main entrance, with families pushing this way and that, determined to pay their shillings and get inside.

'Do you think that children might possibly be half price?' I asked Kitty. 'Couldn't we just have a *little* look at the Exhibition before we think about performing?'

'We're here to make money, not to spend it!' Kitty said sternly.

'Oh!' I said. I couldn't say anything else. I wanted to see the elephant so much.

'Oh, Lucy, don't look like that! I'm sorry to be so fierce. My goodness, if it wasn't for you I could still be locked up in that wretched bedroom! All right, we will have a look round the Exhibition first. I'll be able to tell Gaffer about it when – when I next see him.'

I didn't see how she could possibly do that if he was dead and buried, as I suspected, but I couldn't press her further, because I could see she was near tears. She cheered up enormously however when we tagged onto a large family with six children in their wake like little ducklings. We got whisked past the pay booths with them and entered the Exhibition without paying a penny.

The palace was even more impressive inside. The sun poured through the shining glass and made pools of light on the pale wooden floor. There was greenery everywhere, as if the park outside had crept in with us. Real trees reached right up the arch of the Transept, and water spurted from an immense glass fountain. White marble statues twice life-size peered down upon the crowds below, unabashed by their own nakedness.

I asked an attendant if there was a gallery especially for animals and he directed us to the Eastern Nave. We saw two huge Arabian horses rearing up on their white marble legs, and a great Bavarian lion so realistic that we backed away rapidly, scared it would pounce on us. But where was the wondrous stuffed elephant?

We wandered through gallery after gallery looking for him, and saw furniture, ornaments, jewellery, lace and vast gleaming machinery. Miss Groan would have wanted me to stand and watch and listen and learn – but I skipped along with Kitty scarcely paying attention, stopping willy-nilly and then dashing on again.

We were stopped occasionally and told that unattended children weren't permitted in the Great Exhibition, but we pretended our parents had gone ahead to the next great gallery and scurried off to join them.

We saw a vast metal bedstead with curtains of the same crimson velvet as Kitty's acrobatic costume.

'It's *my* bed!' said Kitty proudly. 'And when all these thousands of people have traipsed back to their own homes we shall jump up into it and close the curtains and sleep in splendour all night long.'

At last we came across a bizarre collection of stuffed animals, and thought the little frogs very comical, especially the barber frog supposedly shaving his customer – but there was no sign of any elephant.

I began to think I had imagined one, but then we found ourselves in the gorgeously ornate Indian gallery – and at last, there was the elephant! He was enormous, richly clothed in fine embroidered hangings, with a carved gold carriage as big as a hackney cab balanced on his vast grey back.

'There's my elephant! Oh, look at him, Kitty, isn't he splendid! And so lifelike! When we have the Crystal Palace all to ourselves I'm sure he will come alive and we will climb right up to that carriage and sit there like sultans. The elephant will take us for a tour of the Exhibition and then ride us round Hyde Park by the light of the moon. Won't that be marvellous!' I cried.

'It will indeed,' said Kitty, rubbing her ankle. 'But now you've seen him we'd better get to work.'

'Don't you think we'd better have a little rest first? Is your ankle very painful?' I asked.

'It aches a little,' said Kitty. 'But when I do the tumbling boy I'm mostly doing handstands and cartwheels so I won't be standing on it.'

'I should think up another song especially for the Exhibition. I wish I could think of a good rhyme for elephant,' I said, as we made our way to one of the exits.

We badly needed refreshments as it was long past dinner time by now. We shared a ham sandwich and a piece of currant lardy cake and took turns sucking at an orange. Then we had a little rest under the shade of a tree. Kitty slept a little and I lay on my back, composing.

I made up a variation of the National Anthem as everyone seemed in such a patriotic mood, blessing Queen Victoria and Prince Albert.

God save our gracious Queen
Long live our noble Queen
God save the Queen.
Make it your mission
To see the Ex-hi-bi-tion
The greatest there's ever be-ee-n
God save the Queen!

Kitty and I could hold hands and sing it together. She was wearing red and I was wearing blue. I picked the daisies in the grass and made two white daisy chains. Now we would be dressed in the colours of the Union Jack!

I told Kitty my idea when she woke up and she was impressed.

'Though I can still do the tumbling boy, can't I?' she asked.

'Of course, Kitty. That's our best act ever,' I said.

It seemed a great effort to walk all the way round the enormous palace so we decided to place ourselves near the exit. There were only a few performers there, though there were many souvenir sellers. I still hankered after a commemorative medal, silver or not, and I wanted to buy a little glass model of the Crystal Place *and* a china figure of the Queen and Prince Albert, but Kitty frowned at me.

'We're not punters, Lucy. We're performers,' she said. She took hold of my hands. 'Let's start right now!'

My stomach lurched. I'd got used to singing in front of ten or twenty people in a park. But we were at the Crystal Palace now and there were huge crowds milling around everywhere.

My throat dried so I could hardly speak. 'I don't think I can!' I whispered.

'Swallow. Take a deep breath. We'll start with the tumbling boy, seeing as we know that best. Come *on*!' Kitty implored.

So I swallowed, I breathed, then I opened my mouth and started singing.

'See the little tumbling boy,' I quavered, and Kitty turned herself head over heels and landed lightly on both feet without wincing. We'd begun!

No one seemed to notice at first. We just looked like two children larking about. So I sang louder and Kitty shouted '*Hey!*' each time she tumbled. The souvenir sellers stared, a large family stopped and smiled, then another – and suddenly we had a little crowd around us. I sang out and Kitty cartwheeled round and round. When

I began the last verse I cupped my hands hopefully for money and the crowd responded generously.

Kitty stuffed the coins in her pockets and then we stood together and sang the anthem about going to the Exhibition. This went down so well that the crowd grew and started throwing more coins at our feet. As soon as we'd finished the verse they shouted for us to sing it again – and the third time most of them joined in too.

They sang it as they drifted off on their way home, but we attracted fresh people and another shower of coins. Kitty's pockets were now so full that they were weighing her down and she could barely keep her puffy trousers in place.

'I'd better look after the money!' I said. 'We don't want your trousers falling round your ankles!'

I searched for some kind of container in vain while Kitty stood on her hands and waggled her feet in the air.

'Don't worry, little missy,' said the man selling the miniature Crystal Palaces. 'You can use one of my empty boxes. I'll look after it for you. My, you two tiny kiddies are making a fortune! And no wonder! I've never seen such a novelty act before.'

'That's so kind of you, sir,' I said politely.

He chuckled. 'You've got a sweet tongue in that pretty head. Do you like my little palaces? If I've got any left at the end of my stint I'll give you one for free,' he promised.

I thought him a lovely man and sang out happily after that, collecting coins after each song and depositing them in his box. They made a satisfying clinking sound as they tumbled into it.

'Making a fortune, you are!' he repeated admiringly.

We sang on and Kitty tumbled and after a long while we started improvising, doing a little dance between numbers. The crowd clapped and cheered appreciatively whatever we did and threw more coins. We really *were* making a fortune.

'Oh, Kitty, isn't this amazing?' I said.

'It's marvellous. You've had the best idea ever!' said Kitty. 'You're the cleverest girl in the world!' She smiled at me, her eyes sparkling, her cheeks flushed, though she was limping now as she ran about.

'Perhaps we ought to take a rest now,' I said.

'Not when we've gathered such a good crowd!' said Kitty. 'I can't wait to count up all the coins! Where are you putting all the tin?'

'That kind man's lent me a box. He's keeping an eye on it for us,' I said.

'What man?' said Kitty, suddenly frowning.

'He's just behind us. He's selling those little Crystal Palaces and he says he'll give me one for nothing!' I said.

I looked round to point him out – but I couldn't see him.

'He was just there!' I said, puzzled. I dodged in and out of the crowd, searching for him.

But he was gone, with his tray of little palaces – and our box full of money!

15

'I can't believe you could be so foolish!' Kitty exploded.

'But he was so kind! And he promised me one of the little palaces!' I said.

'And I said you were the cleverest girl in the world!' said Kitty. 'Oh, Lucy, I despair!'

Some of the crowd had drifted away, but there were still a great number staring at us impatiently. I had to try and save the situation.

'Ladies and gentlemen, as you can see, we are distraught,' I said. I opened my eyes as wide as possible and the tears started flowing. 'We've been hard at work performing all afternoon, but we've just discovered that a wicked man has stolen all our money. It wasn't for ourselves. Our poor dear mother is languishing at home, sick of a fever, and unless we can pay for a doctor we fear for her very life. I know some of you have already been generous, but could I beg you to spare us a few more pennies?'

I looked at them imploringly. A few shook their heads and backed away – but others seemed concerned. Several gentlemen searched their pockets and emptied all their loose change at my feet, and one white-haired elderly lady pressed a florin into my hand, though her companion remonstrated.

'It's a confidence trick, my dear! The child is doing her best to wring your heartstrings when I daresay she's telling us a string of lies,' she said, accurately enough.

'Look at her poor little innocent face with the tears running down her cheeks! No child would be capable of such guile,' the old lady insisted, and gave me *another* florin to show her friend she had a mind of her own.

I thanked her kindly, curtsying, and managed to get more folk to make their contributions.

'My, you can charm the birds from the trees,' Kitty muttered admiringly, when they'd all gone. 'I take it all back. You were brilliantly convincing. You should go on the stage.'

'As if Papa would ever let me become an actress!' I said. 'He'd sooner see me dead!' Then I realized that Papa wouldn't be seeing me any more, dead or alive. I could do as I liked. It felt so strange.

'What would you do if you suddenly saw your pa here, come to see the Exhibition? He might recognize you now, in your new blue frock,' said Kitty.

I tried to picture it. What would Papa do? Would he open his arms wide and pull me into a warm embrace? Would he burst into tears and tell me I'd broken his heart? Would he take his elegant ivory cane and beat me with it for running away? No, Papa wasn't a man of passion. He would look at me with cool distaste and hand me over to Miss Groan, while he went off with the New Mother and Angelique. I would be kept upstairs in permanent disgrace, peering out of the window until my own face melted like Ermintrude's.

'I do not think Papa has acted like a true father,' I said. 'But you are like a true sister, Kitty, even though we're not related. So I would run away with you.'

'That's the correct answer!' said Kitty, eyes shining. 'Let's go and celebrate our success. And tomorrow we'll do our act all over again. We will have a pitch here day after day, week after week, until the Exhibition has ended. But we'll look after our tin ourselves in future!'

We had a cheese-and-pickle sandwich and a slice of gingerbread cake and an orange and a ginger beer *each*, because we had been working so hard. Then we wandered off to find the best place to sleep for the night. We decided to stay in Hyde Park so we could start our act bright and early when the queue first started forming at the main entrance of the exhibition.

We were both footsore and weary now, but at least the grass was soft to walk on. We trudged the whole length of the palace, turned the corner, walked along the side, and then approached the entrance. The main crowd had trailed home, but people too poor to manage the shilling fee were peering through the glass walls to have a free glimpse at the wonders inside.

Many were children on their own like us, some much smaller, tugged along by older sisters, and gangs of boys larking about, tussling with each other, suddenly darting for lost handkerchiefs and coins and purses lying in the grass.

'That's what we need – a purse to keep our own tin in,' said Kitty. 'Keep your eyes peeled, Lucy.'

We kept our eyes on the ground, sifting through the rubbish stirring in the breeze. So many people had lost property in the vast crush to get in the Exhibition. There were several shawls that had slipped off shoulders, though none as fine as the paisley cashmere we'd found in the church. We found a woollen one though that would do as a bedcover at night.

'And we can spread it out in front of us during the day for people to throw their coins on,' said Kitty. 'But we could do with a big fat purse to keep about our persons so no thieving pedlar can get his dirty hands on it.'

'We really need one of those pocket purses that you tie round your waist. You know, like our rhyme. *Lucy Locket lost her pocket, Kitty Fisher found it, Nothing in it, nothing in it, But the ribbon round it!*' I chanted.

'Well, I'd better find something of the sort for you,' said Kitty.

She was staring at a circle of boys surrounding two wrestlers, betting on who might win. I saw her eyes narrow when she looked at one particular ragged boy with his cap on back to front. He had a little edge of fine leather sticking out above the waistband of his tattered trousers.

'Aha!' Kitty murmured, and moved closer.

'Kitty, you can't!' I hissed.

The boys were all much bigger than her, really young men. If she tried to snatch that wallet from them they'd all set about her and she'd end up with more than a twisted ankle.

'Watch me,' she murmured.

She walked forward boldly, turning her head this way and that, acting as if she simply wanted to watch the fight. They elbowed her out the way impatiently, and after bobbing here and there in vain, she came back to me, shrugging.

'Them stupid boys wouldn't let me watch,' she said loudly. 'Come on then.' She linked arms with me and we walked off.

'Never mind,' I said consolingly.

'What do you mean, never mind!' she whispered. She glanced over her shoulder, making sure no one was watching. 'Guess what I've got in *my* pocket!' She patted the side of her little red trousers.

I saw it was bulkier than usual. 'You didn't get the wallet!' I gasped.

'Course I did,' said Kitty, grinning.

'And that boy didn't even notice?'

'I'm an expert,' she said.

'But . . . isn't it thieving?' I wondered.

'Not if it's been stolen already. You can't tell me that ragged lad would own a fine leather wallet like this one,' Kitty said firmly.

I wasn't sure she was right, but I didn't want to argue with her, especially as she was so proud of herself, though she was annoyed to find it didn't contain so much as a brass farthing. Then she picked up a lost top hat from the grass. It was bent where someone had trodden on it. She stuffed her little cap up her other trouser leg and stuck it on her curls at a rakish angle. She found a cigar end next and mimed smoking it, which made me laugh so much I got a stitch in my side.

Some of the performers and souvenir sellers had set up a makeshift camp beside the palace, clearly going to spend the night in the park too. Kitty seemed intent on joining them.

I pulled at her arm. 'Don't let's go near them, Kitty. Some of them look so rough. And even the nice friendly ones can turn out to be really mean. Think of that horrid souvenir seller who stole all our money!'

'That's who I'm looking for!' said Kitty. 'I want to get it back before he drinks or gambles it away!'

'But how are you going to do that? You only come up to his waist! He'd be far stronger than you,' I said.

'Gaffer taught me how to fight,' said Kitty.

'Yes, I'm sure you're really good at it, but you can't always win. Look what happened when you got set upon last Sunday.'

'There were six or seven of them lads then,' Kitty retorted. She clenched her fists. 'There's only one of that pedlar and I'm younger and quicker and know just where I have to aim my blows.'

I knew there was no point arguing with her. I was mightily relieved when there was no sign of the thieving pedlar. Some of the performers nodded at us, and chuckled at Kitty in her battered top hat and red velvet jacket and trousers. Many of them were wearing outlandish costumes too, dressed as harlequins and clowns. Two boys were sporting acrobat outfits like Kitty's. One man was wearing a huge crinoline and had a crown on his head, pretending to be Queen Victoria. Another sported a frock coat and trousers in red white and blue stripes. But the most extraordinary was the man in a leopard skin: a giant with great arms bulging with muscle. He wore white trousers as tight as stockings and soft calf boots as delicately fashioned as ladies' footwear. He was eating an enormous pie big enough to feed a family of ten.

He saw me staring and grinned at me, flexing an arm until the huge muscle seemed about to bulge through his skin.

'Kitty, just look at that man! He looks so strong!' I murmured.

'Gaffer's nearly that size and as strong as an ox,' said Kitty. 'Stronger than him I'm sure.'

He must have heard her because he finished his pie in three more gulps and then got to his feet.

'Stronger than The Muscled Marvel, the strongest man in the world?' he said. 'That's a bold statement from a tiny scrap of a girl.'

He glared at her as if he were annoyed – but you could tell from his twinkling eyes that he was only joking. He flicked Kitty's top hat from her head, caught it deftly, and planted it on his tousled mane, where it looked ridiculous. Then without warning he seized Kitty in one great hand, me in the other, and *lifted us both high in the air*!

He laughed when we squealed and waggled our legs, and the rest of the camp cheered and clapped when he set us on our feet again.

'Perhaps you're just a tad stronger,' Kitty conceded, joining in the fun.

'So what are you two little girls doing here by yourselves? Shouldn't you run home to your ma and pa?' he asked, offering us each a hard-boiled egg from a stack of them in a big brown paper bag.

I didn't know how to eat an egg without an egg cup and a little spoon, but Kitty was an expert and tapped the egg smartly on the ground, peeled off the shell and started eating.

'We ain't got no ma and pa. We're not little girls anyway, we're performers like you,' she said, with her mouth full.

I copied her and started on my own egg.

'I've got a little twist of salt here, if you'd like a bit of flavouring,' said The Muscled Marvel. 'So, you're performers, eh? What do you do then?'

'We have a unique song and dance act,' said Kitty proudly.

'Show us it then! We'd like a little entertainment,' he said encouragingly.

'Show us your act first then, mister!' said Kitty. 'Or do you simply snatch little children like an ogre?'

'Yes, and if they give me cheek I snap off a little arm or leg and chew it up like toffee,' he said. 'And I also lift any grown man who challenges me, and strike poses to show off my muscles and then I whistle a tune and make them dance.'

'Dance?' I said.

'Yes, little miss – like this.' He threw out his chest and made his muscles move rhythmically in turn while he whistled a polka tune.

We burst out laughing at such a comical sight and clapped our hands. He swept us a deep bow.

'Your turn now,' he said.

I hung my head shyly, but Kitty was keen.

'We'll show him the tumbling boy,' she said. 'I want him to see my handstands and cartwheels.'

So I sang the song while Kitty spun round and round upside down. When we'd finished The Muscled Marvel cheered mightily, and many of the performing folk joined in too – though a few looked disconcerted, and the acrobat boys glared at us.

'I reckon your act is a nice little earner,' said The Muscled Marvel. 'Don't you dare come and take a pitch anywhere near me tomorrow. You'll take all the attention away from me!'

'As if anyone could fail to notice you! No wonder you're called Mr Marvel,' I said.

'You've got a sweet tongue in that pretty little head,' he said. 'Now if you're intending to stay the night here I have to warn you it gets pretty raucous at times. You two stay close to me. I'll protect you.'

It did get very noisy and rowdy, with a lot of drinking and laughing and shouting, and then sudden fierce quarrels and fighting, but Kitty and I curled up close to The Muscled Marvel and he rolled up his own dressing gown to serve as a bolster for us. When he settled down to sleep himself he started snoring like a steam train, but we were so tired by now we were quickly lulled back to sleep.

We woke up very early and crept away to relieve ourselves in the bushes and then wash in the Serpentine and tidy ourselves for the day. There was already a long queue forming at the entrance to the palace, and the food stalls were all open, so we bought two mugs of coffee and a bag of buttered rolls. The coffee was very bitter, but it cleared my head remarkably. We ate a roll each and then took the rest back to The Muscled Marvel to thank him for his protection.

Then we walked up and down the queue, trying to find the perfect place for our act, wanting to try it at the front this time.

'We'll try performing halfway down the queue when their legs are getting tired and they're wondering just how long they have to wait. They'll welcome a little diversion, and be happy to see our act,' said Kitty.

'And reward us appropriately!' I said. I had the fat wallet stuffed down my dress for safe keeping. I patted it every now and then to make sure it hadn't slipped down past my chest.

The performers were already starting to line up. We saw the two boy acrobats practising their act, one of them leaping upwards, turning head over heels in the air and then landing neatly onto the other boy's shoulders.

'I wonder if I could do that,' Kitty murmured, looking as if she might attempt the trick.

'No! You could easily break your neck! Or break *me*! Look, they might be able to do all kinds of fancy tricks, but they don't have songs. Our tumbling boy act is far more amusing – and we have our *God Save the Queen* too. Think how that went down yesterday! We'll be far more popular than those boys – but we'd better keep away from them all the same.'

We decided it would be a sensible policy to find a spot where no one was singing either, so eventually settled between a woman selling oranges and a poor old blind man, very dirty, with two monkeys on chains. The sad little creatures were dressed in tiny velvet costumes very similar to Kitty's, but they had strange fat gloves over their paws. They didn't seem to be doing very much, just sitting hunched up beside their owner.

'Please sir, may I stroke the monkeys?' I asked politely.

He turned his head towards me, his black spectacles glinting in the sunlight. 'I wouldn't do that if I were you, missy,' he said. 'They're quarrelsome little things. It's the way I've trained them. They're novelty animals.'

It turned out their novelty was boxing. When the blind man clucked his tongue the monkeys flailed at each other with their bound paws. They didn't land any serious blows so they weren't hurt, but it seemed a horrid act even so.

It would hopefully be easy to grab the crowd's attention. Kitty crammed her top hat on her head and squeezed my hand.

'Let's get started!' she said.

I took a deep breath. 'Ladies and gentlemen, boys and girls – let us entertain you while you queue! First we will perform the tale of the Little Tumbling Boy!'

I nodded at Kitty and she flourished her top hat and then set it down on the grass by my feet.

'*See the little tumbling boy,*' I began, and Kitty sprang into action.

When I got to the last line of the final verse I grabbed the top hat and held it hopefully towards the large family who were clapping the hardest. The gentleman delved deep in his pockets and produced a handful of coins. I thought he might simply select a penny, but he chose a yellow threepenny piece, and he let each of five children take a halfpenny each and sprinkle them into the hat too.

It was an excellent start! It also encouraged other parents to let their children contribute too. Then when the majority of the folk near us shuffled forward in the queue I started speaking again.

'Ladies and gentleman, boys and girls, isn't it wonderful to be here today at the Great Exhibition opened by our own dear Queen.' Then I flung back my head and sang, and Kitty joined in too. Folk in the crowd stood straighter and started singing along too, but then faltered when we changed the words. They listened, they chuckled, and when we finished and I ran round with the top hat they *all* threw in some money – even people further up the line who had already contributed when we performed the tumbling boy.

And so it went on. We seemed to be the main attraction in the queue. Some folk stood circling us for ten minutes or more, lagging behind, delighted with our performance, watching our routine twice, even three times. They had no eyes for anyone else. No one bought a single orange but perhaps it was too early in the morning for folk to need their thirst quenching. Several children were attracted to the monkeys and watched their half-hearted boxing for half a minute, but soon lost interest. The blind man only earned a few pennies – whereas we stood to earn *pounds* if we worked hard all day long.

We didn't tire as the morning wore on. We'd never been such a success! It buoyed us up and made us sing with more expression, improvising new gestures, enjoying a little chit-chat with the crowd. Kitty lost her limp altogether and danced between tumbles, and performed a little throwing routine with her top hat whenever I emptied its contents into the wallet. It was almost too full to fasten now. We'd have to go in search of another one soon.

Kitty declared she was thirsty and tried to spend two pennies on oranges.

The woman glared at her. 'You can suck on your pennies to quench your thirst!' she said angrily, and stalked off to find another pitch.

The blind man and the boxing monkeys stayed where they were. The man was frowning at us malevolently, his dark glasses glinting. The monkeys had to be prodded to perform, and they started screeching, showing their teeth. I hoped they wouldn't really bite.

I turned my back on them and Kitty and I carried on with our show. The queue had got much thicker now, and more quarrelsome, because some people did their best to join it halfway up instead of starting right at the back. Two gentlemen began shouting at each other, and suddenly one of the wives swung her picnic basket at her husband's opponent. The queue surged forward in a rush, eager to see what was happening. A proper fight started and several people called for a policeman.

A couple of men in uniform came running from the main entrance. I leaped backwards out of their way because I was mortally afraid of police officers now. My hands went to my mouth – and I felt something slip inside my dress. The wallet full of our hard-earned coins!

I ducked down, searching for it, and was nearly bowled over by the crowd. Kitty was beside me, realizing at once, her hands scrabbling amongst the multitude of feet. But another hand reached out too, an old freckled hand with grimy nails. The fingers were surprisingly nimble, grabbing the wallet before Kitty or I could reach it.

I grabbed at the wrist desperately, and a sharp pain suddenly shot up my arm. A tiny mouth had sunk its teeth into me, biting so hard it drew blood. It was one of the monkeys – and his old wizened master was the thief! He wasn't blind at all!

Kitty dived after him, grabbing him by his grimy coat tails. She hung on, and even though the monkeys on his shoulders squealed at her, teeth bared, she somehow managed to prise the wallet from his fist.

'I've got it!' she shouted in triumph.

But the man flailed at her furiously, shouting in a reedy voice, 'Help! Stop this thief! She's snatched my wallet! Police! Arrest these wicked urchins!'

We were both so astounded Kitty and I stood staring at him. All the folk around us shook their heads, and a stout gentleman seized us by the shoulders.

'For shame! Stealing from an old blind man! You should be taught a lesson!' he said. There was a murmur of assent amongst the crowd.

'I am not a thief!' Kitty said furiously. '*He* stole the money from *us*!'

'A likely story! How could the old gent steal anything when he's blind?' someone else said.

'He can't be blind – he's only pretending!' I said. 'He's angry with us because we made more money than him. And he set his monkey on me, look!' I held up my bleeding wrist, but no one had any sympathy for me now.

'They're bare-faced liars, both of them. What would they be doing with a gentleman's wallet like that? They're little cut-purses, trained to thieve! Police, come and arrest this pair!' the old man shrieked, and the two monkeys echoed him, waving their tiny boxing gloves in the air.

'He's the liar, I tell you!' Kitty insisted. 'Look, we earned all the money honestly with our act. You must have seen us performing! Some of you gave us the very pennies in this wallet!'

But those people were much further up the queue now, taking advantage of the fight to gain places nearer the entrance. The crowd surrounding us hadn't seen us – and it was clear they didn't believe us. A man twisted Kitty's thin arm until she had to unclench her fist, and our precious wallet was handed over to the old man. Worst of all, further policemen came running up, waving their truncheons.

'Run, Lucy!' Kitty shouted, but I was held fast and so was she, though we both struggled frantically.

Then an arm went round my neck, practically choking me. 'Help! Someone's trying to murder me!' I gasped.

It was one of the policemen! Kitty set about him furiously, punching and kicking him, trying to rescue me. Another policeman seized her and shook her hard.

'Quit that, you little varmint! Right, sir, if you'd care to make your statement then we'll take this brazen pair into custody,' he said.

The old man said a whole torrent of lies, and when Kitty interrupted him the policeman holding her cuffed her on the head, knocking her precious top hat off.

'How dare you hurt her like that! And give her the hat back!' I shouted.

But the policeman kicked it hard and it rose up in the air and disappeared into the crowd.

'You should be ashamed of yourself! You're an officer of the law! You're not meant to treat children like that!' I said furiously.

'Hark at this one! She's got all the airs and graces of a little lady, and yet she's just a thieving little urchin!' said the policeman, laughing at me in a horrid manner.

We were dragged off – though a gentleman from the top of the queue ran after us.

'Wait, officers! Tell me why you're taking these children into custody. I'm sure they're the pair that were entertaining us most splendidly earlier,' he declared, like our very own wonderful knight in shining armour.

'They're a pair of accomplished little thieves, sir – and perhaps you're all too aware of that? Do they work for you? Do you train them up and then pocket all their cash?' Kitty's policeman demanded.

'How dare you suggest such a thing!' the poor gentleman spluttered. 'I shall report you to your superior!'

'You can report for all you're worth – but I rather think you'll end up in jail yourself for your pains,' the policeman retorted. 'I suggest you mind your own business or it'll be the worse for you – and your family.'

Our knight decided he'd lost the battle and stopped protesting.

Kitty and I were frog-marched across the park to the police station specially erected for the Exhibition. There was a large red-faced sergeant sitting at a desk – and behind him a very large barred cell full of people, though it was only mid-morning. Some were slumped in corners, staring straight ahead without focus. A woman was sitting on the grimy floor with her apron over her head, weeping and lamenting. Several men grasped the bars and shouted aggressively, using the most terrible language. One man seemed utterly demented, and growled terribly like a wild beast.

I was appalled at such sights, too shocked to cry – and Kitty looked utterly despairing.

'Don't worry, they must have somewhere separate for children,' I whispered, trying to be reassuring – but then I spotted a little boy not much older than Tommy Magpie right in the midst of them, gnawing his knuckles with fear.

'Right, you two, what have you been up to then?' the desk sergeant enquired.

'Simple case of thieving, Sarge, sir,' said the policeman.

'Taken down a statement from the aggrieved person, Sarge, sir, and returned his wallet full of coins,' said the second policeman.

'And how many coins would that be?' said the desk sergeant.

'I reckon around ten shillings,' said the first policeman.

The desk sergeant whistled. 'My, my! Right, lads, off you go. Well caught.'

'Please, Sarge, sir, might I say a word?' I asked.

'It's Desk Sergeant Peters to you, little girl, and I advise you only to speak when you're spoken to. This is a very serious state of affairs. A theft of ten whole shillings – plus the leather wallet containing them. We arrested a child your age for stealing a penny orange last week, and the Beak sent him down for two years' hard labour just to learn him not to steal.'

I wondered if he was just making this up to frighten us. He was certainly succeeding.

'Was it Pentonville?' Kitty asked. 'Oh, will I be sent there?'

'*Pentonville?* Nah, not even a wicked little imp like you would be sent to a place like that,' he said, chuckling. 'Right, tell me your names and addresses, quick sharp, and no lying now or it will be the worse for you.'

I took a deep breath. I had to tell the truth and save us from languishing in prison.

'My name is Lucy Alice May Browning, and I live at five Yewtree Crescent. I am a gentleman's daughter. Please contact my papa as soon as possible. He will vouch that I am not a thief. This is all a most terrible mistake,' I declared.

He raised his eyebrows – and then peered at poor Kitty.

'So *she's* the thief, is she?' he said, his eyes narrowing.

'Oh no sir, not at all. She is Kitty, and – and she's my little maid. She's as honest as the day is long,' I said.

'According to my officer's notes it was her who snatched the wallet from the victim,' said the desk sergeant.

'No, sir, *we* were the victims, and that terrible gentleman accusing us was the actual thief, I assure you,' I said, opening my eyes wide.

He stared back at me. I thought his expression softened a little.

'Well, when we're not so busy I'll send one of my lads to your address and see if your papa will come and pay a fine to release you. Meanwhile you'll have to stay here – though I can see that the main holding cell isn't quite the place for a gentleman's daughter,' he said. 'Or her little maid or whatever you are.'

I glanced at Kitty, hoping she'd be impressed by my quick thinking. But she looked furious.

'I'm *not* your blooming maid!' she mumbled.

16

The desk sergeant took us into a bleak little room with two hard chairs and a table.

'Here, you can stay in my interview room for now,' he said.

'Oh, thank you very much indeed, Desk Sergeant, sir,' I said, though he was hardly offering us luxury accommodation.

We sat on the chairs and Kitty watched hopefully as he marched out of the room – but then we heard the key turning outside, locking us in. She put her head on the table and started sobbing.

'Oh, Kitty, don't. I just said you were my maid on the spur of the moment. I didn't mean to upset you,' I said.

'I'm not crying about that,' said Kitty, wiping her eyes – and her nose – with the back of her hand.

'Is it because I told that horrid sergeant where I lived? I was just trying to find a way of getting them to release us. I'm sure Papa won't mind paying a fine. I think he is very rich,' I said.

'He won't pay a fine for me too,' Kitty sniffed.

'Yes he will!' I insisted – but I could see Papa might be likely to blame Kitty. Maybe he *wouldn't* pay for her. 'But if he won't then I will take money from home, or go out and perform all by myself until I have enough money to free you,' I said.

I expected her to be impressed but she shook her head wearily. 'I won't be here. They'll have carted me off to the Beak and sentenced me and then I'll be in prison,' said Kitty.

'Then I'll stay with you whether Papa pays the fine or not, and we'll both go to prison and no matter what it's like at least we'll be together,' I said stoutly – though inside I was quavering.

We sat there on the hard chairs for hours and hours. The desk sergeant brought us a morsel of old cheese, a small chunk of bread and a tin mug of water for our dinner.

'Is this for the two of us to share?' I asked when he'd gone. 'It's not very much.'

'I daresay those other folk in the big cell won't be getting anything at all,' said Kitty.

'Then let's pretend it's a wondrous feast,' I said. 'Pray try this fine portion of . . . peacock, Princess Kitty.'

'You can't eat peacocks, you noodle!' said Kitty, but it made her smile. 'Very well, may I help you to this sweet barley sugar twist?' she said, offering me a crust of bread.

'Let us wash it down with our fine wine,' I said, taking a sip of water.

'Delicious!' said Kitty, taking her turn to sip. 'Oh my, it's gone straight to my head. I'm drunk, look!'

She slid off her seat and staggered round the room, playing the fool. I copied her, and we swayed about, bumping into each other, laughing hysterically.

'We'd better stop this or they'll lock us up in the madhouse instead of prison – and they say it's even worse there,' said Kitty.

'Do you think the desk sergeant really has sent someone to tell Papa?' I asked.

Kitty shrugged. 'Maybe. He seems to like you. Everyone does.'

'No one really liked me at home,' I said. 'I'm sure my New Mother secretly detested me. And Miss Groan was very strict and irritable all the time. And I don't even think Papa cared for me very much – though fathers are meant to love their children, aren't they?'

'Gaffer loved me immensely and he wasn't even my father,' said Kitty.

Nurse wasn't family either, I thought, but I knew she loved me immensely too. I felt a sudden pain in my chest because I still missed her so much. Was she missing me badly too? Or was she settled down in her country cottage now, tending the roses round the door and eating the beans from her vegetable patch? Did she spend every evening rocking comfortably in her chair with a stray cat on her lap? Or would she have had to find another job? Perhaps she was in another nursery now, cuddling some other child and calling it her own little darling?

I felt a stab of such jealousy that I clutched my chest.

'Have you got a pain, Lucy?' Kitty asked anxiously.

'No, it's just because I'm missing her so much,' I mumbled.

'Mrs Chubb?' Kitty asked. 'If it wasn't for me you could still be with her and be her little girl and live happily ever after. You're thinking this and yet you're too kind to blame me and say it's all my fault.'

'No, not Mrs Chubb!' I said. 'I *liked* her at first, but not when she started plotting against you. We were only with her a few days anyway, not enough to really care about her.'

'*We've* only been together a few days too,' said Kitty.

'But it feels as if we've known each other for years and years, you know it does. I love you best in the whole world, apart from Nurse,' I told her. '*She's* the one I'm missing.'

Kitty bent her head. 'I love you best in the whole world, apart from Gaffer,' she said.

We pushed the two chairs together so that we could hold hands comfortably as we sat. And sat and sat and sat. We sometimes heard the cell door clanging as prisoners were pushed inside. Someone started screaming and didn't stop. Someone else started hitting the wall repeatedly, over and over again.

'I do hope that little boy's all right. They won't *really* put him in prison, will they?'

'They could. And they could put us in prison too. It don't look like your papa is coming with that fine, does it?' said Kitty.

But at last the desk sergeant came back into the room. He stood there, hands on his hips, his big stomach straining the brass buttons on his navy tunic. I smiled at him cravenly, but he didn't smile back.

'Don't you flutter your eyelashes at me, you scheming little minx,' he said. 'My young runner's just reported back to me. I know the whole truth now!'

'I – I don't know what you mean,' I quavered. 'What did Papa say?'

'Your pa's away on business, but my boy spoke to your so-called mother,' said the desk sergeant.

'She's not my real mother!' I protested.

'Exactly! The good lady said that your pa had a little girl once, but she'd run away from home,' he said.

'Yes, yes, that's me!' I cried.

'Oh no, *that* poor little girl has never been seen since. They've sent out search parties and advertised in the newspapers, but now they feel she's lost for ever. Only the other day *another* girl turned up on their doorstep, an impudent ragged urchin who claimed *she* was their daughter – and she had an accomplice with her, a dark curly-haired street child with barely a stitch on!' He pointed at Kitty.

'Yes, that was us, but I'm sure she *knew* it was me. She hates me and was glad to see the back of me,' I said. 'Papa didn't recognize me then because I was so dirty and was wearing dreadful rags—'

'My frock!' Kitty interrupted indignantly.

'But he'd know me now I'm decently dressed, and although I daresay he's still very vexed with me I know he'd pay the fine, Desk Sergeant, sir,' I said.

'You're expecting me to believe your father didn't recognize his own flesh and blood?' he said incredulously. 'You're a clever little liar, but that's much too far-fetched!'

'Indeed, sir, it isn't! I swear I'm telling the truth. And Papa mistook me for another child when we were at the seaside together several months ago,' I said. 'He does not see very clearly,' I continued, because it was so humiliating having to admit that my sharp-sighted papa was so disinterested in me that he'd simply failed to recognize me.

But the desk sergeant was shaking his head at me. 'The lies that come flowing out of those rosy little lips! You need a good birching to teach you a lesson!' he declared. 'And I daresay you'll get one where you're going.'

'We're going to prison?' Kitty asked.

'It would do you both good – but there's been such a multitude of felonies today that we've had word that the courts can't deal with any more tomorrow. So you two are in luck,' he said.

'You're letting us go? Oh, thank you, thank you, Mr Desk Sergeant, sir,' I began fervently, but he was shaking his head incredulously.

'You can't think I'm letting you waltz out of here scot-free! I can't send you home, because it seems clear you ain't got one, so you're going to a place where you'll be looked after,' he said.

'The workhouse?' said Kitty.

'The workhouse!' I echoed. I didn't know anything about workhouses and what happened there – just that they were very bleak places for very poor people.

'You can't send us there!' Kitty insisted.

'Oh yes I can!' said the desk sergeant, enjoying himself. 'Come on, up you get. Your carriage awaits, young ladies.'

'But we're too little! We're not nine yet! I'm only . . . seven, and Lucy is rising eight,' Kitty gabbled.

I stared at her. I knew she had no idea how old she was and she knew I was nine.

'I daresay they'll make suitable provision for you. It's up to them. Come along, let's be having you,' he said, seizing us both by our wrists and pulling us towards the door.

There was no point struggling. He had us in an iron grip, and then a horrible burly gentleman in a fancy uniform took over. He seemed to have the strength of Mr Marvel, because he tucked us under each arm as if we were piglets, and deposited us in the large open cart waiting outside the police station. There were handcuffs bolted to the wood inside the cart, and we were firmly attached by one wrist. The boy was caught there too, and the weeping woman, and several bold girls with face paint, and an old man with a long beard who stared in front of himself blankly, out of his wits.

The burly man got up in the driver's seat and took up his reins. His old thin horse tried to bend his head in protest, but the man gave him a sharp flick with his whip. The horse lumbered forward wearily.

'Did you see him whip that poor horse!' I said indignantly to Kitty.

'Ssh now, or he'll whip you too,' Kitty whispered.

'Why did you say I was rising eight when I'm not. And I'm sure you're much older than seven even though you're so little?' I whispered back.

'You're supposed to be nine or older before you're put in a workhouse. Gaffer always said they're terrible places. You have to pick oakum,' Kitty said.

'What's that?'

'It's some sort of old rope and you have to unpick all the strands,' said Kitty.

'I don't think that sounds too bad. I quite like unpicking things,' I said. I had once pulled the end of my woollen muffler and felt a wicked delight in unravelling an inch or so.

'You have to sit still on a hard bench with all the other inmates for twelve hours a day and pick it until your hands bleed,' Kitty whispered darkly.

'Well, we'll have to make sure we sit next to each other and then we can play our pretend games,' I said.

'You're not allowed to say a single word. You get severely punished if you do,' Kitty hissed.

I wasn't sure I wanted to ask what kind of punishment. I imagined various dreadful possibilities as we were driven along at a snail's pace, all the poor horse could manage. This was punishment too, because the crowds drifting away from the Great Exhibition all stared and pointed, and some rough boys actually threw stones at us. It grew worse when we were out of the park and driving along the main thoroughfare. It was dreadfully crowded and we felt very small and vulnerable in the midst of great omnibuses and grand carriages, with every eye upon us.

Some people exclaimed in horror: *Oh, dear heavens, look at those wretched souls!* Some recoiled: *Avert your head at once. You don't want to see such dreadful folk!* Some looked sad: *Poor devils! What a motley crew! See the handcuffs, even on the little children! Surely they're not all destined for the workhouse?*

We were driven across a great bridge over the Thames, where the streets were smaller, the buildings more decrepit, the people poorer. We didn't attract so much attention here. Then we turned into a cobbled street that made us bounce in the cart, and as we were joggled up and down we saw a large bleak brick building along the way. We didn't need to be told. We were approaching the workhouse.

The burly man jumped down from his driver's seat and rapped sharply at the formidable door. Another man in uniform appeared, and between them they seized the women and the very old man, whose knees buckled so they ended up practically carrying him inside. Kitty and I and the small boy were left shackled to the cart, all three of us trembling.

'Perhaps we can make a bolt for it when that man comes back to undo our cuffs?' Kitty suggested.

But when the burly man emerged he got back in his seat and whipped the horse into action again. He drove us right past the workhouse and round the corner, to a low red brick building with a name carved into the plaster above the door: *Junior House of Correction*. I wasn't sure what that meant. Miss Groan had corrected all my lessons, scratching rueful comments in the margins of my workbooks. So was this some kind of school? Perhaps we would do lessons all day? Although they could be boring, at least they weren't as tedious as picking oakum all day long. And I might shine. Miss Groan had despaired of my Arithmetic and General Knowledge, but she'd acknowledged that I was a very good reader and my compositions were well-written, if a little fanciful.

The burly man rapped at the door and an enormous woman answered it. She had to turn sideways to step outside and take a look at us. Mrs Chubb had been well covered, Nurse had been plump, but this person seemed practically the size of the stuffed elephant at the exhibition. She wore a black bombazine frock that strained at every seam and a white apron large enough to sail a boat. She had a white cap on her head, with a few sparse ringlets dangling around her ears as if she were still a young girl. She dimpled at the burly man in a flirtatious manner.

'Why, Mr Barrow, what have you brought for me today?' she said, rubbing her swollen hands as if she were expecting presents.

'Two girl thieves, and a surly young pickpocket,' the burly man said, gesturing at us.

'We're not thieves,' Kitty said through gritted teeth.

'That one's very wild,' said Mr Barrow. 'I'd keep your eye on her especially.'

'I keep my eyes on all my little charges, don't you fret,' she said. They were very small eyes, sunken down into her face, but she batted her eyelids and dimpled all the more. 'Release the little chicks and bring them indoors, if you please.'

Together they herded us through the door, down a dark corridor, and into a very large room set with long tables and benches. Children sat stiffly side by side along each bench, some so small they had to be tied into position to stop sliding underneath. They looked like one enormous plain family, because they all had brutally short haircuts and ill-fitting grey uniforms. There was a terrible stench of damp dish rags and unwashed bodies, and an overwhelming sour milk smell wafted from a collection of tureens on a table at the end. There were many tin bowls and spoons and a strange wooden trough that didn't seem to have any purpose. Did they keep an animal in this nightmare dwelling?

The huge woman dallied with Mr Barrow while the children in the room stared at us newcomers. A few little ones fidgeted and whimpered, but the others were weirdly silent, glancing every now and then at the great bulk of bombazine. Kitty tried poking her tongue out at one of the boys on the front bench. He blinked in alarm but didn't pull a face back.

Then the two adults said their farewells and the elephantine woman glided over to us, surprisingly light on her feet, her hem swaying as she walked.

'I am Mrs Turnover, the matron of this fine establishment. I'm sure you will benefit from your time here, so long as you keep quiet, work hard, and pay attention at all times,' she said in a girlish little voice, smiling. Then she suddenly thrust her head nearer and shouted, 'So what is my name, children?'

It was such a shock that I could barely stutter 'Mrs Turnover'. Mercifully Kitty and the small boy managed to mumble it too.

'That is correct. Well remembered,' she said, softly now. 'So tell me *your* names, chickies. Boy first!'

'Bertie Woodfield,' he said.

'Bertie Woodfield *what*?' Mrs Turnover demanded.

'There ain't another bit,' said poor Bertie, mystified.

'You should say Bertie Woodfield, *Mrs Turnover*,' she shouted at him. 'So say it!'

He had to gabble it five times before she was satisfied.

'Enough!' She turned to me. 'First girl. Name?'

'Lucy Alice May Browning, Mrs Turnover,' I said, and I bobbed her a little curtsy, though my legs were trembling so much I very nearly fell over.

'*Lucy Alice May Browning, Mrs Turnover,*' she said, in a cruel childish mimic of my voice. 'Oh my, who have we here!'

I didn't know if she was asking a question or making a statement. I repeated my name in a whisper.

'What's that? Speak up!' Mrs Turnover commanded, putting her hand to her ear in a pantomime of deafness.

My mouth was so dry I could hardly stammer it out a third time.

'And who exactly *are* you, Lucy Alice May Browning?' she said, clasping her hands over her enormous aproned stomach.

I knew who *she* was. She was the most hateful woman in the world, and no wonder every child in the room was cowed into silence.

'I am a little girl, Mrs Turnover, falsely arrested,' I said.

'A little *lady*, with big blue eyes and dulcet tones. Oh my, we're lucky to have you here, in my little nursery workhouse. Falsely arrested, are you? Tut tut, such a shame! Are you expecting me to beat my breast at the injustice?' she asked.

'No, Mrs Turnover,' I murmured.

'You don't belong here, do you, little Lady Lucy?'

'Not really, Mrs Turnover,' I said in a mouse squeak. 'I haven't done anything wrong, and neither has my friend here. We haven't stolen anything! A wicked man stole from *us*.'

'Such brazen lies – and you a little lady! You must be especially wicked and depraved to end up in this situation, when you've had every advantage. It's clear you were once used to a privileged life. A wealthy papa, a mamma clad in silks and satins, maids running to please her every whim, whilst you get pampered by your nurse and governess?' Mrs Turnover gave a contemptuous sniff. 'So I take it you'll be expecting me to bow and scrape and curtsy to you, your little ladyship?'

'No, Mrs Turnover, not at all,' I said.

'Ha! She thinks I *meant* it!' she declared to the room of children, and they tittered nervously. 'But she's very much mistaken, isn't she?'

'Yes, Miss-us Turn-o-ver,' they chanted bleakly.

'*You* will do the bowing and scraping and curtsying, little lady Lucy Alice May Browning, and if you fail to please me I will have to introduce you to my little friend,' she said, nodding towards the corner of the room by the door.

I couldn't see anyone standing there at all. Then I realized what she meant. There was a walking stick propped up in the corner, very sturdy and well-polished. The room seemed to be spinning round me now, but the stick stayed sharply in focus, looking ever more menacing.

I wondered if Mrs Turnover meant I should literally start bowing and scraping and curtsying. I knew how to bow, I knew how to curtsy even if I wobbled, but how on earth could I demonstrate scraping? Should I prostrate myself on the floor and pretend great deference?

But before I could attempt such a terrible task Mrs Turnover had started interrogating Kitty, seemingly forgetting all about me.

'Second girl! Or are you perhaps second *boy*, seeing as you are dressed so outlandishly in velvet bloomers?' she said, pointing at her mockingly.

I prayed Kitty wouldn't give her any cheek. It would be madness to defy such a terrible woman. I was beginning to wish I'd told my true age earlier to the desk sergeant. I would sooner pick oakum twelve hours a day *and* twelve hours a night than stay here in the Junior House of Correction.

Kitty stood up straight. 'I am a girl, Mrs Turnover. I am wearing this outfit because I am a street performer.' She said it proudly, her chin up.

Mrs Turnover's tiny eyes gleamed. 'Oh, pray enlighten me, girl. What exactly do you *do* when you are performing in the street?'

'I sing, Mrs Turnover. And I tumble.'

'Aha! Well, I daresay you will have the opportunity to do both in this establishment. You will sing loudly when my little friend warms your back during the day, and if I catch you out of your bed at night then I will set you tumbling all the way down the stairs. Do I make myself plain, second girl?'

'Yes, Mrs Turnover,' said Kitty, her fists clenched.

'So what is your name? I daresay it is something outlandish and theatrical,' she said disdainfully.

'It is simple, Mrs Turnover. I am Kitty,' said Kitty.

'Kitty . . . ? Every child has a surname.'

'I'm afraid I don't,' said Kitty.

'Then you shall be called . . . let me see. What would suit you? Kitty Uglyface! Do you think that a fine surname for this little wretch, children?'

They sniggered obediently and nodded.

'Then Kitty Uglyface you are, from this moment on, and I shall take great pains to tell your name to the Beadle of the adult workhouse when you progress there,' Mrs Turnover threatened. 'It's a name you'll never forget. Or have you forgotten it already. *What's your full name, second girl?*'

Kitty's face was as red as her velvet costume. I was terrified she'd say something defiantly rude and end up beaten half to death. But common sense prevailed.

'I am Kitty Uglyface, Mrs Turnover,' she said in a monotone.

'Kitty Uglyface!' Mrs Turnover repeated. 'Did you hear that, children? *Kitty Uglyface!* What kind of a name is that? It's very comical, isn't it?'

There was forced laughter. Kitty grew even redder. I burned for her. I stood alongside her while Mrs Turnover had her fill of fun. Then she suddenly stopped the goading and glared around the room.

'What's this? Why aren't you eating your lovely supper? Your porridge will be cold by now, you naughty children!' she said, and stomped to the serving table where the tureens were.

They had stopped steaming. Mrs Turnover shouted, 'First row!' and the children stood in a line and shuffled forward.

Each was given a ladleworth of porridge in a tin bowl. It smelled terrible and it looked terrible too, but the children started eating it quickly, even scraping their bowls. I didn't know if they were half-starved or terrified of causing offence.

'You three new inmates! Bertie Woodfield, Lucy Alice May Browning and Kitty Uglyface! Come and get your nourishing supper and then sit in the front row where I can keep an eye on you,' Mrs Turnover commanded.

We were given our portions and tried hard to fit into the first row. The other children squeezed up as best they could, but the three of us were woefully squashed at one end. The porridge was even worse than I'd imagined. It bore no resemblance whatsoever to the dish I'd been served every morning at home. It was thin grey slimy stuff with a rancid reek. I tried the tiniest taste. It was barely lukewarm and coated my tongue. I did my best to swallow it down but a lump made me retch.

Mrs Turnover was watching me with her horrid hawk eyes. 'Don't you care for your porridge, Lady Lucy?' she asked, putting on her little girl voice.

'It's very good, thank you, Mrs Turnover – though I'm not actually very hungry,' I said.

'Perhaps it needs a little seasoning?' she said. 'Do you like sugar on your porridge, child?'

'Yes, Mrs Turnover,' I said.

'However, I hear the Scots put salt on their porridge. Shall I fetch the salt shaker and see if I can make it tastier to tempt your appetite?' she said, eyes gleaming.

I imagined her shaking salt over my bowl until it was snow white, and then commanding me to eat it up.

'I think the porridge is perfectly pleasant as it is, Mrs Turnover,' I said, and I forced myself to take another spoonful. I had to tighten my stomach to stop myself bringing it right up again.

Mrs Turnover took her eyes off me while she supervised the bowl filling of the second, third and fourth rows. Bertie Woodfield ate his own porridge, though he pulled a few faces. Kitty ate hers too, surprisingly rapidly. When Mrs Turnover was busy scolding an unkempt girl Kitty swapped my full bowl for her empty one and ate mine too. She bolted her second bowlful, her eyes watering, but she managed to get it all down for me. I reached for her hand under the table and squeezed it hard, overcome with gratitude.

I had a quick glance around. The children were all eating, except for four children at the back who didn't have a place on any bench or a porridge bowl either. They were standing still, looking wretched. When all the rows had been served, Mrs Turnover peered at them. She tapped her serving ladle on the tureen.

'Your turn to be fed, animals!' she called.

The four children shuffled forward, heads bent.

Kitty turned to the girl on her other side. 'Why does she call them *animals*?' she hissed.

'Because they wet the bed,' the girl whispered back.

Mrs Turnover scraped the contents of the last ladle into the wooden trough. 'Feeding time!' she said.

The four children all knelt and then put their heads in the trough and had to gobble the porridge as best they could. We watched in horror. When they were allowed to take their heads out they had the disgusting porridge all round their mouths, on their cheeks, on their chins, even on their ears.

I felt the tears sliding down my face. I felt so sorry for them – and also so scared. When I was little I had sometimes wet the bed myself, but it was a secret between Nurse and me. It had happened several times when she left, but I had got up very early and bundled my wet sheet into the laundry basket, praying the maid wouldn't tell on me. I would have died if Miss Groan had found out.

'Oh, Kitty, what if *we* wet the bed?' I whispered.

'We're not going to,' Kitty murmured. 'Because we're not going to *be* in bed.'

'What?'

'We're not staying,' said Kitty. She stood up, seized her porridge bowl, and hurled it across the room. It went flying through the air and landed smack on Mrs Turnover's temple, making her stagger.

'*Quick!*' Kitty hissed, seizing my hand.

We leaped off our bench and ran helter-skelter for the door. The children gasped in shock.

'Run too!' Kitty yelled. 'Bertie Woodfield, all of you! Come with us!'

But they stayed glued to their benches, too scared to move. We couldn't wait to encourage them further. We got to the door – but Mrs Turnover had recovered and was charging towards us, black skirts flying. Kitty seized the 'little friend' walking stick and held it with both hands. Mrs Turnover rushed at her, and Kitty poked her hard in her enormous stomach.

She gasped and then collapsed onto the floor. I got the door open and we ran hard down the dark corridor. The front door was bolted but we tugged together and turned the handle hard, wrenching our wrists, getting it open just as Mrs Turnover came in view, advancing on her knees, screaming threats.

We were out of the front door and running, running, running, with no idea where we were going. I think we would have run into Hell itself rather than stay in Mrs Turnover's Junior House of Correction. We ran until we couldn't draw breath, and then dodged up an alleyway and leaned against the dank wall, panting.

'Oh, Kitty, you were magnificent!' I said, when I could speak at last.

'That sound she made when she sank to the floor. *Oooof!*' said Kitty. She said it again and again, and I did too, and then we both collapsed with laughter, clutching each other to stay upright.

'Ssh now!' I gasped. 'She might still be coming after us!'

'On her knees!' said Kitty. 'Oh, glory! How I wish I could have pushed her horrid head into that awful trough. What a wicked old biddy!'

'She looked so angry – she'll kill us if she catches us!' I said.

'Yes, all she has to do is hurl herself upon us and we'd be squashed flat,' said Kitty, laughing.

'But seriously, what are we going to do? She'll tell the big burly man with the cart and he'll come after us. And they'll tell the police too, and they'll *all* be looking for us,' I said, starting to panic.

'I'll whack them all with my stick,' said Kitty, waving it in the air. 'You wait, they'll all go down like ninepins. Whack, whack, whack!'

'But they'll be so many of them and they'll all be furious because we've outwitted them. They'll spread the word to policemen everywhere. Two girls, one fair in a blue frock, one dark and wearing red velvet bloomers – we'll be pretty obvious. We'll have to find some different clothes, Kitty,' I said.

'I'm not ever, ever, ever wearing anything but my acrobat costume,' said Kitty.

'Well, you'll look a bit silly when you're an old woman of fifty,' I said. 'Oh, Kitty, it's not a joke! It's really scary. They'll catch us in the end. They always do.'

'I know,' said Kitty, suddenly serious. She put her hand to her throat in sudden despair. 'What are we going to do?' she whispered.

'We can't stay round here. We'll have to go far away. Go to the country! Oh, Kitty, we'll go to Sussex and find Nurse!'

'I can't leave London, I told you,' said Kitty.

'But we have to! If we stay they'll catch us. I know you'll fight and I'll try too, but we're little and they're big, and the police all have truncheons. They'll beat us and lock us up and maybe – oh, Kitty, maybe they'll say you were trying to murder Mrs Turnover and then they'll hang you!'

'I wish I *had* murdered her,' said Kitty. 'Hateful, hateful, hateful woman! *She's* the Uglyface, not me!' She hit the wall hard with the stick, again and again, and then stopped, in tears.

'We have to get right away from London,' I persisted.

'I know,' said Kitty, in a very small voice. 'But tomorrow's Sunday. I need to stay until eight in the morning. And then we will try to get to the country.'

'But that's madness! We need to get away *now*!'

'I *have* to wait till eight. I must let Gaffer know. *Then* we'll be off,' said Kitty, and I knew there was no way on earth I could make her change her mind.

17

At least Kitty agreed that it would be wise to get as far away from the Junior House of Correction as we could. After the brief rest in the alleyway we set off again. I knew how much Kitty loved her red velvet, but I wished she was still wearing her ragged brown dress. People stared at her so. We would be so easy to track down if the police came after us.

I had no idea which district of London we were in, but Kitty kept forging ahead determinedly. She kept looking around her to see if she could find somewhere she recognized.

'Where are you making for, Kitty?' I asked her.

'Just somewhere,' she said.

'Well, obviously – but *where*? Near Yewtree Crescent where I used to live?'

'No, of course not,' she snapped. 'Do stop asking stupid questions.'

I was so tired and scared that I burst into tears at her terse tone.

'Oh, stop it,' she said impatiently.

I took a deep breath and tried hard, but I couldn't prevent the tears rolling down my face. It was twilight now, but the street lamps were lit, so I couldn't stop her seeing.

'Don't cry,' she said, more gently. 'You don't *want* to try going back to your home, do you?'

'There's no point, not if Papa's really away on business. I'm sure the New Mother would go on pretending even if she recognized me. No one wants me there,' I said mournfully.

'Yes, you keep saying, sounding so sorry for yourself,' said Kitty. She paused. 'Mrs Chubb wants you. I'm sure no one would go looking for you there. You could live with her and Mr Chubb and Tommy Magpie and all them other boys. You'd be part of their family. No need to worry about me. I can look after myself. I even got the better of Mrs Turnover, didn't I? I'll be fine. It's the two of us together they'll be looking for. We stick out too much. We're too different. In fact, I'll be better off without you.'

'You don't mean that, do you?' I asked.

'Yes, I do,' said Kitty. She paused. 'No, I don't,' she added in a tiny voice.

'We're sticking together, you and me,' I said.

'I feel so bad, making us wait till the morning, but I have to tell him,' Kitty said, and now she was the one nearly in tears.

'Tell Gaffer?' I said softly.

She nodded.

'You know where he is?'

'Yes. But – but I can't see him,' she murmured. 'I just have to *tell* him.'

'And he's . . . under the ground?' I said delicately.

She stared at me. 'They don't keep them under the ground,' she said. 'They're in cells.'

'Oh my goodness! Gaffer's in *prison*!' I said, the penny dropping at last.

'Don't say it like that! I can't bear it. I haven't told a single person before because they'll think the worst. Gaffer's not a common criminal. He shouldn't be locked up, especially in Pentonville. It's the hardest prison of all, kept for the worst cases. He doesn't belong there. He's the loveliest, kindest, most gentle and honest man in the whole world,' said Kitty, her voice rising.

'Ssh!' I said, scared that someone would hear her. 'So what was he accused of?'

Kitty took a deep breath. 'Murder.'

'*Murder!*'

'Only attempted. It's so unfair,' she said. 'It wasn't his fault! We'd walked all the way to London, because Gaffer had heard an old travelling friend of his was dying there in dire poverty. Gaffer had money from working in the fields, and wanted to make sure his friend had a decent burial and wasn't just flung into a pauper's grave.' Kitty was walking quickly now, getting more and more worked up.

'After the funeral we held the wake at an inn. There was a man called Jasper there, who seemed nice enough at first, and he made a great fuss of me, calling me Gaffer's pretty little girlfriend.' Kitty shuddered. 'It's all my fault. I wasn't used to anyone calling me pretty and I liked him making a fuss of me, though it made Gaffer frown. Jasper and his cronies had me singing a few ditties for them and that made Gaffer frown more. He said it was time we were going and went to settle the drinks bill at the inn. Jasper took me on his knee and asked me why I wanted to stay with such a surly fellow. I didn't like him saying that and tried to wriggle off, but he held me tight.'

'Oh, Kitty!' I had to run to keep up with her now.

'I started crying and Gaffer came back and pulled me away, and then yelled at Jasper. He said dreadful things about Gaffer and me and so Gaffer hit him. And then Jasper took out a knife and tried to stab him but Gaffer was too quick for him and – and somehow he got hold of the knife, and it all went wrong and then, then Jasper just lay there.'

'He was *dead*?'

'I wish he was! It was only a little wound, though it looked so much worse – but the innkeeper had called the police and Jasper said Gaffer had tried to murder him. And all the others said he had too. I tried to get them to see that it hadn't been like that at all, but no one would listen to me. They all thought that it was Gaffer's fault because he looked so big and fierce. Gaffer was taken away and sentenced to seven years' hard labour and sent to Pentonville.'

'Have you visited him, Kitty?' I asked.

'They won't let me see him in there, though I've begged and begged. But every Sunday at eight o'clock the prisoners are taken out of their cells and cross the yard to go to chapel – so I stand outside every Sunday and shout to Gaffer than I love him and I'll wait for him for ever,' said Kitty.

'Can he hear you then?'

'I'm sure he can,' said Kitty. 'And now I have to shout one more time to tell him I have to stay away for a while, but I'll be back one day. You do see, don't you, Lucy? I can't let him think I've given up on him.'

'I see,' I said, because I had to. I didn't think it at all likely that Gaffer *could* hear her, but I saw that she badly needed to believe it. 'So where is it, this horrible prison?'

'It's up the Cally Road,' said Kitty, which meant nothing to me. 'I'm sure it can't be too far away from here. So you'll stay till eight tomorrow, so I can explain to him?'

I nodded.

'Oh, Lucy, you're the best friend in all the world. I love you the *same* as Gaffer,' said Kitty. 'What would I do without you now?'

'What would I do without *you*? I'd still be stuck in that other alleyway without any clothes! So where shall we sleep tonight? Are we going to this Cally place now?' I asked.

'It's not a good place to sleep. A lot of rough folk live round there,' said Kitty.

'Then shall we just stay somewhere here?' I peered round hopefully. 'Maybe in that alley over there?'

'No, it's too near that awful Mrs Turnover. And alleys aren't good either. We don't want to be lying there so that some drunken fool can lurch in and tinkle on us! No, we'll walk on. Don't worry, I'll find us a safe place, I always do,' said Kitty.

We felt too conspicuous in the lamp-lit main streets. We did our best to stick to the shadows, scurrying along like little rats. I felt so tired I could have lain down on the pavement and slept there, but we had to find somewhere hidden. Kitty had started limping again but she didn't complain.

We found a park, but it was fenced all around with high railings with sharp ends, and the gates were padlocked. We found several churches, but the doors were all bolted. We found many shop doorways, but all the ones with dark porches were already occupied with street folk with flimsy beds of rags and newspapers, and they cursed us if we tried to squeeze in beside them.

Eventually we found a mansion block of flats stretching the length of a quiet street. All the entrances were securely locked, but each had a large whitened step.

We sat on the furthest one simply to have a rest, but we were so exhausted we huddled together, heads nodding, and spent the whole night there.

I woke with the sound of a distant clock chiming. I had a cricked neck and was chilled to the bone from the stone step even though it was summer. I took a few tentative steps, walking like an old lady. Kitty woke too, suddenly fearful.

'Gaffer!' she said, jumping up, wincing when she put the weight on her ankle.

'It's all right, we've got all the time in the world to get to him. It's only six o'clock, I just heard it chiming. Goodness, I ache everywhere – and I'm so thirsty. Let's find one of those coffee stalls,' I said. 'We'll feel better after a bit of breakfast.'

'What are we going to buy breakfast with?' said Kitty, rubbing her ankle. 'We haven't got any tin, they took it from us.'

'Then we'll have to earn it,' I said. 'We'll find a likely spot and sing.'

But there seemed no likely spot nearby, and no audience either. People were still in their beds or eating their own breakfasts. We had to trudge on, hungry, thirsty and sore-footed.

Kitty plunged down this street and that, seemingly almost at random.

'Are you sure you know where you're going?' I said timidly.

'Of course I do,' said Kitty. 'I go there every week.'

'Yes, but you've never been *here* before,' I pointed out. 'I think we're lost.'

'I swear to you I know exactly where I am,' said Kitty, but I didn't believe her.

People were starting to emerge from their houses – children scurrying on errands; young boys walking dogs; poor families in drab Sunday best going to early Communion.

'Let's ask if any of them know the way to Pentonville,' I suggested.

'No!' said Kitty, outraged. She had started using the correction friend as a proper walking stick, and made a tap-shuffle, tap-shuffle noise on the pavement.

So we blundered on and on. I grew scared we were going round in circles and would suddenly find ourselves all the way back at the Junior House of Correction. Maybe there would be a whole posse of policemen ready to catch us because we seemed to have committed any number of crimes since we met in that alleyway when my clothes were stolen.

It seemed so extraordinary that the only crime I'd committed up till then was standing my doll in bright sunshine and letting her face melt. I'd become another Lucy altogether now, in less than two weeks! I'd never been allowed to walk to the end of the Crescent alone before, and now here I was wandering all over London with a street child, looking for the worst prison in England where her adopted father was sentenced for attempted murder.

I gave a little shiver – and Kitty saw.

'Oh, Lucy! I'm sorry. I didn't mean to drag you into all this,' she said, nearly in tears. 'Look, we'll find a safe place for you to wait, and I'll go to Pentonville myself.'

'It's all right. Truly. I don't want to be left behind. I'm going to stick with you for ever now,' I said.

'Then you are a very mad girl,' said Kitty, but her eyes shone.

We walked on hand in hand – and then Kitty suddenly strode forward purposefully.

'There's the river! Look, it's Blackfriars Bridge! Come on, Lucy!' she cried.

'Are we nearly there?' I asked.

'Well, we've a little way to go yet,' she said. 'But I recognize everything now, I promise.'

I didn't remind her that she'd sworn the same just twenty minutes ago. We walked over the bridge together, peering down at the river. It smelled so bad we had to hold our noses, and the water was foul and murky, and yet it glinted in the sunlight. A big boat sailed underneath the bridge, causing a creamy wake in the dark water.

'Maybe we could jump into it,' I said. 'We could make friends with the sailors and they'd take us far away in their boat. We could go all the way down the river, miles and miles and miles, until we reached the sea.' I wasn't sure this was possible. I hadn't got to grips with Miss Groan's Geography yet. I was only pretending but Kitty stared at me as if I was serious.

'Could we sail all the way to Australia?' she asked.

'Yes, of course, we'll go all round the world and see the kangaroos and the koala bears,' I said, remembering *The Child's Book of Wild Animals* on my nursery shelf at home. Angelique's nursery now.

Kitty's brow wrinkled. Perhaps she didn't know about foreign wild animals.

'A kangaroo is a curious animal, very big, and it bounces along on its great feet. And a koala bear is the dearest little thing—'

'Never mind them animals. You think we could *really* sail to Australia from here?' she said urgently.

'Yes, I suppose so,' I said. 'We could be the cabin boys on a ship. You would be really good at that, Kitty. You'd clamber up all the ropes like a little monkey and sort out all the sails. I'm not sure what I'd do. Perhaps I could help the cook, and we'd make big stews together and I'd butter all the ship's biscuits. And sometimes we'd dive into the sea and swim along with the dolphins,' I said, getting carried away. When I'd been to the seaside with Papa I'd been dunked in the water by the big fierce lady who owned the bathing hut and I'd screamed my head off.

Kitty was looking at me so hopefully. 'And is Australia a good place?' she asked.

'I'm sure it's a splendid country,' I said. 'Maybe we'll really go there and we'll build a little house together, just for you and me.'

'Gaffer could build it for us. He built us little hideaways when we travelled, plaiting rushes to make a proper roof so we didn't get wet when it rained,' said Kitty.

'But Gaffer's in prison,' I said gently.

'Yes, but I was talking to these boys last week and I said I'd wait for Gaffer for seven years, and one of them laughed at me and said I'd be waiting in vain because prisoners at Pentonville get sent to Australia after nine months. I thought he was lying to torment me so I fought him – and all the others – and I tried hard not to believe it, but now . . . now I'm wondering,' said Kitty.

'*You* fought *him*? So those boys didn't set upon you when you hurt your ankle? You started the fight? Oh, Kitty!' I said, shaking my head.

'And I'd have won it too, if it was just with that one boy,' Kitty said fiercely. 'Lucy, do you think he was right? Do they send convicts all the way across the world?'

'I don't know,' I said. 'We could ask someone.'

'Who? A policeman?' said Kitty, sighing.

'My papa would know – he knows everything. He always says *I'm* a dunderhead,' I said.

'I think your papa's a dunderhead for not recognizing you,' said Kitty.

A gentleman was walking briskly over the bridge towards us, swinging his arms, obviously enjoying the exercise. He had a fresh complexion and a little beard, and he was dressed like a dandy, wearing a velvet jacket, and cream nankeen trousers. He nodded at us.

'Lovely morning, children. What are you up to, peering down at the water so earnestly? You're not about to take a dip, are you?' he enquired.

'No sir, it stinks!' said Kitty.

'Yes, it does, rather,' he agreed.

'We were having a conversation about Australia, sir,' I said suddenly.

'Were you indeed!' said the gentleman.

'And we were wondering – is it true that – that convicts can be sent there?' I asked.

Kitty winced at the word convict, but didn't try to stop me.

'My my, you're strange little girls wondering about such things! Well yes, I believe it is true. Capital idea, I think. Give them a new chance in a new land,' he said.

'But do they have to leave their families behind?' Kitty asked desperately.

The gentleman looked at her. 'Oh dear, don't let it upset you. If people only knew how little children agonize over the slightest things! Here, my dears. Cheer yourselves up.' He dug deep in his pockets and produced a small packet of sultana biscuits. 'I munch them as I march. You do the same!'

We took one each and thanked him, and he went off on his way.

'Can you just tell us the time, mister?' Kitty called after him.

He stopped and consulted his gold pocket watch. 'A quarter past the hour,' he said.

'A quarter past which hour, sir?' I asked.

'Seven, my dear. Farewell!'

'We must hurry!' said Kitty.

We set off again at a smart pace. Luckily the roads were straightforward, one leading into another, and Kitty knew where she was now, but she seemed more and more anxious. By the time we reached the Caledonian Road she was running and I could barely keep up with her.

There was the prison – a vast brick building with a clock tower – brand-new and ominous, seeming to suck the very air from the street. I stood still, gasping, clutching a stitch in my side. The hands on the clock showed ten to eight, and Kitty breathed out and leaned momentarily on the wall opposite.

Then she gathered herself together and pulled me along the street, stopping where the main building finished, though the high wall continued.

'I think this must be where they're taken out for exercise. And then can you see the smaller building with the pointy top? I'm sure that's the chapel. The men are led in there. No one ever talks, they're not allowed, but you can hear their feet shuffling, and some of them cough. So if I can hear that then surely they can hear me. Gaffer's always had excellent hearing – he can tell if a fox or badger or stoat is a hundred yards away even in the pitch dark, and he knows each bird's individual song. He heard *me*, when I was mewling in a ditch, abandoned as a baby. He must hear me now, mustn't he?' Kitty asked urgently.

'Yes, of course,' I said, badly wanting to reassure her.

'He can't answer back because he'd get punished. I understand. Just so long as he can hear. I shout as loudly as I can. I'd better stop talking now, so I don't run out of voice!' Kitty said.

We were both a little husky from the very long walk and we hadn't had a drop to drink since yesterday. Kitty earnestly swallowed and coughed and did her best to clear her throat. She stood tensely, watching the hands of the clock. At the precise moment it struck eight we heard the creak and snap of heavy locks, the bang of doors, and then suddenly the sound of men walking, more and more of them, there just beyond the forbidding wall. I could even smell them, a stale stench of hundreds of men confined to their cells for twenty-three hours a day.

Kitty breathed in deeply and then shouted: 'Gaffer! Gaffer, it's Kitty. I have to tell you that I shall be gone a while. I'm going to the country as I'm in a spot of bother here, but you mustn't worry. I shall come back when it's safe and I'll be thinking of you all the time. And – and if you get sent to Australia, I shall sail there too and come searching for you, because I love you. I will always always always love you!' Her voice gave out and she leaned back exhausted.

Then I heard another voice, deep and cracked from lack of use: 'I love you too, my Kitty!'

'Oh!' Tears poured down Kitty's face, but her mouth was stretched wide with joy. 'Oh, Lucy, did you hear him? He did say I love you, didn't he?'

'Yes, yes! He said, "I love you too, my Kitty." I heard him clearly!' I said.

'He sounded strange, not really like my Gaffer, but it was him, I'm sure of it! He's answered me at last. He'll understand if I can't come for a while. Oh, my own dear Gaffer! If only he wasn't locked up in this awful place!' Kitty cried and cried, even when I gently led her down the road.

'Come, Kitty. We must get away from London altogether now or we'll be locked up too. Which way is the country, do you think?' I asked.

Kitty shook her head. 'I don't know. I used to know all the country roads and lanes, as Gaffer and I would walk miles and miles each day, but I don't know how to *get* there,' she said. She was still crying helplessly, suddenly seeming so lost and little.

'Well, let's just walk, but not back the way we came. And we'll ask folk and look for signposts. We'll find it, you'll see,' I said.

So we walked on, and when we found a drinking fountain at last we both drank thirstily and then washed ourselves as best we could. After a long while we came across a small market, and scavenged in the gutter for bruised apples and softened oranges. There was a very sunburnt woman sitting at one end wearing an old-fashioned black straw bonnet and a faded cotton frock, a tray of small pink flowers on her lap. They were tied into tiny bunches, fastened with pink ribbon, with a pin at the back.

'Would you like to buy your mamma or papa one of my rose nosegays, little girl?' she asked. 'Or perhaps you'd

285

like one for yourself to pin on your pretty blue frock? Only a penny and it will last for days. They're freshly picked this morning, lovely wild roses and they smell so sweet.'

I stopped still. Kitty bent her head over them, breathing in deeply.

'Do you mind telling me where you picked the roses, madam?' I asked the flower seller.

'Up on the Heath,' she replied. 'I goes there for my flowers every day. Why go to Covent Garden when you can go to God's own countryside and pick them for nothing at all, that's what I say.'

'Please could you tell us the way to the Heath, madam?' I said eagerly.

'Fancy you keeping on madaming me! What a pretty tongue you have, child. It's a long walk to the Heath. You go north from here, up the road, down the road, this way, that way—' She took one of her own nosegays and made it walk through the air as if it were a little pink girl.

I tried to follow what she was saying, but it was impossible to remember it all, though Kitty was paying attention now, concentrating hard.

'It's the real country, not just a park?' she asked.

'It's country, all right. Stretches for miles and miles, trees and bushes and flowers and ponds and the air is fresh and the roses smell sweet in the hedgerows,' said the flower seller.

'Thank you, madam,' said Kitty, giggling a little. 'Can we have one of your nosegays if we sing you a little song? We haven't got any money.'

'Songs don't butter no bread,' said the woman, but when we sang the Great Exhibition song together she clapped us heartily. 'Well, you two should go on the stage. Bravo! Here's a nosegay each, you've certainly earned them,' she said.

We thanked her earnestly and pinned the nosegays in place. Kitty kept her head on one side, snuffling the scent.

'I didn't know you liked flowers so much, Kitty,' I said.

'Gaffer used to stick them in my hair, calling me his little flower fairy. Daisies, buttercups – but the wild roses were best of all because they smell so lovely. I can close my eyes and pretend I'm walking along with Gaffer down a country lane, both of us free as birds,' Kitty said dreamily.

'Well, can you keep your eyes open whenever we get to a turning, because I couldn't figure out what the flower seller was saying at all,' I said.

'We just walk this way, that way, turn here, go down there,' said Kitty, pointing in the air with her finger.

I suspected she was making it all up – but allowed her to lead us. She smelled her nosegay wistfully for a while, daydreaming about Gaffer, but then she straightened up, rubbing her neck, and walked more purposefully.

We had a terrible fright when we turned a corner and saw a policeman in his dark serge uniform and domed helmet lecturing three ragged little boys who were taking turns swinging from a lamppost.

'Quick, run!' Kitty hissed.

But luckily for us the biggest boy up the lamppost couldn't resist swinging out and giving the policeman a big push in the chest. It couldn't have really hurt because the boy was barefoot, but the policeman's dignity was severely wounded.

'You little varmints! I'm arresting the lot of you!' he shouted, trying to grab hold of them.

They were far too quick on their feet and tore up the road, laughing. The policeman lumbered after them, shaking his fist – giving Kitty and me a chance to saunter along demurely, unnoticed.

'The sooner we get to the country the better!' I said. 'I wonder how many other policemen are lurking round all these corners.'

'I wonder why they wear such pointy helmets,' said Kitty. 'Maybe they've all got especially pointy heads.'

'Our cook is stepping out with a police officer and I caught her having a cup of tea with him in the kitchen one time. He had red marks under his chin from the strap of his helmet, but his head was the usual sort of shape,' I told her.

'You had a special lady to cook for you?' Kitty asked curiously. 'And a maid to clean and tidy the house?'

'Yes, lots of maids, and a cross old gentleman butler, and a boy to run errands and brush the boots. My New Mother had her own maid, and the baby had a nurse. I had Miss Groan my governess, though I used to have my own lovely Nurse who looked after me.' It was my turn to sigh now, fingering the soft blue material of my frock.

'We'll go and find her in the country,' Kitty said. 'Though you don't really need her to look after you now. *I* look after you, and *you* look after me.'

'Yes we do,' I said.

We smiled at each other, suddenly so happy, though we were tired and hungry and footsore, and still in grave danger of being captured.

'What do you think Mrs Turnover would do to us if we were caught and sent back to her?' I asked.

'She'd beat us with a new little friend and then dunk our heads in that beastly trough of slime porridge,' said Kitty.

'Maybe she'd stuff us into a great big pot and turn *us* into porridge,' I suggested.

'Maybe she'd just lie on top of us and squash us flat,' said Kitty.

We amused ourselves inventing new and terrible Turnover tortures, snorting with laughter.

'We'll always get the better of her,' Kitty insisted. 'We'll beat *her* with her horrid "friend" until the stick snaps in half.'

'We'll make her eat out of that trough and her whole head will be dripping with porridge, imagine!' I said.

'And we'll buy one of those great big pots we saw at the Exhibition and boil *her* into porridge!' Kitty declared.

'And we'll make the stuffed elephant come alive and he'll squash *her* flat,' I laughed.

We turned a corner as I said it and saw a big hill in the distance – and there at the top was a dark silhouette of a creature almost as big as the trees surrounding it. It was round, with great legs yet a very small tail. Its vast head had enormous ears – and its nose spread down and down and down until it nearly touched the ground.

'Kitty, look! *Look!* It's an elephant! A real elephant!' I gasped.

'How could it be an elephant, you noodle?' Kitty said. Then she looked where I was pointing and gasped too.

'And it's alive, see, it's walking!' I said. 'Do you think it's in the Zoological Gardens? I always longed to go there, but Papa thought it too vulgar a venue for a carefully brought up little girl.'

'I don't think you were carefully brought up at all. They didn't seem to care in the slightest,' said Kitty.

'Let's go and see the elephant properly! Oh, how wonderful! Do you think it will let me stroke it?' I said, skipping along.

'You can't just go up to a wild animal and stroke it! Hello, Mr Bull, what a big fellow you are, pawing the ground so furiously, let me stroke you on the nose! Hello, Mr Wolf, smiling at me with your big yellow teeth, let me pat you on the head!' Kitty mocked, hurrying beside me.

'It's not wild, it's on a lead, look, and there's a man walking him along,' I said, squinting into the distance. 'There's another man too, over there, a huge man, even taller than Mr Marvel!' I said.

He seemed to have a normal-sized head and body and arms, but the longest strangest legs ever, which made him stride with the oddest gait.

'Do you think he's a monster?' I asked Kitty. 'Look at his legs!'

'They're not his real legs. He's strapped each foot to a long stick hidden inside those huge baggy trousers. I've seen street performers walking like that. Maybe I could learn to do it! How I'd love to be the tallest girl ever instead of the smallest!' said Kitty.

'How *I'd* love to ride an elephant!' I said. 'Then I'd be even taller!'

We hurried on, and when the hard pavement became soft grass as far as we could see we knew we were on the Heath at last.

'It's not the *real* country though,' said Kitty. 'Look, you can still see London all around us.'

'Yes, all right, but *please* let's go and see the elephant first before we try to find the country,' I begged.

'Of course we're going to have a proper look at the elephant,' said Kitty.

We weren't the only ones. There were many folk walking in the sunshine on the Heath, and those with children were all heading the same way, towards the elephant. The giant man had vanished out of sight but the elephant was still standing proudly at the very top of the hill, his head back now, his long trunk curled – and then he suddenly bellowed!

We were still quite far away but we both heard him distinctly.

'My goodness, he's calling to us!' said Kitty, and she imitated him accurately.

He made several more bizarre noises, and then slowly and majestically started walking over the brow of the hill, gradually disappearing.

'Wait for us!' I shouted. 'Please come back, Mr Elephant!'

A young couple passing us laughed at me. 'Don't worry, dear, he's part of the circus. They're here for another week, though there's no show today because it's Sunday. You can still have a look at all the animals though, taking their exercise,' said the lady.

Her companion was looking at Kitty, taking note of her red velvet jacket and bloomers.

'Ah, lad, I see you're actually part of the circus! A young acrobat, by any chance?' he asked.

'Yes, indeed I am,' said Kitty, tremendously pleased, and she stood on her hands and waggled her legs in the air.

They laughed and clapped. I wondered about breaking into song to do a little performance for them to earn some money. There was a wonderful savoury smell in the air, making me hungrier than ever – but I also wanted to catch up with this wondrous elephant in his circus. I wasn't quite sure what a circus *was*. I hadn't read about one in any of my storybooks, but if it contained an elephant *and* a ten-foot-tall man then it was not to be missed.

We hurried to the top of the hill, and there was the circus itself spread out on the flat grass below: a circle of brightly decorated caravans and wagons with folk cooking their suppers over little fires, and a huge red tent at one end. There were great sturdy horses eating grass at the other end of the meadow, clearly used for pulling the circus vehicles. The elephant was led to join them and taken to a big tub of feed. He ate in a mannerly way, dipping his trunk into the tub like a spoon and then lifting it to his mouth without spilling a crumb. More horses were being exercised beyond the circle of caravans – white ones like Mr Chubb's Nelson, but these seemed a different species altogether: fairy horses, sleek and dainty, galloping round in unison, while a beautiful young girl rode the first bareback, her long red hair flying out behind her.

I stared at her in wonder. 'Look at that lady, Kitty!' I exclaimed. 'Isn't she marvellous!'

Kitty only gave her a quick glance. She was too busy looking at two men – one was balancing upside down on the other one's head!

'Oh, Lucy, do you think we could ever do that?' she asked. 'All you would have to do is stand very still – and I don't weigh very much.'

'Still far too much for me!' I protested.

We walked nearer, until we could read the lettering on the side of a big wagon: *Tanglefield's Travelling Circus*. I said the words aloud, and Kitty murmured them after me, transfixed.

Then a boy walked up to us with a swagger, a whip in his hand. He wore a jersey and jodhpurs and long black boots and looked very fierce.

'We're closed. It's Sunday. Come back tomorrow, little girls,' he said curtly.

'Who are you to tell us what to do?' Kitty said defiantly. 'You're not any older than us.'

'I am Sam Tanglefield Junior – my father Samuel owns this whole circus. It will all be mine one day. It's our property and you're trespassing, so clear off before I take my whip to you,' he said, and he cracked it in the air menacingly.

I took a step backwards, and pulled Kitty with me. 'Please, Mr Tanglefield Junior, we don't mean any harm. We just think your circus is so splendid,' I said politely.

'It's the best British circus you'll ever find – but we ain't got no time for ragamuffins plaguing us, even pretty little popsies like you, wanting a free show,' he said rudely. 'Now, scarper!'

'We want to be *part* of the show,' said Kitty. 'I'm an acrobat!'

I stared at her. Surely she wasn't going to desert me!

'So what's your name and which circus family do you come from, boy?' he said.

'I'm actually a girl and I'm just called Kitty and I happen to be the child of the Great Gaffer, the strongest man in the world,' said Kitty.

'Never heard of him,' said Tanglefield Junior.

'Then it proves you don't know nothing about circuses,' Kitty retorted. 'Watch!'

She stood on her hands and circled him, and then did six or seven cartwheels in succession. He didn't look particularly impressed.

'Elementary! I could do likewise by the time I was five.' He nodded at me. 'So let's see you strut your stuff too.'

I took a deep breath. I couldn't possibly pretend to be an acrobat, when I couldn't turn so much as a cartwheel.

'She's Lucy Locket, the little nightingale, known for her sweet singing,' Kitty said. 'Sing him a verse, Lucy.'

'Nah, we don't need no singers at the circus. Clear off, both of you. Do you think I was born yesterday? You're just little street kids, not circus folk at all,' he said, and this time he cracked his whip at Kitty, lightly flicking her nose with it.

She cried out in shock.

The Tanglefield boy sniggered unpleasantly. 'Be off with you!' he said.

We had no choice. We backed away, poor Kitty rubbing her nose.

'What a beast! Oh, Kitty, he's made your nose *bleed*,' I said.

'Doesn't hurt,' said Kitty, though her eyes were watering. 'Come on, let's go and look at that old elephant up close.'

'But he told us to clear off his property!'

'It's not *his* circus, he's only a hateful boy. And anyway, the circus is on the Heath, and heathland belongs to everybody, Gaffer told me. We've got a perfect right to be here,' Kitty insisted.

She took care to walk round the *outside* of the caravans though, keeping well away from the other circus folk. We reached the field and crept as close as we dared to the elephant. It was tethered, but it could still move about on its enormous feet. It could clearly squash us flat with one small stamp. But it didn't seem at all threatening, standing there placidly eating out of its tub.

'Hello, Mr Elephant,' I said, and he swung his huge head round and peered at me with his surprisingly small eyes. He raised his trunk.

'He's waving at us!' said Kitty.

The beautiful red-haired girl came cantering up to the field, jumped off her glorious white horse, and opened the gate to let the other five trot through. She didn't have a whip. She didn't glare at us. She smiled.

'Are you saying hello to Elijah?' she said.

'We're very sorry to trespass, miss,' I said quickly. 'We just think he's so magnificent.'

I thought *she* was magnificent too, her hair glowing in the sunlight, her pale skin flushed with exercise, her slender figure lithe in her riding breeches.

'Elijah and I are old friends,' she said. 'I sometimes ride him as well as my horses.'

'How on earth do you get on his back?' asked Kitty.

'I fly through the air,' she said, grinning.

'That's a fib!' said Kitty.

'I'll show you!' She gave her horse a pat. 'Wait there, Prince!'

Then she stood in front of the elephant, put her head on one side, and said, 'Hup!'

Elijah took his trunk out of his tub, coiled it round the girl's tiny waist, and lifted her high in the air, right up above his head, and then with a delicate twist deposited her safely onto his back.

'See!' she said triumphantly.

'Oh, how wonderful! Oh please, please, please, will he do it to me too?' Kitty begged.

'I don't think he should. You might fall and take a terrible tumble,' she said.

'I don't mind. I *am* a tumbler, look!' Kitty sprang forward and did a handstand and then another and another and another, hands feet, hands feet, hands feet, hands feet until she blurred. I should have started the tumbling boy song, but I was suddenly too shy in front of the red-haired girl.

She laughed and clapped. 'So you are! You should join our circus!' she said.

'I want to! Perhaps I'm still at the elementary stage, but I'd work so hard and get better and better, and I'd train Lucy here too, and I'm sure we could even do that act where I balance on her head,' said Kitty.

'I don't think we could,' I murmured, but Kitty was showing off her cartwheels now, going round and round us until we were dizzy. The white horse Prince started fidgeting nervously, so I stroked his beautiful head to calm him.

The girl nodded at me. 'That's right! It looks as if you understand horses,' she said approvingly.

'Oh, she does! She's an absolute wizard with horses,' said Kitty. 'She used to ride this huge big powerful horse Nelson, a great brute of a creature, ready to bolt as soon as look at you, but Lucy made him as docile as a little lamb.'

'My goodness, is that true?' the girl asked, looking at me. She was smiling a little. It was clear she didn't believe Kitty's outrageous fibs.

'Oh, Kitty! No, ma'am, it isn't true,' I said, blushing painfully. 'And Nelson wasn't a brute, he was a poor old nag who had to pull a hackney cab, and he had a lovely nature.'

'But you rode him?'

'A little. I liked him very much,' I said.

'Would you like to ride Prince?'

'I – I would love to,' I said.

'Very well. Come here!' Her arms were slender but she seemed very strong. She picked me up easily and sat me on Prince's smooth pearly back. I seemed suddenly very high up, and didn't know how to hold on properly without a bridle or reins. Prince shifted slightly, sensing my anxiety. I had to grip with my knees to stop myself sliding right off him.

'That's right. Try to sit upright. There you go!' She swung herself lightly up behind me, holding me so that I immediately felt safe. She clucked her tongue at Prince and he stepped daintily forward, going very slowly, and I gradually relaxed and got used to his movement. She clucked again and he broke into a smooth steady trot. I laughed delightedly and we circled the field, while Kitty ran along beside us, clapping.

'There, you're a natural,' said the red-haired girl, jumping off Prince and then helping me down too. 'So you're Lucy? And you're Kitty? I'm Addie, though I'm Miss Adeline when I'm performing.'

'And can we be performers too?' Kitty begged. 'I'm sure you could train Lucy in a few days.'

'I think it would take a lot longer than that, even though she shows such promise,' said Addie. 'But child performers are always a big draw. Folk love them.'

'I'm sure they'd love us!' said Kitty. 'And I already have my costume!'

'So you do,' said Addie. 'It suits you wonderfully. What would your parents say though, if you ran away with the circus?'

'We haven't got parents and we *need* to run away,' said Kitty.

Addie nodded as if she understood. 'I needed to run away once upon a time, so that's how *I* joined the circus. It's a hard life though, especially for girls. We have to do all the cooking and the cleaning and the sewing and we have to look our very best when we're in the ring. Yet we're expected to join in the heavy work too, the raising of the Big Top and the big clear-up before we move on. You two will be expected to run all the errands and help sell the tickets and the sugar-candy and gingerbread in the interval. Could you cope with all that?' she asked.

'It sounds marvellous!' said Kitty.

Addie turned to me. 'Do you think it would be marvellous too, Lucy?'

'Yes, very much so – but Sam Tanglefield Junior said we couldn't possibly be part of his circus and told us to clear off!' I said.

'That wretched boy, forever swaggering around and telling people what to do!' said Addie impatiently. 'It's not *his* circus, not yet. It's his father's. Come with me, girls. We'll ask him.'

She left Prince grazing with his sleek white companions and took us to the biggest caravan, painted a bright canary yellow. A middle-aged man was sitting on the steps smoking a cigar. He wasn't wearing a shirt, just a vest and jodhpurs and he'd kicked his boots off and was barefoot. Even so, he had an air of authority, and we knew at once that he must be Mr Tanglefield. He looked a stern man – but his face softened when he saw Addie.

'Hello, my dear,' he said, puffing at his cigar. 'So who are these little waifs?'

'Two talented little recruits for our circus, boss,' said Addie.

'We don't need any more mouths to feed, girl, you know that,' he said.

'They're very small girls with scarcely any appetite,' said Addie. 'Both seem very promising. I reckon I could work with them to perfect two pretty little acts—'

'I won't need much work at all. I'm already an excellent tumbler,' Kitty interrupted.

Mr Tanglefield chuckled at her cheek but didn't seem convinced.

'They'll work hard. It'll be like having an extra adult hand about the place – only they won't require any wages, not till they're grown,' said Addie.

'Not even sixpence each?' said Kitty.

'My, this one's a cheeky little baggage,' said Mr Tanglefield. 'I'm not sure. They could be more trouble than they're worth. What about family? We don't want to be accused of kidnapping them.'

'We haven't any family, sir. We're just us, Kitty and me. She truly is a great tumbler and I do love horses – Miss Addie says I'm a natural,' I said, blushing again.

'Well, where can they sleep? We haven't got any spare vans,' said Mr Tanglefield.

'We could sleep *under* a caravan. We're used to roughing it,' said Kitty.

'They're still only babies, for all their cheek. Who's going to look after them?' Mr Tanglefield asked.

'We look after each other, sir. We don't need anyone else,' I said.

'I still don't know. Children can be a wretched nuisance. Look at my boy,' said Mr Tanglefield, shaking his head.

As he spoke his son came to the caravan door, peering out. He glared ferociously when he saw us. 'You two again! Go away before I give you a real whipping! I ordered them to clear off, Pa!' he declared.

'Did you, my boy?' said Mr Tanglefield, and he deftly twisted round, seized his son, and turned him upside down. 'You ordered them, did you? Who *actually* gives the orders round here, eh?' He shook him hard.

'You do, Pa!' the boy gasped, purple in the face.

'That's right – and don't you forget it!' said Mr Tanglefield, setting him on his feet again. 'These two little girls are part of my circus now. You treat them with proper respect!'

'Yes, Pa,' said the Tanglefield boy, and ran off, mortified.

'So we really can stay?' Kitty asked.

'If you behave yourselves,' said Mr Tanglefield.

'We will, we will!' she promised.

'Come along then. I'll make you some supper and find you some bedding,' said Addie, taking us both by the hand.

We passed the big wagon with the message painted on it.

'Tanglefield's *Travelling* Circus,' I read again. 'Miss Addie – where does the circus travel to? Does it go to the country?'

'The *proper* country?' Kitty added.

'Yes, it travels all over the south east of England,' said Addie. 'We're off to Surrey next.'

'I don't suppose – perhaps it's unlikely – but does it ever go near Sussex?' I asked, scarcely able to breathe.

'Yes, we travel right across the Sussex downs,' said Addie. 'We spend a couple of months there so all the village folk get a chance of seeing us.'

I hugged Kitty and she hugged me back. We might find Nurse! And now we were part of this travelling circus. Not just Kitty – me too! I wasn't little Lady Lucy from five Yewtree Crescent any more, captive in a schoolroom, in silk and a starched white pinafore. I remembered the little muslin fairy dresses I'd seen in Monmouth Street. Would I be able to wear one of those when I rode Prince? Perhaps I'd learn to stand on his back and wave to everyone watching. Then Kitty would tumble round and round the ring in her red velvet before leaping onto Prince's back too, while the crowd cheered.

We'd be *Kitty and Lucy Locket*, circus stars! It looked as if this was the start of a whole new adventure . . .

ABOUT THE AUTHOR

JACQUELINE WILSON wrote her first novel when she was nine years old, and she has been writing ever since. She is now one of Britain's bestselling and most beloved children's authors. She has written over 100 books and is the creator of characters such as Tracy Beaker and Hetty Feather. More than forty million copies of her books have been sold.

As well as winning many awards for her books, including the Children's Book of the Year, Jacqueline is a former Children's Laureate, and in 2008 she was appointed a Dame.

Jacqueline is also a great reader, and has amassed over twenty thousand books, along with her famous collection of silver rings.

Find out more about Jacqueline and her books at www.jacquelinewilson.co.uk

ABOUT THE ILLUSTRATOR

NICK SHARRATT has written and illustrated
many books for children and won numerous awards
for his picture books, including the Children's
Book Award and the Educational Writers' Award.
He has also enjoyed great success illustrating
Jacqueline Wilson's books. Nick lives in Hove.

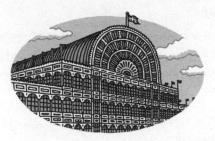

THE GREAT EXHIBITION

Lucy and Kitty's story takes place during Victorian times. Did you know that the Great Exhibition was a real event that happened during that period?

1 May 1851 was a very exciting day for Great Britain – the Great Exhibition opened in London! From May to October, anyone could come and for just a few pennies see wonders from all around the world, including exciting new modern technology like the facsimile (the fax machine) and one of the biggest diamonds ever, the Koh-i-Noor.

The Great Exhibition, or its official name, 'The Great Exhibition of the Works of Industry of all Nations', was the brainchild of Queen Victoria's husband, Prince Albert. He wanted to show the world that Great Britain was the best at everything! The exhibition was going to be so big they had to construct a brand new building to house it – the Crystal Palace. It was a majestic sight, made of glass and so tall it towered over everything. An architectural marvel and an engineering triumph, London had never seen anything like this before.

Over six million people came from far and wide to see the displays. There were flags everywhere, and richly coloured ornate carpets hanging from the ceilings. Huge statues dotted the halls and lavish fountains gushed water, but most magical of all were the real and enormous elm trees that grew inside the palace.

The western side was filled with exhibits from all over the British Empire, like manufacturing machinery, microscopes and never-before-seen inventions like flushing toilets. There was a whole section just for India, with a stuffed elephant decked out in magnificent cloths (the very one that Lucy was so eager to see!), an ivory throne and clothes embroidered with pearls, emeralds and rubies fit for a maharaja.

Visitors could even get up close and personal with precious diamonds like the Daria-i-Noor, a very rare pale-pink jewel, or watch the entire process of cotton production, from spinning to the finished cloth.

The eastern half boasted glorious sights from foreign countries, like gold from Chile, Cossack armour from Russia, porcelain from Paris, vases from China and luxurious cloths from Turkey.

The Queen herself visited the exhibition with her family several times and even famous people like Charlotte Brontë, Charles Dickens and Lewis Carroll attended.

The event was a huge success and the profits were used to fund the Victoria and Albert Museum, the Science Museum and the Natural History Museum – three famous places that you can still visit in London today! You can even find a memorial to the exhibition, a monument with Prince Albert atop, just south of the Royal Albert Hall.

Welcome to the
Wonderful World of
HETTY FEATHER

HETTY FEATHER

Victorian orphan Hetty
is left as a baby at the
Foundling Hospital – will
she ever find a true home?

SAPPHIRE BATTERSEA

Hetty's time at the Foundling
Hospital is at an end – will
life by the sea bring the
happiness she seeks?

EMERALD STAR

Following a tragedy, Hetty
sets off to find her father –
might her sought-after
home be with him?

DIAMOND

Life at the circus is too much for Diamond to bear. Could her beloved Emerald hold the key to a brighter future?

LITTLE STARS

The bright lights of the music hall beckon – will Diamond and Hetty become real stars?

CLOVER MOON

Clover's chance meeting with an artist gives her an inspiring glimpse of another world – but will she have the courage to leave her family and find a place that really feels like home?

HETTY FEATHER'S CHRISTMAS

An unexpected gift leads to trouble for Hetty on Christmas Day – will she be allowed to take part in the celebrations or will mean Matron Bottomly get her way?

YOU MIGHT ALSO LIKE

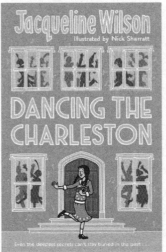

HAVE YOU READ THEM ALL?

LAUGH OUT LOUD
THE STORY OF TRACY BEAKER
I DARE YOU, TRACY BEAKER
STARRING TRACY BEAKER
MY MUM TRACY BEAKER
WE ARE THE BEAKER GIRLS
THE WORST THING ABOUT MY SISTER
DOUBLE ACT
FOUR CHILDREN AND IT
THE BED AND BREAKFAST STAR

HISTORICAL HEROES
HETTY FEATHER
HETTY FEATHER'S CHRISTMAS
SAPPHIRE BATTERSEA
EMERALD STAR
DIAMOND
LITTLE STARS
CLOVER MOON
ROSE RIVERS
WAVE ME GOODBYE
OPAL PLUMSTEAD
QUEENIE
DANCING THE CHARLESTON

LIFE LESSONS
THE BUTTERFLY CLUB
THE SUITCASE KID
KATY
BAD GIRLS
LITTLE DARLINGS
CLEAN BREAK
RENT A BRIDESMAID
CANDYFLOSS

THE LOTTIE PROJECT
THE LONGEST WHALE SONG
COOKIE
JACKY DAYDREAM
PAWS & WHISKERS

FAMILY DRAMAS
THE ILLUSTRATED MUM
MY SISTER JODIE
DIAMOND GIRLS
DUSTBIN BABY
VICKY ANGEL
SECRETS
MIDNIGHT
LOLA ROSE
LILY ALONE
MY SECRET DIARY

PLENTY OF MISCHIEF
SLEEPOVERS
THE WORRY WEBSITE
BEST FRIENDS
GLUBBSLYME
THE CAT MUMMY
LIZZIE ZIPMOUTH
THE MUM-MINDER
CLIFFHANGER
BURIED ALIVE!

FOR OLDER READERS
GIRLS IN LOVE
GIRLS UNDER PRESSURE
GIRLS OUT LATE
GIRLS IN TEARS
KISS
LOVE LESSONS